Abel's SAVIOR

Abel's Savior

Mongoose Security #1

Flo Journey

FD press

Abel's Savior © 2025 by Flo Journey

Paperback ISBN-13: 978-1-965176-18-4

Ebook ISBN: 978-1-965176-17-7

For information, please contact publisher at faireydragonpress@gmail.com

Acknowledgements

Thank you to my wonderful PA's Crystal and Dreamweaver for helping to get this book to the finish line. Also thank you Loreweaver Books LLC for the perfect cover and Mongoose logo.

About This Series

This and the rest of the Mongoose Security books have strong male characters and women who won't let them get away with being jerks.

This book

Death, Kidnapping, PTSD, Stalking, Torture, Panic Attacks

Table of Contents

CHAPTER ONE

I forgot just how humid Kansas City can be, with the humidity slapping me in the face the minute I stepped off the plane. It clings to my skin like a second uniform. I was finally out of my first uniform. I didn't need another. Reaching the terminal, I paused, taking in the airport. It had been nine months since I last visited. It felt both like coming home and the end of an era. The first stop was baggage, where I had hoped to avoid most of the travelers, but when I arrived, there were already two rows of people waiting for their bags. Leaning against a column, I pulled out my phone.

"Hey, I'm on the ground, no surprises, just waiting for my duffel." I pressed the phone against my ear, sidestepping a family with their assortment of rolling suitcases. Mike's familiar laughter greeted me.

"I was hanging out in the cellphone parking lot. Let me know when you get your bags, and I will loop around."

"Thanks." I hung up and stayed away from the carousel while still close enough to grab my bag quickly. The sky was still dark, an hour before dawn, and the humidity was already hinting at what type of day it was going to be. I fidgeted, walking back and forth in my area near the carousel. The closer people got to me, the more anxious I became. Thankfully, I traveled light and saw my duffel dumping onto the carousel. A few people nudged, and a young girl stepped on my toe, grabbing her princess bag. The tension in my jaw increased as I worried about what I could possibly say. I took a deep breath and waited for the duffel to circle around to me. Once it did, I grabbed it and moved toward the glass entry doors. I needed to get away from the crowd, the people, the noise. The faster the better, some may call it avoidance, but I call it preservation. As I touched the glass door, I thought I heard my name.

"Abel!" The call was faint, somewhere amid the clusters of travelers all seeking their luggage or a coffee from the local shop. I didn't turn around; the voice wasn't familiar, and if it was, I still didn't want to know who it belonged to. Not yet anyway.

"I finally got my bag." I voice-texted Mike before stepping out into the Kansas City weather. Instantly, I began sweating, thankful I had taken off my thin jacket on the plane. Less than five minutes later, Mike's red Chevy Caprice pulled up to the curb. Stepping out, I never knew how his six-foot-two-inch frame fit in the car, but somehow it did and had since we were young.

Hugging me, "Welcome home, Abel." I hugged him back.

"Thanks, so far it is good to be back, but let's see if that changes." Mike looked at me knowingly before nodding and opening the trunk. Sliding my duffel into the trunk, I shut it before going to the passenger side.

"Where to?" Mike asked out of the corner of his eye as he navigated traffic around the airport.

"I bought a place in Lee's Summit."

Mike's eyebrows raised. "You aren't returning to Independence?"

"Not if I can help it. In fact, Lee's Summit is close enough. Some of my unit also moved to the Kansas City Metro area, so I think I'm close enough to KC but also away, you know?"

"I do know, I am out in Raytown with the wife and kids. So how are you?" Mike didn't turn as he asked, possibly afraid of what my facial expressions might show.

"Good, bad, depending on the day."

"Well, you know if you ever need anything, I'm just a phone call away."

"I know, thank you."

***

The drive to my new house only took 40 minutes, given how early it was. The ribbon of highway was a stark contrast to the brightening horizon. As we turned off the freeway, I could see the traffic slowing. Rush hour in Kansas City is not my favorite time of day, in fact, if I can avoid it, I will. I could also breathe, as if the city was watching and waiting for something. I let out an exhale that I felt in my feet, although my heart still hadn't gotten the message that everything was okay. It continued to hammer in my chest. As I took deep breaths, my heart slowed down. Looking over at Mike to see if he noticed, he didn't seem to.

"So why out here?"

"I am starting a security company, and I wanted to have my own space."

Mike and I watched as the short gravel driveways disappeared into trees. I knew there were houses back there, because this is exactly what I had been looking for when I had my realtor put in offers.

"It's this street up here, Gryphon Drive." I pointed at a small sign.

"Fitting." Mike laughed as he pulled onto the street.

I don't know why it had a name, there was only one house on it, but I wasn't going to complain. The large trees appeared as if they were threatening to take over the gravel road. The road was dark, and my heartbeat faster, as if warning me that something might be out in the trees. I dug my fingers into the palm of my hand and reminded myself that I wasn't in Iraq anymore, that I was in a peaceful suburb. It seemed to help as Mike pulled out of the trees onto a large, paved driveway.

As the house appeared, I closed my eyes. This was precisely what I wanted, exactly what I needed. I felt the briefest sense of optimism that this place that I spent everything on would be my refuge, or just another façade. One that breaks down at the slightest hint of wind. It was a beautiful single-story building with weathered cedar siding. It may not look like much from the outside, but I knew what I was getting.

"This is nice." Mike whistled as we pulled up to the door.

"I hope so, I paid a lot of money for this place to be quiet."

Mike killed the engine, and we both listened to the quiet for a minute.

"I would kill for this much quiet," Mike commented before stepping out of the car.

"Don't speak things like that to existence." I reminded him. He was right, though; the stillness was more profound than anything I could remember. It was quiet, untouched by the constant hum of duty or command. The sun peeked out from behind the trees, setting everything aglow with a fiery intensity. I could hear the birds waking up, seeking that worm. Finally, I reached for the door handle, ready for my next adventure.

With the slam of the car door, it felt like the house was turning its attention to me. After grabbing my duffel bag, I looked around. This was all mine, and having paid for the entire thing upfront, it would never be taken away.

"You need help or anything?" Mike asked as I stood, as if waiting for something.

"No, the moving trucks already dropped off my meager belongings, so I think I am set. Thank you again for driving me. Say hi to Margie and the kids."

Mike patted me on the back, "Will do, take care of yourself, and I'm serious, call if you need anything."

"I will." My smile didn't quite reach my eyes, but Mike didn't notice.

I stood there on the porch, which creaked under my weight, watching Mike drive down the road. Once I couldn't see him anymore, I turned and really looked at the house. From the outside, it looked like nothing special. It was mine, and this was the first thing that I could honestly say was mine. It felt good, but also sad. Before I joined, I figured I would live in Independence my whole life, get married, and have some kids. Life has a funny way of making its own decisions. Here I was, 32 years old, buying my first house, with all of my belongings likely fitting into a sprinter van.

I pulled out the single key mailed to me after closing. The door was weathered, but the lock and deadbolt were fresh, and the key slid right in. Turning the key, I felt like my life was about to take a turn. I didn't know if it was a good turn, but a turn, nonetheless.

The door sighed open, but not a hinge squeak was heard. It was as if the door and house were welcoming me in. I paused at the threshold, taking the shadowy rooms in. The living room sat in front, mostly empty, except for a futon that was way past its normal lifespan. I stepped inside and shut the door behind me with the determination of a man needing to start over, to wash the past away. Each room spun out from the living room in a circular pattern, allowing me to meander in a circle to take it all in.

The floors were wooden, and every step brought a faint smell of finish. As I passed the windows, I paused. The house may look old from the outside, but the view that these windows afforded made it all worth it. Well, that and everything has been updated recently. I ran my hand over the built-in bookcases as I walked toward the first door. Opening it, I saw what would become my gym, with windows overlooking the property, but enough space to hold all of my equipment.

I initially thought I would feel the same detachment as I did every time I moved into a new place. Just another place to lay my head. This time, however, it didn't come; instead, I saw my future here, as clearly as I saw the past. "My space, without sharing." The words were strange on my tongue, and I surprised myself when I said them. Maybe this was truly the start of something new.

Walking through the rooms, I saw my new bedroom and the guest bedroom I had planned to turn into my office. The more I ventured from the front door, the more I felt the sharp weight of resolve coming over me. I knew I could do it, no matter what my commander had said, as I processed out. I would not run back to the Army, not if I could help it, not after what happened last time. Throwing my duffel on my bed, I walked back into the office, looking at all of the boxes.

With no sign of what was in them, I began to open them. The past and present blurred as I opened the second box from the tower of packed-away life. One eye was fixed on the bright light coming in from the single window, while the other scanned the jagged edge of the torn lid. Tape crackled as it coughed up old memories and ghosts that I wanted to stay gone. Decorations and commendations were the first thing I saw, but before I closed the lid, my fingers found the letter.

It wasn't your fault.

Like hell it wasn't. I was the senior NCO; everything that happened was my fault. I placed the letter down, but as I did, the folded photo floated to the top, as if fate wanted to force me to see my failures. It felt like a landmine. As I reached for it, my hands trembled, but no matter what I did, I couldn't stop them from grabbing it. I wasn't worried about damaging the photo; it was seared into my brain. No, I was worried about the moment it opened, the explosion in my mind before I could stop it, gunfire tearing through my mind.

The sounds erupted from the edges of my consciousness, deafening. Everything compressed, the room disappeared. Screams sharp near me, tracer rounds bright as they skimmed the air around me. My heart slammed in my chest, knocking the breath from my throat. I doubled down, but knew that if I went to all fours, I would be dead. One hand snaked out seeking something to hold to keep from collapsing. My other hand clamped over my mouth to keep from screaming. The photo fell from my grasp, but I could still see the faces, feel the bonds we had, everyone and everything caught in the frame just before the flash of the camera.

I couldn't stay up any longer, sinking to the floor, unsure if it was from my legs giving out or an involuntary act of finding cover during a battle. I could feel and hear it all, as if my past was no longer in a distant time and land, but in front of me in the present. Time collapsed into nothing as every battle, every fight, every death came slamming back into me as if I was shot. Bits and pieces of words came to me as if they were shrapnel.

"Stay low!" I heard someone yell. The voice was familiar but also not. "Keep moving!" Another voice from the past urged. I didn't know if they were people I knew saying it, or if it was a distorted version of my voice yelling at me. The sense of urgency clawed at me, I struggled against the weight of needing to be out, safe, away.

Suddenly, I opened my eyes, and the walls of the house pulled back into view with a slow, jarring snap. Afternoon light was coming in through the same window that I swore was morning just minutes ago. I grabbed the desk and pulled myself up, trying to get a sense of what had happened while also staying centered. My emotions were still reeling from the brunt of the battle, while my senses were trying to make sense of what had happened.

This wasn't the first time, but this was one of the worst I had had since coming back. I talked to the doctors, I made the appointments, and I stopped short of going on the medications they wanted me to. They said it was all in my head and that it would fade over time. That they wanted me to stay, that I was dependable and needed.

A silence pressed in as the echoes finally faded. Nothing was left but the raw edge of my breathing and my heart pounding against my chest. My hands found the box again, desperate to put the genie back in the lamp. I gathered everything that had fallen out, including the photograph last, and put it all back in the box. I hastily shut the box and placed it on the top shelf of the closet. A place I hope it stays for years, if not forever.

I had thought I could do this, that months after deployment would dim the memories. They lingered, though, ever-present, ready to jump out and remind me of my failures, reminding me of the consequences of my actions. No matter how much I tried to move ahead, they were there, sharp, and always outpacing me. It took five solid deep breaths before I could speak. "Not now." I pleaded with the universe, with the box, with the memories. I wasn't so naïve to think I could run forever, but not now.

Hauling myself to my feet, I felt the tension of the last however long uncoil in my limbs. I needed to get out, do something, anything to get my thoughts away from the box. Determination swelled as I gained distance from my office. Stepping away from the past and its torn corners. I knew I was torn between my past and my current situation, but right now I didn't want to focus on that. By stepping away, I had created an uneasy truce, one that I knew the slightest thing could disrupt. I inhaled sharply, promising myself that I'd hold it together this time, that the flashbacks wouldn't win, because I knew they were just flashbacks, even if my body didn't.

The world finally steadied as I took cleansing breaths. I reclaimed normalcy, at least for a bit. It was the way I always sought to regain myself, especially when the past reared its head, not ugly, just ever-present. I looked at the box on the shelf one more time, "There will be a time when I am ready." But it wasn't now, I turned and walked away. My footfalls echoed in the house, each one more sure than the last until I could reclaim the silence.

Dusk advanced over the house, shadows popping up everywhere. The lights tried, but failed to keep the shadows at bay. I initially planned on unpacking everything, but one box of memories derailed that plan. I sat on the futon, looking at the blank wall where a TV would be later, now than sooner, and considered my day. The air was still, but not the kind that I relished in. In fact, it was the kind that was stifling. I pulled my phone out of my pocket and began dialing her number from memory. My fingers were typing before I could tell them to stop. I was one number from finishing when I tossed my phone next to me and stood up. Not tonight, not ever if I could help it.

Grabbing my keys and treacherous phone, I knew I had to get out, but to where? I walked to the detached garage and opened it to find my BMW M2 sitting there as if waiting to be driven. When we first returned from Iraq, I bought it on a whim. I thought I would drive it more, but between the debriefings, meetings, training, and out-processing, I never really had a chance.

Sitting in the car, I thought about everything, about how the stuff I unpacked seemed not to help. There was a weight from the past, and that weight wasn't in a box, it was a five-foot-two-inch redhead who turned my life upside down. Initially, I thought about reaching out the minute I set foot on home soil, every single time, but then the days became weeks, and the weeks became months, and then years passed. I went from feeling urgent to now feeling uncertain about ever speaking to her again.

I didn't need to know how she was doing; in fact, I would rather not. It took her no time to find the bed of another man or woman when we were together. Why should I expect anything else now? *But you were young,* my inner voice yelled, but I knew it was a voice from the past thinking things could be fixed with a call. Every deployment, she vanished faster and faster until I wasn't able to reach her.

Just one call, ease your mind. The inner voice said, and before I knew it, I was dialing. It rang four, five, six times before the voicemail clicked on. "The number you are trying to reach is no longer in service. Please check the number and try again." Laughing at myself, I put my phone on the seat and started the car.

As I drove, I thought about how easy it would be to find her. Go to her parents' house in Independence, see if her friend still works at Walmart. Even go to the bar we used to get drunk at every Friday night. Maybe I would do that, but not tonight. Tonight I wanted to lose myself.

No! I slammed my hand against the steering wheel. She burned me too many times, and when I wrote that letter, I meant every word. I would not contact her. I wouldn't contact anyone in her circle. With that resolution, I put all thoughts of her behind me. This was a new life, and I needed to move on from the old one. The doctor said that drinking could cause more flashbacks, but in the last six months, the only thing that held them at bay was alcohol. But with my family's past, I made sure not to overdo it.

Finally settling on what I was going to do, I put the car in gear and drove away from my house, my home. Just thinking that made me smile. I turned on the Bluetooth radio and listened to my favorite metal bands as I drove to Overland Park. Since I knew no one I didn't want to see would be there, it was the perfect place to disappear. I let myself drift to the music as I drove, enjoying the feel of being behind the wheel.

CHAPTER TWO

The bar's parking lot was full, which is a good indicator of either good food, good booze, good music, or good women. I was in for all four if they presented themselves. I rarely dated, especially since every time I tried, it ended badly, so I would opt for quick hookups to take my mind off whatever was bothering me, which worked well enough. This was especially true near military bases. Any bar or club within walking distance had many women and men looking for a one-night stand, hoping it would lead to something longer and more lucrative.

Walking in, I looked around. Money was flowing just as the drinks were. A full live band is playing, which is a good sign. This is definitely not a dive or your run-of-the-mill country bar, no, these people had money, influence, or wanted it. I walked up to the bar and waited for my turn. A bartender who is probably five years younger than me came over. After looking me up and down, she smiled.

"Your turn, what can I get you?"

"Whiskey Sour, none of that egg white crap if you do that here, and half ice please."

"You look like a man who likes specific bourbons, got a favorite?" The bartender batted her eyelashes at me. It would not get her a bigger tip.

"Elijah Craig, if you have it, Woodford Reserve if you don't."

"We have Craig, let me get that for you, are you opening a tab or just a single drink?"

"It depends on how fast I find what I am looking for."

She leaned against the bar, pushing her tits together, "and what are you looking for?"

"Similar but older." I winked as I gave her my card to start the tab.

She smiled as she walked toward the register. I looked around the room as I waited for my drink. Putting it on the bar near me, I took a sip and nodded to her. It was a good whiskey sour, not the best I've ever had, but not the worst by any stretch.

Just as I was about to turn to put my half-empty glass on the bar, I saw a group of women walk in. They are all dressed as if they had just left work. As they laugh about something, they find a table near the dance floor. I sit there watching them as the server goes over to get their drink order. Of the six women, five are eagerly ordering drinks and small food items from how much the server was writing. The sixth woman, though, said two words and then looked at her phone.

I was immediately intrigued by the woman as she looked toward me and smirked. Lifting my glass slightly, I smiled back before turning around and asking the bartender for another.

"Oh, you find something you like?"

"Maybe, you know anything about the group of women over there?"

"The boss babes?"

"Boss babes?" I must look like a deer caught in the headlights because she laughs.

"That's what we call them. Every Friday night, they come here. They all have corporate or professional jobs. They come in, get absolutely wasted, tip well, and leave."

"Any specific information on the taller brunette with them?"

"She doesn't come every Friday, and when she does, she doesn't drink as much. I haven't seen her talk much, unlike the other ones who yap all night long."

"You know how old she is?"

"Early to mid-30s for sure, I know I carded her once."

"Gotcha, thanks."

"No, thank you. This may be the most enjoyment I have had all week."

"What do you mean by that?"

"Oh, every week some tweedle dee douche canoe tries to hit on them, and every week they take their money in the form of drinks before they push him to the outskirts."

"Interesting."

"Right on time." She points to the group as a man is approaching them.

I turn and watch as the man swaggers toward the group. The women are not paying him any attention, but the brunette, I can tell, is watching him. Not overtly, but more of an always watching, always calculating way. I can't get enough of her.

"What is the brunette drinking?" I ask the bartender when she is close.

"Look, if we are going to be friends, you should at least know my name." She laughs as she fills a glass of beer.

"Fine, I'm Abel, and you are?"

"Katie, and she drinks Jack and Diet Coke."

"Seriously?" I am surprised; she doesn't look like a Jack and Coke type of woman.

"Yup, for all of this information, I'd better get a nice tip."

"Katie, you keep feeding me information I want, and you will get a great tip."

"Consider me your spy then." Katie laughs as she walks away to help other customers.

After another drink, I notice that the woman's drink is almost finished, so I wave over Katie. "Send her another drink, please."

"Sure thing." She rings it up and hails a server to deliver it. When the drink arrives, the lady looks straight at me, cocking her head slightly before smiling. Step one complete. Now for step two. After a bit, I walk over and ask her for a dance on the next song. All of her friends are well on their way to being trashed, so they giggle like middle schoolers. I hate when grown ass women act like teenagers.

Smiling, she says yes, and I hold out my hand. Taking it, she lets me guide her to the small dance floor. Katie may have clued me in on what the next song is, a song perfect for the Texas two-step, one of the dance styles I actually know.

"You know how to two-step?" I ask.

"Yes, but you are suppose to be the one leading me." She smirks.

"Well then, let me lead you." I swing her around and we dance the entire song. Every time I bring her close, she seems to get closer, which I take as a good sign.

At the end of the song, I hold her hand as we walk back to the table. Two men are trying to get the attention of the women, but I can tell they are going to end up with less money and blue balls.

"Ms., I will be at the bar if you want to dance again." I kiss the back of her hand to the oos and ahhs of her friends.

"My drink is almost empty, since you bought the last one, let me buy you one." She says.

"I won't say no to a drink, but I have expensive taste."

She looks me up and down before biting her lip, "as do I." Chuckling, she walks to the bar where I had been standing. Raising two fingers, Katie walks over after helping a customer.

"What will it be?" She winks at me.

"I would like another Jack and Coke and give him another of what he is drinking." The lady holds out her card.

"By the way, I am Annie." She holds out her hand to me. Taking it, I respond, "I'm Kevin." I know she is lying, but I also never give my real name, so it doesn't bother me. Looking at her, she is only a couple of inches shorter than my five nine. Looking down, I notice she is wearing flats. I like a woman my height or just a little shorter; it makes many things very convenient. I also noticed that while we were dancing, she wasn't wearing a ring, but sometimes when women are out with their friends, they don't. Not my problem if she is stepping out on her partner.

Katie brought the drinks and set them down before leaving.

"I haven't seen you in this bar before. You new to the area or new to the bar?"

"Both, I guess, and also neither."

"Cryptic."

"I can be." I wink as we clink glasses.

"So, you don't seem like your friends, not in a derogatory way, just different."

"You are perceptive. We all went to school together, we come out together once in a while, they do every Friday, but I can't."

"Business or personal, keeping you away?" It is a game; you talk about things, but you don't talk about things.

"Both at times, separately at others. You know how it can be."

"I definitely do." I reply, watching how 'Annie' surveys the crowd and the group of friends. She is definitely a former military member or in a field that requires attention to detail. I thought about calling the evening off, but the powerful woman standing near me pulls me in. I don't know what it is about her, but I can't keep my eyes off of her.

Finishing my drink, I put it down. Now to up the game. "Well, I should go, this is my third, and I need to drive."

"Why so soon? I am on my third as well. I won't be drinking more, but let's go dance some more." Annie grabs my hand and pulls me onto the dance floor.

"Does this mean you are going to lead this time?" I laugh.

"I mean, if you want me to." Annie says as she wraps her arm around my neck.

"No, I think I got it." I run my hands down from her shoulder blades, one resting on the small of her back and the other resting on her ass. I expect her to say something, but instead, when the song starts, she rubs against me.

One song turns into four, and we have another drink. "Do you want to wait? I need to get the girls in their Ubers," Annie says as one of her friends almost falls over.

"Go, help them. I will be here." My dick is hard just thinking about Annie pressed up against a wall or a car. I watch as she guides them out one by one, alone, much to the chagrin of most men in the bar.

While she is helping the women out, Katie brings over water and my tab. "Figured you wouldn't be drinking anymore." She says.

"You figure right, and as promised, here is your tip." I lay down a fifty and sign my name to the tab.

"Come back any time, 'Kevin'." She smirks as she walks away, quickly putting the crisp money in her pocket. If I have to guess, they pool tips here, but what they don't know doesn't hurt them.

"They are all in Ubers on their way home," Annie says as she rests her hands on my shoulders.

Rolling my neck, I turn to face her, "Did they drive here?"

"No, they all Uber together here, and then take separate Ubers home."

"Well, at least they are safe." I wrap my arms around her and kiss her neck.

"Want to go outside? It is hot in here." Annie steps back toward the door.

"Absolutely." I down the water and follow her to the parking lot that is still full of cars. She pulls me against the side wall of the bar, her lips crash into mine, hard and needy.

"You have protection?" She asks as she comes up for air.

"Always," I say as I whip her around and push her against the wall. Pulling her shirt off, I step back quickly to admire her figure. Before I step back, I unbutton and slowly lower her pants. She is wearing a matching lace bra and panty set, which, with my basic knowledge of women's intimates, I know is expensive. Carefully, I slide her underwear off before using one hand to unhook her bra while I kiss her neck and chest. My other hand runs through her slick folds, slowly entering her while my thumb rests on her clit.

"You don't get to have all the fun." Annie pushes me back and gets down on her knees before unzipping my pants. I watch her as she pulls my hard dick out and covers the tip with her tongue before she takes my entire length in her mouth. My head falls back as I brace myself on the wall with one hand while the other is in her hair.

"Fuck, if you want to be fucked, you need to sto—" before I finish, she stands back up, wiping her mouth.

"What are you saying?"

"Oh, you are something, aren't you?" I slip the condom on before pushing her against the wall, and I place both my hands on her hips as I lift her up. She wraps her legs around my waist as I slowly enter her. Her arms wrap around my shoulders as I pound into her. My fingers dig into her hips as she bucks against the wall. Annie isn't petite, but with my years of special forces training, I hold her with one hand while my other finds her clit. Slowly rubbing a circle, I could feel her tense up. Placing my head near her ear, I whisper, "Come for me, come on my dick." She throws back her head and screams, and I feel her tighten around me. I ride her orgasm as I thrust two more times before coming myself.

Holding her as we breathe, I slowly let her down on her feet, where she is unstable initially. I kiss her lightly on the mouth before kissing her on the forehead.

"That was—" I start to say.

"Great. Well, Kevin, have a good night." Annie quickly puts on her clothes before walking away. As she gets near the parking lot, she turns and waves before leaving.

"Incredible," I say to myself. I have been with women before, usually younger than my 32 years, but never one like Annie. I never go back for seconds, but Annie was making me question myself.

As I drive home, I can't stop thinking about her legs wrapped around my waist, or that I didn't care if anyone walked out and sees us. It is primal, and it is so fucking hot. Kansas City is a big place, especially since I am not even in Missouri, so the chances I will ever see Annie again are few and far between.

Reaching the house, the memories of what happened earlier are gone, the overpowering need for sleep and thoughts of Annie run through my mind as I strip off my clothes before falling into bed.

CHAPTER THREE

The following month, I just shuffle around the house. Breakfast, working out, walking the property, lunch, dinner, repeat. I think total freedom to do whatever I want to do would be nice, but instead, I am bored. The Friday after the bar where I met Annie, I thought about going back, but I didn't want to seem needy, and Katie had said that she didn't show up every Friday. So instead I stayed at my house and read.

On a Monday morning, I can't take it anymore. After getting up, I decide to drive into Kansas City and have a coffee and maybe at least some second-hand human contact. The drive into the city is as expected, with the morning unfolding with the same urgency as the other drivers. Getting to the coffee shop, I find a spot less than a block from the shop, which I feel is a sign from the universe that I am meant to have a coffee.

The inside was no less hectic than the outside. I snag a table and watch the crowd—light carves through the windows, highlighting hungover faces of young professionals trying to get their morning fix. Placing my backpack on the table, I join the rat race that is the line for coffee.

"What can I get you?" Says the barista with hair coming out of a bun from too many hours already.

"Black coffee, large, and a chocolate muffin if you have any more, please."

"That will be 6.50, cash or card?" She asks without even looking at me.

"Cash, keep the change." I hand over a ten and move quickly out of the way.

As I wait, I can hear the espresso machine churning out orders while employees yell at each other over the constant conversational level of customers.

I can appreciate this ordered chaos. Everything is a well-oiled machine, and most of the customers know their duty. As I wait, an order is handed over that is wrong, and a brief conversation results in apologies without raised voices. Finally, I hear, "Abel, black coffee and muffin?" I look up as the young man places both things on the counter and turns to work on another.

"Thank you." I raise my voice just slightly, in hopes he hears. Heading back to my seat, I sit looking out through the windows. Taking a sip of my coffee, it warms my throat, causing my nerves to come alive. It is strong, similar to what I drank during service, and for a minute, I just savor the bitterness of the coffee before even considering taking a bite of the muffin.

Just as I am unwrapping the warm chocolate muffin that I know will pair perfectly with the coffee, the din of conversation ebbs and flows. Standing out from the rest are two men huddled over a laptop, sitting two tables away. One is tapping furiously as he speaks. "Another one last night. Can you believe it?" Even though his voice is not pitched differently, I hear him plain as day, as if he is sitting across from me.

"Same MO?" The other man asks, taking a sip of his coffee. My internal antenna tunes to their conversation as I mindlessly eat my muffin, my coffee pushed to the side.

"Back door forced, alarm tripped at midnight, but by the time the police showed up, the house was secure other than the slight sign of damage to the back door."

"That is what? Four in the last week."

"Yeah, and everyone is just chasing their tails." The man with the laptop is bringing up floor plans. He turns the laptop just slightly, enough for me to see for a brief second before it is moved again.

My posture shifts, a change barely perceptible but all-encompassing. I pull out a pen and pad from my backpack, something I learned to carry when I was an 18-year-old fresh out of basic. My breathing quickens slightly, each inhale drawing in more than just air, but a future. The details flow onto the paper without conscious thought. They fit together like battle plans. I see connections before I write them down, but only barely. Security concerns, gaps, vulnerabilities, it is everything I know, a language drilled into me when I served. As the pieces fall into place, I smile as my concentration grows. This is what I am intended to do, and I am going to make it work.

I let the voices wash over me as I sit in the coffee shop, and a barista comes up to ask if I want more coffee on the house. I barely acknowledged her presence, nodding to let her know I would like a refill. My pen brings order to the chaos forming in my mind. Every new piece of intel sharpens my focus, transforming possibility into concrete action. My brain continues to take in all the voices, as it infuses them with the framework of my plan—pages upon pages filled with notes. I finally see a path, a place where I could operate on my own terms. Maybe it won't stop the memories, but I hope it will help to stop them.

CHAPTER FOUR

We are supposed to be on the same side, but the business advisor I hire is supposed to help guide me. He has a disarming confidence I can't trust. During the last week, I set up my office and create a professional business plan based on the notes I made at the coffee shop that one morning. Every day, my brain is creating new connections, and I can't wait to implement them.

His pen sweeps through my business plan like an insurgency. Circles and arrows, words like intel: Radio. Demographic. Pricing. Taxes. I sit in his office with military posture, back straight, and eyes sharp. The walls are crowded with diplomas and commendations for being Kansas City's best business advisor. They are all territories he's already conquered.

Finally, he looks up, "Consider local media channels."

"What does that mean?"

"Radio, TV, Newspaper, Social Media. Things that people look at now. Stay away from billboards; the return on investment isn't there. Start small and cheap, get a few clients, and work up from there."

"I can do that." I can, at least with his help.

He bends over the papers again, barely making a noise as he marks them. I grow restless, studying the exits, waiting for him to launch the attack.

After what seems like an eternity, he pushes the papers back to me. Steepling his fingers on his desk, he looks at me with the conviction of someone who's never heard the word no. "Overall, it is okay, but your pricing needs refinement." I sit there listening. He pauses to let that sink in before he continues. Then, in rapid succession, like a machine gun, he keeps talking. "Target broader. Business and residential, there are people who have money here who would want private security. You need additional package options; nothing is one size fits all anymore."

"That is doable." The plan is to take his suggestions and leave. My body is ready to escape, the room's walls are closing in with each passing minute.

"I don't think we will need to see each other again until you expand. Take this suggestion through, hit the radio advertising hard. You have seen the traffic here, everyone listens to the morning news. Radio is the way to penetrate the market." His words drive in. "98 percent of individuals who work in the Kansas City metro area commute." I nod, just a quick jerk of my head as I gather the documents.

"Thank you, I will do that. Do you have a suggestion for the radio station I should advertise on first?"

He smiles like a shark smelling blood. "Absolutely. KMBZ-FM is the biggest and best for your money."

"Thank you, I will reach out to them."

"You need a business name before you advertise." I hear him say as I am walking out the door.

The tension follows me out—the tension of knowing what I want to do mixed with the tension of worry. I am riding high, ready for the next adventure as I leave the building toward my car. Then the sound hits. Sharp and Sudden. A car backfires, its explosive retort sending me into a spiral. My body freezes, breath locks in my throat. The city shifts around me, past and present collapsing into one.

Everything surges and blurs. Everything talked about with the advisor fades, overtaken by commands. A voice from the past drags me back into the fight. I stumbled on the cracked sidewalk, caught between here and there. The memory rises, uncontainable, a tide of sound and color. Faces from that fateful day—the soldier whose luck has run out, bloodied and still, because of my arrogance.

"It wasn't your fault." Whispers a voice from the past.

"The hell it wasn't," I say, not knowing if it was out loud or just in my head.

My heart pounds a brutal cadence, fighting for control, for air. I struggle against the weight of it all, my thoughts like hair caught and tangled in barbed wire. A single, desperate effort to stay grounded, stay present. My chest heaves with quick, shallow breaths, each one a brutal reminder of where I am. Street in Kansas City. Home. Alive. Not gone, not battling.

The scene shifts again, slower now, and I pull completely free from the past. Reality anchors me, the street, the office, the plan, a firm grip in my head. I steady myself, inhale with focus, and count the breaths I take. It takes everything I have not to continue looking back, not to let the past pin me again. My failures, my decisions, ultimately the life that was taken. The urge to run is powerful. The desire, however, to win, to push forward, and try to escape the past, is more so.

I catch my footing, one step at a time. The adrenaline slowly fades. I let the last bit of it fuel the resolve I need. This was another ambush, another memory to outmaneuver, to overcome. I keep

moving, leaving the echo of gunfire and doubt in my wake. This time,
I won't allow the past to trail behind me home.

CHAPTER FIVE

The radio station sprawls ahead like a small and foreign nation. Phones ring out as if they are crying children. Staff in t-shirts and denim move between offices. Either by nature or training, I scan each chaotic scene, how they worked together like a unit, never stopping but always achieving their goal. I can hear the broadcast equipment humming behind the voices and footfalls. I arrived 15 minutes early, never one to arrive on time. The wait seems longer than it should be. I adjust my collar, and I sit up straight, uncertainty creeping in. She catches me off guard, her voice like a quick burst of a memory, and it goes straight to my dick.

"Abel Williams?"

Here she was, standing in front of me, the same but different, now saying my real name. I look up, willing my body to listen to my brain, to not make a fool out of me.

"That's me."

A small smirk crosses her face as she takes a step closer, holding her hand out, "I'm Stacy Reynolds." Oh, she knows who I am, fuck. Here she is standing as a walking contradiction from the last time I saw her in bohemian pants. The harsh lights that normally age a person does the opposite; she is as beautiful as that fateful evening in Overland Park. I catch a scent of citrus, bright against the station's office antiseptic aroma. She smiles with an assurance of someone who knows what she wants and knows how to get it, much the same way as that night. Only this time, I understand her a bit more. I stand with controlled precision, taking her offered hand. The shake was brief, firm, her eyes holding a glint of mischief along with a cool assessment.

"Glad you made it in today," she says, her voice carrying the same familiarity from the bar but with an edge of professionalism and confidence. It slips right through my defenses and lands a bullet straight to my heart.

"Yep," I reply, aware of my curt response. I soften before speaking again, "Thank you for having me."

She laughs, the same light musical sound that comes from that night, a sound I would love to hear at my house. *Where did that come from? Calm the hell down, Abel.* "Follow me," she grins as she turns, her words punctuated by the sway of her hips. The same hips my fingers itch to grab again.

I hesitate, just long enough to know it. I feel as if I am entering her space, a space that I may not come out of the same. Her walk is the opposite of mine; casual, inviting, and unconcerned with the thoughts raging through my head. Or maybe she is aware of them. She pulls me in, and I watch her back, wondering if I should leave, but I stop. This isn't because of my ego, this is my need to help, and so I trail after her, leaving the safety of the waiting area behind.

Stacy moves with the confidence of someone who is in her element. She runs this area, and she knows it. It is no different than when I was giving orders, but it feels different. We make our way through the controlled chaos of the station, the noise of phones, production rooms, and talking unyielding. I feel it press in on all sides, but I ground myself the best way I know how, watching Stacy walk in front of me. Her brightly colored shirt and pants keep me in the moment, and what a wonderful moment it is. Finally, she stops, and I survey the area around us. Beige walls with a door, opening the door, she stands to the side and gestures for me to enter.

As she follows me, I look around. It is a glass-walled room that feels both expansive and confining, a mix of being exposed but also intimate. I can see technicians hurrying past through the window, carrying cords, clipboards, and headsets. I stand looking at the machinery in the room until I hear her chuckle.

"It won't bite, you can sit here." She motions toward a seat with a microphone and headset, and nothing else. The other side is full of buttons, another microphone, a headset, and a phone. Sitting down, I take a deep breath, my back straight and my mind ready.

Looking at me one more time before putting on her headset on in one fluid motion, she cocks an eyebrow. "Ready?" She asks, already knowing from the paperwork I sent in for the interview that I am always ready.

CHAPTER SIX

The "On Air" light flashes red, and a surge of adrenaline hits. The familiar kick of a mission to launch, this time it isn't jumping out of planes, but talking about myself. Stacy's voice comes through my headphones, playful and assured, carrying none of the tension I feel in this moment. "Good Morning, Kansas City! This is Stacy Reynolds with KMBZ's Reynold's Reveals, a look at what is happening in Kansas City. Today, we have a special guest, one of our own, Abel Williams."

As Stacy goes through the initial intro and reads the current weather and traffic, I sit there and watch her. Her voice curls through the microphone, a smooth blend of invitation and curiosity. It fills the small place, and her voice rivets me. She could have been reading off the back of a shampoo bottle, and I would be as enthralled. The entire room leans into her confidence, her command of the airways. I square my shoulders and wait for her.

The 'On Air' light blinks off, and she stretches after taking her headphones off. "We have a one-minute commercial break, and then when we come back, it will be your turn, okay?"

I silently nod, unsure of my voice as I look into her eyes. There is a tapping on the glass, and she places the headphones back on. Looking at me, she nods.

Her entire demeanor shifts as the 'On Air' light blinks back on. "Welcome back to Reynold's Reveals," she announces to an unknown number of listeners, her smile clear through her voice. "Earlier I mentioned we have a special guest, Abel Williams, a former soldier who's traded in his uniform to return home and take up entrepreneurship. With his expertise and experience, he is starting up his own security company right here in Kansas City. Welcome, Abel!"

Her focus on me is absolute, her eyes are peering into my soul in a way that no one ever has before. "Thanks," I let the word stand alone, "I'm glad to be here." It is a calculated response, noncommittal and safe. I feel her energy shift as she leans into the microphone, ready to pursue any sign of weakness.

"We're excited to have you, so I am told you are from the area?" Her enthusiasm was like a warm interrogation lamp, one that I am familiar with.

"Yeah, born and raised in the Independence area."

"That's fantastic, it is always great to have people who are from here come back to settle down. So you've made quite the transition from the Army to civilian life. What's been the biggest challenge in getting your company started?"

"Adjusting back to civilian life definitely has been interesting, no more morning PTs or commanding officers. Also, learning the ropes of how to run a company, I went from running a unit to now running a company, and they aren't the same. Marketing is definitely something I struggle with."

"You mean like radio advertising?" she teases, her eyes sparkling. I know a prod when I hear one, the echo of the advisor's suggestion still fresh in my mind. I nod, careful not to concede too much.

Her eyes thin slightly, and the distance between us feels less like a gap and more like a thin line. One that I feel she is about to exploit. I watch her closely, seeing what direction she is going to take. For one, I am in a cat-and-mouse game, but I am the mouse. This woman already closed the distance once before, and it is only a matter of time before she does it again, but this time it likely won't be as much fun. Stacy's gaze meets mine, steady and daring, waiting for me to react.

Her questions pick up pace, each one stepping closer to the territory I mentally mark as off limits. The company, the strategy, and how I apply my training to a new, but different mission. "It's all about finding the gaps and covering them," I reply, hearing my language softening under the weight of her interest. It isn't fake. I can see she has a legitimate interest in what I have to say, and it makes me sit up straighter, to take notice of just what questions she is asking and when. As I change my posture, so does she, mirroring mine. Mentally, I tell myself I am going to stick to the business side, nothing about my past.

"What has surprised you about starting this venture?" She asks seemingly innocently, but I know she already has a list of questions lined up, ready to ambush me if needed.

"Everything, I just incorporated last week, so I am still getting my feet under me." I left it open, enough for her to fill the space with no need to ask questions. Her fingers trace the outline of the microphone, a small seductive gesture that makes me rethink the line I am holding. Her eyes meet mine, playful but calculating, inviting the kind of questions I am not ready to answer.

Stacy's questions stayed neutral, back and forth, my answers melding with her questions in a strange dance, one that I know is going somewhere, but I am not sure where. I relax, as does she, as our banter becomes friendly. I keep my rehearsed script about my business, safe answers that require little exposure. Her persistence and smile wear me down as I remember how her mouth felt around me. As if she knows, she leans forward, elbows on the table, her hair tumbling over her shoulder as she switches tactics.

"Do you think your military experience gives you a unique perspective?" Her voice is smooth but piercing.

It is a shot at something deeper, a line of questions I don't know if I can answer. I think about all of the boxes, especially the one in the closet, still left to be unpacked. Thinking of the box unleashes the ghosts, the screams rattling through me. My jaw clenches against the memory, trying to stay present. "It helps with operations." Managing, I can see she sees more, sees the internal battle. Continuing, "I did a lot of strategic thinking and planning while I served, and that has transitioned well." I keep it short, to the point, fighting the urge to let her see how deep it all goes.

She doesn't flinch. If anything, my clipped response causes her to be more intent, to focus more on me. Her presence steadies mine in a way that is impossible to ignore. I feel like it would be okay to give her the answers. Her warmth and seemingly genuine curiosity edge into places I've kept under lock and key for a long time. My military past was something I've learned to contain, to hold at bay with discipline and distance. It doesn't always work, but I am making progress. Yet here it is, leaking out, amplified on at least a regional scale, and unmistakable.

Her expression was open, caring, guarding, drawing me in with its unexpected sincerity. "And how do you handle the transition? You have been out what, two months now?" she asks, like she can see right through my façade, through all the layers I built since leaving the service.

"About that, and I'm working on it," I admit, a hint of the unexplored and unscripted in my tone. A stray sense of possibility, of the unknown, hangs on the edge of the words. Her interest in me, or at least my words, leaves no room for ambiguity, and my answer sits thicker than it means to. I breathe out, a tension of unsaid things stretching out between us.

She lets it sit for a minute, neither of us filling the space. I expect her to say something, to lighten the mood, instead she regards me, not as something broken, but as something stronger. I stop short of saying more, remembering how words have the power to outflank intentions, and my intentions are my business. As I watch her, the sudden awareness of something more hits me right in the middle of my chest.

"I have worked alongside many veterans, regardless of where or how they served, and I know that transition can be difficult. Sometimes, it sadly can be near impossible." The haunting look in her eyes tells me all I need to know. There is someone, even if just an acquaintance, in her life who didn't make it. She clears her throat before changing gears.

"So our time is about over. Before we talk about how you can be contacted, do you have a business name? It doesn't appear in my notes."

Laughing, "That is probably the hardest part of opening a business, but yes, I do, it is—" I pause and, without thinking, "Mongoose Security." Trying not to think about the implications of that name as I wait for her to ask me another question.

"Great, so how can interested parties contact you?"

"Well, check back in about an hour, and I will have a website and email. In the meantime, you can contact me directly at Abelwilliams at gmail dot com."

"Thank you, so listeners, if you need personal security or just a fresh look at what you have, contact Abel Williams at Mongoose Security." As she speaks, I quickly buy the domain and create an email account before some random listener beats me to it.

"Thank you for having me, Ms. Reynolds." I smile, and the glint in her eye tells me this isn't the end of our conversation.

"You've certainly given our listeners a lot to think about," she says, her voice rich and welcoming as it is at the beginning, void of the intensity while asking questions. "And maybe even a little inspiration."

"Maybe," my voice is lighter than it has been in a long time. The burden of holding back has lifted. It is as if Stacy sees without me speaking and understands without judgment. Even fellow soldiers judge, but here, a woman that I thought I would never see again is sitting in front of me, accepting me for what she knows. I'm not sure how it happened, or what I'll do now that I have briefly opened up. All I know is she has found a way through, past the lines that I carefully crafted and drawn since leaving the military.

Stacy's outro matches the intro, a quick look at the weather, current events, and traffic. It is precise, driving, and engaging. It is an impression that isn't soon to leave. Her gaze lingers in a way that suggests she has more questions she wants to ask. I thought I was prepared, coming in to talk to a radio personality, but I obviously have not done my research, and I swear it will be the last time I am caught unaware. As she signs off and the 'On Air' light dims, I realize I may have underestimated not only 'Annie' from the bar, but Stacy sitting across from me. She takes her headphones off and walks to the door.

CHAPTER SEVEN

Before I can move, Stacy is out of her seat. I think she is opening it, but I hear the faint click of the lock engaging. Stretching as she walks back to the desk, she flicks a button, and the windows go dark. Her grin as she steps toward me is both frightening and fucking hot. I roll back slightly as the room changes, with an energy that differs from during the interview. Her laughter breaks through as her hands rest on my shoulders. I feel the corners of my mouth lift; her laughter is infectious.

"Abel, you did great." She says as her fingers brush my cheek. The enthusiasm in her voice is as genuine as her earlier interrogation. "I bet the listeners love hearing you speak. I know I do."

"Thanks, um, should I be going?" I reply, trying to reconcile the difference between the sharp edge of her questions and the warmth of her presence as she runs her fingers through my hair. The way she shifts so easily from one to the other catches me off guard.

"No, I usually take about an hour to myself after the show. I am the only one who uses this sound booth, and I had blackout windows put in. Sometimes my shows can be…difficult."

"Do you only do the morning show?" My brain cannot latch on to her actions, but my dick is fully ready for whatever she has planned.

"No, Reynold's Reveals is both live in the mornings, and I do a separate section that usually airs in the evenings. They are much darker in nature." She leans over, her hand running from my hair to rub against my dick as it strains against my pants.

"Should we be doing this? Do you do this a lot?" I stammer; I am acting like a 20-something-year-old.

Leaning down, she whispers in my ear, "Why, don't you want a replay of that night, Kevin?" My eyes roll back as she grips my dick. "To answer your question, I have never done this or that night before, and honestly, I haven't planned on doing it until you walked in the studio." Sitting in my lap, she licks my ear and lightly runs her tongue down my neck.

I didn't know whether or not to believe her, but a round two with this woman, I will not turn down. Picking her up off my lap, I stand up. "I am never one to tell a woman no. Hard or soft?" I ask as I pull her shirt off.

"You choose, I have the time." She laughs as I slide her pants down. Wearing nothing underneath, I look at her with a smirk.

"I thought you haven't done this before?" Not unsure but also a bit wary.

"Unless it's for a business meeting, I don't wear underwear."

I pick her up and put her on the desk before getting on my knees.

"Well, since you got to taste me, I guess it is time to taste you. You aren't loud are you?" Pushing her legs apart, I ask.

I can tell she shaves, but not everything. The front is trimmed with the point directing me straight to her clit. I don't take the bait, though, instead starting at her left knee. I kiss and lick up her inner thigh before going back to her right knee. As I kiss and run my tongue in lazy circles, I use one of my hands to knead her other thigh. I am in no hurry, and there is a part of me worried this is the last time, so why not make it last? Her hands are in my hair, trying to pull me to her core, but I am resisting the urge, even as every fiber of my being wants to be face deep in her folds.

No, I am going to tease, at least a little. Taking my time, leaving her legs to stand up to kiss down her neck and across her chest. Nibbling at her hip bone, my fingers play leisurely in the trimmed hair at the apex of her thighs. I feel her wiggle under me, and I place both of my hands on her upper thighs. "What do you think you are doing?" I question.

"Trying to get in a better position." She smiles, trying to be sweet, but I know what she is doing. I yank her butt off the desk as I kneel again. She yelps as the only thing holding her up is my arms around her thighs.

"Now where was I?" I pull her up slightly as I lick at the crease between her thigh and torso. I can see her glistening as I run my tongue straight up from her hole to her clit. She gasps as she tries to hold my head on her clit.

"Oh no, it is my turn." Using the flat of my tongue, I lick her again before diving in. My dick is straining on the seams of my pants, but I want to feel her come on my tongue before I join.

Pushing her back on the desk, her butt barely on the surface, I insert a finger in her as I concentrate on her clit. It throbs slightly, and I move to the sides of her folds, alternating between slowly licking and flicking with my tongue as my finger thrusts in and out. When I feel she is wet enough, I pull my finger out to the sound of her complaining before I thrust two in. Without knowing for sure, other than what I experienced at the bar, I figure she is the type who likes external orgasm versus internal, so while my fingers continue to thrust in and make a come-hither movement slowly, my primary focus is on her clit and the surrounding skin.

I suck on her clit softly before pulling away to focus on another area. She holds my head on it. "Right there, just like that." Now I am not a man to tell a woman no, so I stay, alternating between flicking and sucking. I can feel her walls tighten against my fingers, but I keep thrusting them in as deep as I can. I look up to her, and her head is thrown back, her eyes closed as she holds perfectly still.

Using my other hand to pull back the skin covering her clit, I suck deeply, and she comes hard around me, sucking my fingers in while her clit throbs against my tongue and lips. She barely lets out a yelp as she comes. I hold on as she rides out the spasms, each one gradually decreasing. When she is done, I pull out my fingers and put them in my mouth, sucking off her juices as she watches me through tented eyes. She leans on her elbows, watching me step back and adjust myself.

As much as I want to be balls deep in her tight pussy just this moment, I regain my composure.

"Aren't you going to fuck me?" She says as she sits there with her legs spread, inviting me in for another round.

Stepping in between her legs, she has a victorious grin on her face until I kiss her forehead. "As much as I want to be in you all day long, I need to take care of some things."

She doesn't glare, she doesn't throw things, instead she nods, picks up her clothing, and puts it on. She is back to Stacy Reynold's professional radio personality.

"When you get your business fully up and running, we should grab coffee sometime," Stacy says, her voice bright and without malice. I expect anger like I experienced before, but not with her.

"Honestly, I'd love to hear more about how you plan to tackle security in KC." Her eyes meet mine, but it is only truthfulness.

It is a straightforward invitation, nothing that I can tell is amiss, the kind that has no right to be as complicated as it feels, especially with what just happened. I hesitate, this is a woman who is quickly burrowing through my last defenses, and at this point in my life, I do not need the distractions, no matter how nicely they are presented. Before I could formulate a plan to excuse myself, my brain answers for me, "Sure, why not?" I feel a shift in my tone, one that I plan on beating out of myself the minute I get home.

Stacy opens the door and stands there as I leave the room. She walks me toward the front door, all the while talking. "Thank you for going off record, explaining in depth more about your business and past. I hope that eventually you will detail some of your abilities on the record." Her voice is loud enough for others to hear, and I know exactly what she is doing. She is setting the stage so no one can question what transpired in her booth. Reaching the waiting room, she smiles and offers her card. I take it, looking down at the script with a written phone number below the name. Looking up at her, her smile is genuine, a lightness that I would just soil if I get too close.

She does not seem to notice my change in expression. "Thank you, Ms. Williams, that is much more than I expect. I am not sure how much you would talk about your past, and I am glad that I didn't scare you off with my questions."

"Not yet," I answer.

"Great, so for the coffee shop, there is one right around the corner, and I think you will really like it. It has great coffee, and just the right kind of chaos that allows you to watch people, but also not too much that you can't concentrate on the company you may be with." She winks.

"That sounds great, and like a place I will enjoy. I really appreciate you taking the time to interview me." I say as two technicians walk by. The lobby is busy, the activity I am more accustomed to tracking. The noise level is good enough for a cover for what I want to tell Stacy. For the first time, though, the phones, the equipment, and the talking doesn't seep into my brain as fast or nearly as much. Instead, I can focus on what Stacy is saying.

"There's always a ton going on here." She says as if she notices my concentration slowly slipping. Placing her hand on my arm, she looks up at me. "You have to promise me you won't go AWOL before we get that coffee."

I laugh, surprising myself, "I'll be there," I assure her, more certain of it than I am of my car being in the same place in the parking garage.

My attention keeps returning to her as she talks about her favorite coffee and what she is planning on talking about for the next radio segment. She speaks with her hands, and I watch as her gestures map the air as she speaks. I can't remember the last time I've been this curious about anyone, or the last time I let myself feel this way at all. It was before my last deployment, before everything I knew fragmented both domestically and internationally, before reforming in the desert's unforgiving sun.

I catch myself wondering how soon we can set a time, a question that rises with an impatience I haven't felt since getting off the plane in Kansas City. It is reckless and honest, and not just because I want to explore every inch of her body, but I also want to explore her mind.

I back into the doors and stop. "Hey, Stacy." I stop her mid-sentence, "I have to go, but I will be in touch."

The look she gives is a mix of victory and sadness, as if she has won but also lost.

"You'd better call the number on the card," she replies, her voice carrying as I step out onto the busy sidewalk. I know if I don't walk away now, we will be back in her sound booth, and this time the excuses won't be as justified. I watch as she spins and walks away, with just a knowing swag to her hips. A rare possibility presents itself on her heels, and I know that the future has changed, even slightly, to something I might have no control over.

CHAPTER EIGHT

I know I shouldn't go. I get an email from the VA about how they are having a combat veteran meeting in the basement of a restaurant. The meeting disbands for a break with a shuffle and a cough as if we didn't just sit for an hour saying almost nothing, but the emotions are thick. I slip into the hallway like an overdo ghost. The lights buzz, as if they are full of insects, as I hurriedly made my way past the faces and unanswered questions. I follow the signs of daylight, ignoring the sounds of the others as they reassemble into a group dynamic. The stairwell is unguarded, as if understanding what I need. I take the stairs fast, as I reach the door, I throw it open and take a deep breath, one to not only get my bearings but also to escape the basement.

I let my steps lengthen, shaking the weight of the room. The voices stay with me, though, trailing me down the sidewalk. Keeping my head down, I fight the grip of the meeting that exposes more than I mean to show. I didn't use many words, but the emotions are there. Every single person likely feels the emotions, including the so-called therapist who parades our issues out in front of us.

I thought it might help, hell, I thought maybe some of my old unit might be there. Some settled near Kansas City, if I remember right. Instead, it is folding chairs and harsh lights, eyes locking on me as I introduced myself. The air was full of emotion, some understanding, and some volatility. We were supposed to take a break and have some stale coffee and store-bought cookies, instead, I had to create distance. I knew it was going to be my turn to explain why I was there. It may be easier if I knew, if I understood what drew me to find fellow veterans, but their stories weren't mine. They hadn't seen what I saw, nor do I wish that on them.

As I walk down the street, I breathe in my freedom. Distance is what I need, not to talk about what happened time and time again with people who are there for selfish reasons. Not to be told by some therapist who never served what I need to do. No, I need time and space and silence so deep it could smother the past or make me deal with it.

I will not call Stacy, as much as I am sure she would listen, I need to face this myself, at least for the time being. I want to, though, so badly. To hear her voice, to see her dance, to smell her citrus aroma. I am no good to her like this.

The rest of the afternoon unfolds like a map I know how to read. I make it back to my car, and without thinking, I drive home to the ever-shrinking office. It isn't my imagination that the office is becoming smaller, it is the equipment, the filing cabinets, the surveillance computers, everything is expanding faster than I could anticipate.

As I get home, I decide to walk first, to clear my mind. Every step from my car marks a hesitation. Faces float up, unmoored and insistent. They are always there, but I am not in command of them; they are part of my history, but not my complete history. Some share the same scars, some the same stories. We are all on the same side, but it feels unknown. It feels like I am detached from them.

My pulse slows as I reach the bottom of the hill my house sits on. My hands begin to unclench from the meeting. It is not a request, almost a demand by them to tell my story, about my last deployment, about who I lost. It is not just my last deployment, but a culmination of all of them, putting me on the path I now follow.

As I watch the sun set, my cell rings. Looking at it, it is an unknown number, but since I am using my number for Mongoose until I can get a separate line, I answer it.

"Mongoose Security, Abel speaking." With the way I am feeling, I don't want to put on a mask, but I know this is the first step for my business and for my healing.

"Abel Williams?" A familiar woman's voice asks. It is sweet like honey, but I feel the bitterness behind it.

"Yes, how can I help you?"

"Abel, this is Amanda, you know your girlfriend."

"I don't have a girlfriend by the name of Amanda. I used to, but it was a long time ago. You must have the wrong number." I know she doesn't, but I will not slide back into anything.

"You've always been so funny. I heard you on the radio with that skank. I am sure you tried to contact me when you got home. Sorry, I changed my number."

"What do you want?"

"I want to see you, I want to get back together."

"Amanda right now is not the best time, but I can tell you right now, we are not, nor ever going to get back together. I told you that in my letter to you two deployments ago."

"I just figured that was because of your deployment, and that you didn't mean it." Her voice turns pouty. I can envision it now, her lower lip sticking out, eyes trying to widen and look innocent. I roll my eyes before straightening my shoulders.

"Amanda, I am going to tell you this once, and only once. We are done, we have been done for years. You made sure of that with every bed you jumped into. I need and have a new life."

"What with that brunette slut that opens her legs for anyone?" Her vitriol spits over the line.

Resisting my urge to rise to the bait. "I haven't seen anyone since getting back. I went to an interview for my business, you know the one I answered with?"

"Knowing her, you probably fucked her to get the interview."

My nerves are getting tight, and I don't want to yell at her, that is precisely what she wants. To be the victim.

"Well, that isn't what happened, so unless you have something else to talk about, I am going to hang up."

"I need to see you."

"No, you don't," I respond, knowing exactly where this is leading.

"Just once, I just want to see you again, we had so many fun times."

"Absolutely not, I am hanging up, have a good life." I hang up before she can say something or cry. It is her way; if she doesn't get what she wants, she turns on the waterworks, and I am not falling for it anymore.

I am mad, and for so long I tried to rein in my feelings, to push them back to become a better soldier. As I sit here, some of the fellow veterans carried their pain like badges, proud and defiant, that they had lived through it. I could tell others held it close like I did, not afraid to speak, but knowing what speaking would do. I left before my story could be told. It is my story, and I cannot accept that some of those veterans would take my pain and mold it into their own.

The rumble of a train, along with the whistle, brings me back to my walk. I know I need help. I know that a meeting like that is not the way. Shaking my head, I look at my house, remembering the good, the future, and I push up the hill. I will not let a group of veterans tear me down without me saying a word. We are supposed to be in this together, not separate. I need to find my people. My unit in the civilian world.

CHAPTER NINE

Over the next week, I make it a mission to get out of my house, not just for work, but for my peace of mind. I find a park, creating distance between myself and my work. Between Stacy and me. Not because I want to distance myself from her or from work, but because I know I need it. The gym at my house only further isolates me and I know that is not the best way. It never will be.

Sunlight slices through the branches as I run. I cut deeper into the park every day, further into unfamiliar territory. The pond appearing on my left is an ambush of brightness, small waves striking the edge as if they are cleaning the past. I know when I hit the pond, I am just starting. It is a touchstone, one that I know I can return to when I need peace. I stay on target, instead of pausing at the pond, I continue to move. Every step I run, every thought becomes smaller.

I cover more ground every day as I become more confident in my surroundings. I feel at peace, my mind finally able to untangle some of the past, and slowly I am able to let go of things holding me back.

One day, I am running, and instead of running past the pond, I stop. It feels right at this time to take a break. My mind needs it, and so does my body. I pause near the bench by the pond, the water sparkling in the sun. The wind is just enough to push the ripples higher than usual onto the land. I let my mind free and it scatters in every direction. Leaves rustle above, creating a wind chime discord. Ducks cut across the pond, oblivious to me as they show their young how to dive. My focus even feels the wind, brushing against my sweating arms and legs. My mind is soothing as I focus on the main path, holding onto the awareness. Old instincts take over, my muscles taut, ready to run. I keep my actions slow as I really view the space around me.

The sharp crack breaks through, loud and unexpected. It is the finality of a bullet finding its mark. I don't think, my mind goes from soothing to focused in less than a heartbeat. My body acts on its own, a quick dive behind a bench, my hand trying to find my service weapon, instincts hard-wired and immediate. I hit the ground, I feel the grass damp beneath me, breathing short and fast, but my mind is elsewhere. The chaos has an echo, it doesn't stay in the present. It ricochets inside me, exploding into the sharp angles of memory.

I am fully there again, sounds collapsing in, gunfire tearing through the air. The desert sun is harsh as the sand in my eyes. Everything compressed, the world no longer present, but entirely in the past. My heart beats out a tempo that risks coming out of my chest. I can't outrun the scene, it played out in high-speed clarity. I am helpless but to watch as the voices ring out through the dust and smoke, words fragmented and jagged. *Stay low, Move! Explosions ripped through the rush of the battlefield consumed me completely.*

A name tears from my throat, my voice strange and faraway as if I am hearing it and not saying it. "KESSLER!" The memory pins me, the past, the most real thing I'd known. It is as if the last six months have been a dream. My mind sees what my body felt: dust, sweat, heat, chaos. There is blood on the ground, every sound amplifying until it drowns everything else out. I am out of time, senses slam back into that place, and I know if I don't move, I will be next. The edges of the battle are too sharp, too bright, and it carries with it a terrible weightlessness. It is the moment before we lost it all.

A voice reaches in, cutting and unknown. "Hey man, you're okay, you aren't there, you are safe at home." I blink against the force of the sun. It is a command, one that I am trained to follow. "You're okay, you are home, you aren't in the battle." As my eyes focus, I see it is another jogger, one I have seen before, unarmed and calm. I can see, though the beads of sweat on his brow, the tension in his jaw. He may be relaxed now, but it hadn't been that way.

The past shatters into bits of dust around me. I shake the last of the fragments, disoriented, afraid to breathe as he sits there, just waiting. The quiet stuns me, my body is still in fight or flight, my heart is still pounding, and I am having issues catching my breath. Suddenly, the wind picks up, and I feel the sweat pull from my body.

The jogger doesn't move, slowly, he speaks, slow and steady. "Hey, you're back." He pauses, looking around, "I heard it too, a bullet somewhere deeper in the trees."

My hands are flat on the ground as I process what he is saying. I force myself to focus, to breathe in and out. The pieces reassemble. I had been running, and there was a noise. The other man keeps his distance, worried but not willing to come closer. I understand.

"Hey, I'm Erik. I am near the pond when it hit. I saw you go down, but it took a minute for me to reorient myself. You good?" He asks, his words neutral as if we are both hedging around the truth.

I feel ashamed that someone saw that, and I feel out of control. I nod, a quick and exact gesture, the only thing I am sure I can do in the moment before speaking. "No, but I will be." The words are tight, almost cracking. Even though I know he knew what happened, I cannot explain it. He nods, but doesn't press, giving me the space I need, but I don't necessarily want.

Tipping his head, he takes off, running down the path back toward the parking lot. The look on his face tells me everything. He experienced it too, but neither of us are ready or open to talk about

it. It feels almost relieving to know someone else is out here—
someone who feels the same way. My mind doesn't automatically go
back to the past, instead, it focuses on the feeling of not being alone.
I run a hand through my hair, pushing the bits of memory still
clinging away. The park returns quickly to its pace. The ducks return
to the pond. I stand, tension still running through my hands as they
shake. I thought I could outrun the past, but this time it has pushed
me over.

No, I cannot face this alone, but I am not going back to the
failure; they call a meeting. No, I will not bare myself to the
unknown. I run back to my car, faster than usual, if nothing else to
leave the memory of shaking on the ground like a piece of grass
pushed over by the wind. I am stronger than that. If I am not, then I
will be.

Arriving at home, I look at my phone, debating whether to
call now or wait. Looking down at myself, I decide to take a shower,
peeling off my clothes as I make my way to the primary bedroom. I
ignore my office and the box holding the memories, especially of the
name I screamed. I may not remember everything, but I remember
calling out his name. My failure, my memory to carry forever.

Standing in the shower, my hand flexed on the glass. Tremors
sneak in, betraying me in their subtle insistence. My mind goes back
to how the day spun out of my control. The flashback that dragged
me back to places I couldn't escape. Standing under the water, I let
the hot water clean my skin. Resisting the desire to cry, there is a part
of me that wants to. Without realizing, looking down my skin was
red. I don't know if it is from the hot water or the scrubbing. As I
turn off the water, I lean against the wall. I don't know how long I
stay there until I feel cold, stepping out, I dry off before walking

naked into my bedroom. I stand looking at myself in the glass before pulling on boxer briefs and a pair of sweatpants.

Walking out into my house, I survey it. It's brutal, neat, like a fortress I have fortified against disorder. It is as if I cannot control the disorder of my brain, so I force my surroundings to surrender. My bed is crisp and immaculate, something any drill sergeant would smile at, with its hospital corners dug in with military discipline. Everything outside the office stands at perfect right angles, aligned with the walls or other furniture. I have no decoration, nothing on the walls, and it is a testament to the minimalism of my new life. Or I think it is, now looking at the walls, I feel empty, as if something should be there to keep me in the present.

My chest tightens at how close Stacy is compared to everyone else. The only ones closer were the men I fought next to on my last deployment. Even Amanda, the woman whom I supposedly loved, never understood or got that close. I pull my phone from my pocket, debating what to do. Do I work on my business, or do I call the spicy brunette who, in the course of my time in Kansas City, turned my life upside down? I stare down at my phone, hesitating as if it might go off in my hand.

Without thinking, I pull Stacy's business card off my dresser and dial the number. There is a pulse of recklessness that shoots through me. I lock it down. Once Stacy knows the real me, she will run, it will happen. The line connects, and I hear it ring once, twice, and I almost disconnect. It is no different than the waiting I did overseas, except I need this connection more.

"Hello?" Stacy's voice is bright with an underlying confusion. This is where the disconnect happens. My mind unwinds the fact that she is not halfway across the world, she is in the same town, just beyond my reach.

"Hey, it's Abel, Abel Williams," I say, uncertain if she will remember me.

"I see you finally called." Her voice tinges with laughter. I lower myself onto the futon.

"Yeah, I've been busy, umm." I don't know what to say. This is the first time I am tongue-tied around a woman.

"Same, so you haven't hit up any bars?"

Laughing, "Not at all, I went to one a while ago and there was this woman. I just can't get my mind off her."

"Oh, really? I bet she was something special then." Her voice drops a bit, almost but not quite husky.

"Yeah, she was, but since the interview, I have been working on the business." I let the lightness in, push away some of the dark.

"You take any of my advice?"

"I am getting there, I did some thinking and started running."

"Oh, how is the running going?"

"Well, I guess." As I talk, I look around the room, the stark corners growing softer.

"So when do you want to come back to the studio?"

"I'm not sure, I would like to get established before I come back, but the thought of coming back is definitely growing on me."

"Oh, is that the only thing growing on you? I'm glad, I was worried the red light might scare you off." She laughs at her own joke.

"No, you didn't, did you?" I feel my voice shift from stoic to something more free-flowing. I relax into the futon some more.

"Not one bit, I don't take you for a man that fears a little red light," her response hangs in the air. I smile at her attention to detail.

"So how was your day?" I shut my eyes as I lean back, blocking out the world I have so carefully created and controlled. It is easier this way, instead of looking at the bare walls, letting Stacy's voice anchor me. She tells me about the beginning of her day at the station, and the stories that unfold make me laugh.

I can see her talking, filling the space around her with confident motion, defying every single pattern I am used to. The mental picture is as clear as anything I can remember. Her hair catching the lights as she moves, her hands flow through the sentences, matching the words in an unintended but perfect choreography.

I hear her voice wrap itself around me, persistent, engaging, leaving no room for ghosts or flashbacks.

"Oh, you'll never guess," she says, teasing the words into a long stretch. "I had to call security twice this afternoon. Nothing as sophisticated as what you offer, but still."

I sit up straight, the hair on the back of my neck. "Twice?"

"Yeah, a nutty fan, and a lost delivery guy," she answers, her inflection rising with amusement, "One was looking for me, and the other for cupcakes."

"Not sure which one is worse," I say, a hint of levity easing in. I let the chair hold me, feeling the way my breathing slows.

"It's a toss-up. Between you and me, the fan was easier to handle."

"Doesn't surprise me." I open my eyes, seeing the familiar neatness of my space, but I see it in a different light. It is not as cold as before, but I worry the minute I hang up, it will revert.

She shifts the topic off her with her customary agility. I do not notice the change at first, the way my thoughts loosen as she talks.

"Now that you have had some time after the interview, how is your future looking?"

"I still have some planning to do. I have received some initial requests. Mostly trying not to screw it up."

"You won't," she assures, her tone dipping into sincerity. "It'll be great. You're more ready than you think."

She cannot know how close the truth is, how it carries an impact I am still learning to absorb. Her optimism and faith in me cut through, sweeping away bits of uncertainty that cling to me since the flashback hit earlier.

We talk late into the evening, Stacy's observations spinning into stories that take lives of their own. They draw me in with their unpredictable turns, their lack of agenda or structure. She tells me about upcoming segments and how she thinks I would be interested. She mentions the shooting at the park. My breath catches.

"I was there."

"You were what?" Stacy's voice fills with concern.

"I wasn't at the actual shooting, but I was running and heard it."

"How are you? Why didn't you tell me before? Here I have been rambling on."

"I am better now that we are talking. It was hard, but another veteran, or I assume it was a veteran, was near me."

"I'm glad you weren't alone. My producer wanted me to go down there and interview people, but that isn't my thing."

"Oh, you prefer to stay in your sound booth?" I lighten the mood slightly, remembering the end of our interview.

"Yes, but not for that." Stacy laughs. "You know that was the first time I ever did anything like that in the sound booth. I take my job and profession seriously."

"I can tell that about you, and for what it's worth, I have done nothing like that either."

"As much as I would like to talk to you longer, I have to be up in the morning early." Stacy's voice stops my thoughts.

"I still need to eat and then get some work done, but I have enjoyed this."

"You never called about coffee? Do you want to meet up tomorrow if you're not busy between my segments?" Stacy's voice is hopeful but cautious, as if she is not used to being the aggressor or she is facing down a predator.

"That sounds great." For the first time, I am excited. Her voice soothes parts of me I didn't realize needed it.

"Great, see you tomorrow." Her words are breezy and bright.

We hang up, but the connection stays. I lean my head back against the futon, the last traces of the tension from earlier unraveling as I let it go.

I hear her voice echoing in the space around me, in my mind, in the very air that no longer feels as stifling. Everything is less defined, softer. I feel refreshed and ready to work. As I walk into the office, my eyes dart to the closet. The box doesn't seem as threatening, and the past doesn't scream as loudly. I let my breathing fall into the same pattern, following the lines of comfort she has drawn.

For the first time since stepping off the plane, I feel the full weight of what I have been carrying, and the sweet, undeniable relief of putting it down.

Stacy has got through in a way I'd never expected, catching me off guard and leaving me disarmed. It is not the type of tactical error I am used to. It is the kind I could learn to live with, and it makes me smile.

I see here, in my office, looking over the plans and drifting in the calm, the sense of a new possibility lingering in the atmosphere. I am excited for coffee the next day, and maybe I will not wait long before making the next phone call. The thought crosses my mind like an act of insurgency. I feel hope, pushing forward in ways I never expected. A smile forms as I begin work on finalizing package options.

CHAPTER TEN

I arrive early, a lone figure in the symphony of a mid-morning café rush. I quickly claim a corner table, away from the coffee machines and voices fighting for attention. It allows me a post for quiet observation, to subconsciously watch for danger. Dark roast and ambition fill the air, the scene familiar. I watch as a purple jeep pulls up outside, precise and confident. I watch as Stacy jumps out of the car, luminous in boho pants and a tank top, a renegade among the suits of the nine-to-fivers. My posture softens as she walks in.

The entire energy of the room tilts to her, even as its patrons pretend not to notice. Looking around, she sees me, and her smile lights up her face. Sidestepping tables and patrons, she walks straight to me. We greet each other, warm but awkward, in a new territory with uncertain lines. The red of her tank top pops against the industrial palette of the café. Her hair is a cascade of light as it flows down her back. She floats past the tans and darks of the business suits, her boho pants sweeping a path as curious and jealous eyes follow. She looks both out of place and perfectly at home.

"How was the drive over? Why did you drive over?"

"I have to go meet someone after this, so I drove."

"Nice jeep." I motion for her to sit.

"I will after I get something to drink. Are you drinking anything?"

"Yeah, my order should be up soon," I say with happiness, not for having a coffee, but for being able to spend time with Stacy.

"Okay, I will be back shortly." She places her bag on the table before walking over to stand in the ever-growing line.

I lean back as she sits, tracking the pulse of the room. Conversations buzz in unison, snippets of morning rituals—young professionals hunching over laptops, their coffee orders occupying a prime location on the table. I inhale the scent of new possibilities, the air alive with the urgency of the morning rush—this type of disorder I understand.

As I survey the café, my attention flicks to the street. The sidewalk is full of people in a rush to get somewhere, some on their phones, others carrying briefcases and walking with an urgency that may be fixed by leaving earlier. It always amazes me how people will wait to get somewhere and then blame everything but themselves when they are late. In my experience, running late can mean someone's death, not just a mark against your record.

I catch the red walking back toward the table with two coffee cups.

"You didn't have to get mine." Our fingers brush as she hands me one, the brief contact leaving a warmth that lingers and brings my memory back to how she tastes. I see a flush of her cheeks, wondering if she is thinking the same thing.

"It was there when I picked mine up, so why not?" She smiles.

"I am glad you made it," I say, unsure of what words are coming out of my mouth.

"I told you I would, and honestly, you are enjoyable company." She smiles as she takes a sip of her drink.

"You must not know me that well." I quip.

"So far, I like what I see and feel." She winks, and I swear I blush a bit. She is a woman who has no qualms with going after what she wants, and I appreciate the hell out of that.

I just nod, not trusting my words. We sit, a cautious distance but close without thought. Her presence is vibrant and unpredictable, as it has been before, a counterpoint that fits into the puzzle that is my own measured demeanor. We are both aware of the differences, both stepping beyond boundaries we know.

The café seems to hold its breath, waiting to see who will change the subject first, or to speak both of our thoughts out into the open.

"How are you truly? I know you said you were okay after yesterday, but I know how much it can shake someone who saw combat." Stacy isn't prying to be nosy; she is asking because she cares. The look in her eyes shows she wants to honestly know, without the layers of questions; she goes straight in.

I take a deep breath at how refreshing it feels. "I am okay, honestly. After our talk last night, I felt a lot better, more grounded. You speak as if you know veterans."

"Yes, in fact, I know a lot of them, by either work or happenstance. I can envision the look in your eyes when you told me about being in the park. I've seen it before."

Her candidness pulls me in. I both want to reject the pull but also allow it with my whole body.

"We try to hide it, especially around people who didn't serve, but sometimes it slips through."

"I can understand that, we all have our ghosts." Stacy's eyes have a faraway look to them, similar to one I have seen before.

"Are you okay?" I reach out and touch her hand. She jolts before her eyes focus back on me.

"Yeah, sorry, I got lost in memories." She laughs, trying to clear the air, but it is heavy with untold stories.

Changing the subject, I ask, "Why radio?"

She leans forward, and I mirror her, "I grew up listening to the radio with my dad. I always liked the anonymity. Everyone knows my voice, but no one knows what I look like. Why security work?"

"Familiar territory." Is the short answer, and she knows it.

"Yeah, but there are plenty of jobs out there that I am sure you have skills for."

"That's true, but I know the gaps, the vulnerabilities, and initially, I wasn't going to do anything. But I was sitting in another coffee shop soon after I moved here, and two men were talking about recent break-ins."

"And your company?" She pushes, but gently. "What's your vision?"

Her voice encourages what I haven't let myself say, even to myself.

"I want to help not just corporations, like many private security firms, but individuals as well. Not for profits that can't afford a normal security system. I want it to be a place that is welcoming but also strong and commanding." As I speak, I see the future laid out, vivid and unconstrained. Each word plants a new flag, a claim on a world I am still discovering.

Her eyes stay on me the whole time, a look I am learning not to resist. When I finally say everything I can think of, and some that I haven't, I ask, "So what do you think?" Usually, I don't care what other people think. For some reason, I have this deep need to know what she thinks, to see if she understands the drive, the passion.

"Ambitious," she puts her cup down and takes my hand, admiration unmistakable in her eyes, "but I am not surprised."

I laugh. Finally, my chest feels light. There are so many unknowns about private security, things I didn't even know about. I breathe in the café's air, thick with caffeine and conversation, and feel some of the uncertainty roll back. There are still so many unknowns.

"I know what you are thinking, but there is definitely a need," she says, picking up my thread of uncertainty with a natural ease. "Lots of places in town would want your help." She mentions neighborhoods with security concerns, businesses that can use protection." I absorb it all, feeling her confidence spread through me.

"How do you know all of this?" Her insights surprise me, but they shouldn't. "Right, you know the area."

"Yes, but I also know people and keep my ears open, which makes me very good at my job," she says with a playful glint in her eyes.

"I am sure you do." Winking as I smile. Her lightness fills the space between us, expanding into something larger than the moment. This isn't just business, and we both know it. In fact, I knew it from when I saw her at the radio station; it wasn't just business, but I attempted to maintain my distance, for both of our sakes.

The café noise dims, and I look around and see that most of the morning traffic is gone. I reach for my coffee at the same time she does, our fingers brush, and a spark of electricity jumps between us. It feels less like a connection of skin and more a connection of something more, much more. Something we cannot ignore.

Neither of us pull back; my pulse quickens, a sudden rush in the stillness. Her gaze meets mine, charged and sultry. Neither of us looks away, as if we are in some form of silent staring contest. Every second grows longer, as my body responds to her touch. Closing my eyes, finally breaking contact, I lean back.

I try to resume professionalism, but the smirk on her face shows me she knows exactly the power she has on me, body and mind. We talk until the coffee goes cold. Our conversation tiptoes around topics neither of us wants to broach, but both want to know.

"How long before you need to get back?" I ask.

"Why do you have somewhere you need to be?" Her reply comes off as snarky.

"No, but I thought about showing you where I was at the park." My mouth is running faster than my brain. I just know that I don't want to leave her side, at least not right now.

Picking up her phone, her voice falls for a split second before returning to the happy Stacy.

"Everything okay?"

"Yeah, I got a weird message from my station manager about someone dropping something off for me. Nothing to worry about, anyway, I have about an hour, I can drive if you want, and then I can drop you off before my appointment."

"Are you sure? We can both meet there, so you don't have to drive all the way back."

Looking at her phone again, her face pale, "No, actually, I would like it if you will ride with me."

Something about her demeanor has changed, and I am determined to figure out why.

"I definitely can ride with you. Here, let me take these." I reach for the cups, and she barely acknowledges me, standing up and leaving to throw away the cups.

Getting back to the table, Stacy is rubbing her hands together. "Earth to Stacy, are you okay?" I touch her shoulder, and she jumps slightly in her chair.

"Yeah, sorry, I was just thinking, ready to go?"

I absolutely am going to understand whatever is going on, sooner rather than later, because even though I have known Stacy for a short amount of time, this isn't her.

Stacy stands and gathers her items before walking toward the door. I open it for her, and she walks to the Jeep. I wait for her to get in and unlock the doors before walking around. As I open the car door, I look up and down the streets, not only out of training, but in response to how she is acting. Cars line the streets, and nothing seems out of place, but I still commit to memory the cars directly around the coffee shop, just in case something is amiss.

Stacy says nothing as we drive to the park, so I match her silence, thinking about what may have transpired at the coffee shop to change her mood so drastically. I keep my eye on the mirror for any vehicles that may be following, and while I think a dark colored sedan is a bit too close, they turn off two turns from the park, so I ignore it.

Pulling into the parking lot, I jump out and walk around, opening the door for Stacy as I survey the parking lot. There are four cars, all empty. Recognizing two of them from when I come to run, I study the other two. No one knew we were coming here unless someone overheard us at the café, so I am not worried, but my training kicks in, and I am on alert.

"Thank you." Stacy seems better, a little more color to her face.

Shutting the door, I put my hand on her lower back as I guide her to the path. The route I usually take is a mile to the pond, but I know of another, more direct way.

"Have you been here before?" I ask as I notice Stacy focusing on the ground, her hands not rubbing together as much. I reach for one of her hands, and she tentatively allows me to hold her hand as she steps closer.

"Once or twice when I was younger, but not lately."

"There are a couple of parks between my house and this one, but I like this one more, less crowded, and with multiple routes."

"It sounds really peaceful."

"It really is, in the early morning, the birds are loud, but it is nice, keeps your mind off things." I guide her down the path, knowing the pond with the bench is just around the corner. Slowly, we walk at her pace, as I feel some of the tension fade away, her grip becomes steadier, less shaky. She looks around, at the trees and the flowers, instead of focusing on the gravel and grass sneaking through the hard ground of the path.

"We're here," I say as I stop by the bench.

Stacy's breath catches as she sees the pond. "I don't remember seeing this. It is beautiful."

"Wait until the ducks begin goofing around. I can sit here all day if my mind allows it."

The wind is barely blowing, and the pond is almost glassy as we step around the bench to get closer to the pond.

"It is so serene." Stacy bends down on the edge, her fingers running through the water, creating tiny ripples that spread out. Across the pond, I can see a kingfisher eyeing us up to see if we are going to disturb its fishing. When Stacy stands back up, I point out the bird.

"I bet it is curious if I am going to jump in."

"Maybe or hoping you may have some fish food to help it fish." I laugh, but only a small chuckle escapes Stacy.

I grab her shoulders and turn her to me. "What is going on?"

"Nothing, I am just out of it."

"I know you are out of it; you have been since you checked your phone at the café. Care to tell me?" I deepen my voice slightly, playfully warning her.

"Not really, just stand here with me." Stacy's mouth may have said no, but her eyes look as if they are pleading for help.

"Let's walk over here." I reach for her hand and walk her over to the side of the pond where a large tree is standing, casting a shadow over part of the pond.

"Why here?"

"Because it isn't in sight of the path, and I don't know you well enough to make you talk with people watching," I growl out as I push her against the tree.

"What do you mean?"

"This isn't an interrogation, and I will stop if you tell me to stop. For this, we will not need a safe word, but something is bothering you, and I will not have you going to a meeting or back to work in this headspace, so I am going to change it."

Her eyelids drop slightly before she looks at me. "Why do you want to know so bad?"

"Because no matter what this is." I motion between us. "Something is bothering you, and I can see it. I want you to let me in, let me take some of the weight off your shoulders. Hell, I may be able to help."

"I don't know, you have enough weight, you don't need mine." She says.

Before she can respond, I grab her hands and put them above her head while I separate her legs with my knee, grinding my knee against her. She lets out a small yelp as I look straight into her eyes.

"If I say give me your weight, I mean it." I lower my mouth to her ear as I growl, "Now tell me." I feel her heart rate pick up.

"How do you even know I like this? Maybe I like soft and casual."

I lean back to look at her again, "I guess, and from the way you are rubbing yourself against my knee, I guessed right. I take you for a woman who is in power and has to control everything, so once in a while you want to let the power go."

"Maybe." She will not look me in the eye, which means I am right. I have her pegged as that type of person from the minute I saw her at the bar—the woman who watched her friends, who controlled the situation. I am more than happy to take that power away from her.

"So what is bothering you?"

"Nothing, just something stupid at work." I hold her hands up with one hand as I run my hand down her arm, then across to her breast, before I cup and bring my teeth down to run across her erect nipple. Playing with it slightly with my tongue, I look up at her as she bites her lip, looking down at me. She lets out a soft sigh as I remove my hand.

"If you want more, you need to give me more." I run my hand down her side and across her hip, slightly lifting her shirt to run my fingers across her stomach. I hold her against the tree with my body so she cannot rub against my leg.

"You know the fan I told you about yesterday?"

"Yes, what about them?" I dip my fingers into her waistband, slowly running my fingers over her mound to show her how I reward answers.

"Apparently, a package was delivered to the station. I have someone open my mail."

"Of course you do, what was it in?" I slide them deeper, brushing against her clit. She tries to arch, but I hold her against the tree.

"Nothing, it is stupid, I shouldn't even be bothered by it, I get stupid fan mail all the time." Knowing that isn't the truth, at least the nothing part, I pull my hand back out, resting it on her hip.

A slight hiss comes from Stacy's pinched lips.

"I told you that good girls are rewarded, now tell me what it was," I command, tightening my hand on her hands. The bark is smoother than most trees, but I know it is still digging in. She hasn't told me to stop, and from the way her eyes look at me, this is going to test my resolve. I always had a dominant streak with sex, but most of the women I'd been with didn't enjoy it, and Amanda… No, this is about Stacy.

"It had a picture of me talking to you in the entryway the day you interviewed."

"Strange, has that happened before?" I focus on what she says, along with the implications, while still maintaining a firm grip on her.

"Not to my knowledge, and it scared me. It was just an interview." Tears start welling up in her eyes. I let go of her hand and pull her close. Gone is the time to be rough.

I fun one hand in slow circles as she leans into me. The other hand that is on her waistband slowly runs down, past her mound, and mimics the motion of my hand on her back. Slow and steady. She looks up at me.

"What? Good girls get rewarded, and then we will figure out what to do, if you are okay with that?"

She nods as I pull my fingers off her clit and thrust them into my mouth, tasting her before wetting them. I lick my thumb before moving my hand back to her clit. This time, I use my fingers to run up and down the sides of her folds while my thumb circles her clit. As she moans, I enter her with one finger slowly, enjoying the tightness around it. I pump my finger in and out before pulling it out and putting both in. The entire time I watch her, every subtle flick of my thumb causes her eyes to slightly roll back.

As I feel her tightening, she grabs my arm and stills me. I cock my head at her while she reaches for my other arm. Pulling it from her back, she grabs my hand and puts it on her neck. I wrap my hand around her neck lightly as I speed up my fingers. A flush starts at her neck and runs up toward her face.

"Right there, just like that." Stacy moans. Her hand is still resting on my hand as it sits on her neck. I am afraid of tightening. This is something that I have dreamed about doing but never found someone who wants to.

"Tighter." She says as she moves in motion with my thumb. I tighten my hand as she drops hers and focuses on me.

"Come for me," I say as I speed up my thumb. I feel her tightening, but I keep going. I watch as her eyes roll back in her head, and I tighten my hand on her neck slightly. She explodes against me, coming so hard that I almost lose my balance. I keep thrusting my fingers as her body spasms around them. As her eyes focus, looking at me, I loosen my hand and move it to her waist to keep her from stumbling as I step back.

I put my arm around her waist and lean down to whisper in her ear. "See what good girls get when they tell me what is bothering them."

She is breathing so heavily that all she can do is nod with that sly smile.

We take our time walking back. I mentally clock how long we are out here because I don't want her to be late for her meeting. As we approach the entrance to the park, the three trails split off. I look down one trail and swear I see Nick, but there is no way. My mind must be playing tricks on me, the last thing I knew about Nick was that he was getting dishonorably discharged, and I think he'd moved back to California. When I blink and look back toward the trail the man was on, there is no one. Shaking my head, I try to clear the vision.

"Everything okay?" Stacy, finally finding her voice, asks as I pause.

"Yeah, I thought I saw someone I used to know, but there is no way that it was him."

"Maybe it was just a ghost from the past?" Stacy asks, holding my hand tighter.

"Yeah, it must be." Even though I say the words, they are hollow. I never doubt my sight, even when I was having a flashback, so why now?

Getting to the parking lot, I survey the cars, of the four that were there when we arrived, three are still. There is one new one. It looks like a rental, with shiny rims and not a speck of dirt on the car.

"Get in the car, I want to look at something," I say, a bit more forceful than I intend.

"What happened?" Stacy joins me.

"Please, I just want to check something out, get in the car." I kiss her forehead and push her back toward the jeep.

With a huff, I hear her unlock the doors, and the door open before it slams shut. I quickly walk over to the car. Missouri plates, with a sticker of the Kansas City Jayhawks. Not a rental, just someone who likes to keep their car clean. Breathing a sigh of relief, I join Stacy in the vehicle.

"So what was that all about?"

"That car wasn't here when we arrived, and it looks too clean to be local, so I wanted to see if it was a rental."

Stacy laughs, "Too clean to be local? Have you seen the outside of what you are riding in?"

She has a point; her jeep is immaculate. "Point taken, but not everyone is as organized as you."

She playfully slaps my hand and laughs. "Thank you."

"For what? I mean, other than the mind-blowing orgasm." I laugh, truly not knowing what she is thanking me for.

"Checking the car, making sure I am okay, taking time out of your day to help me."

"You're welcome. Honestly, that is what I would do for anyone that I care about."

"Oh, you just pin people to trees and give them one of the best hand necklaces they've ever had because you care about them?" She pauses before leaving the parking lot to look at me.

"Well, no, I mean the cautious watching of places." I feel myself redden. I have never been physically intimate with someone who is so blunt and outgoing about what she likes.

"Okay, I am about to feel not as special." She remarks as she turns on the street to lead us back into the center of town, and the café where my car is.

I roll my eyes slightly, "You do not seem like a woman who thinks of herself less than she is." I place my hand on her thigh.

"You have me dead right most of the time. I mean, everyone has some insecurities, right?" Stacy responds, laying her hand on mine.

"That they do. Was there just a picture, or did it have anything else with it?" I don't want to change the subject, but for my knowledge, and hopefully her peace of mind, I want to sort out this 'fan'.

"There was a gift card to the café we were at, which isn't terribly surprising, I have said on air how much I like it. In fact, like two weeks ago, I had the owner on about why they opened and how they are settling into the Kansas City area."

"Are they not from here?" I didn't know if Stacy is just that personal with all the places she frequented or if there is a specific reason.

"The owner's husband was a translator in Iraq; he served with a friend of mine. So after the war, I helped my friend get them over here." Stacy says it as if it was helping someone cross the street.

"Wow." My mind races. This woman who walked into my life is much more complex than I initially thought. I mentally kick myself for seeing her as less than she is.

"Good, wow, I hope." Stacy navigates the streets effortlessly.

"Yeah, I'm surprised, I guess. Most people don't go that far for a friend."

"Jealous?" Stacy cocks the eyebrow closest to me.

"No, we all have our pasts. I guess I was more curious." Okay, maybe there is a tinge of jealousy, but I have no room to talk.

She laughs, "We went to school together, and he joined right after high school and served for a long time. During one battle, the translator saved his life, and so he felt it was the least he could do once he got back to the states."

"I understand that we rarely worked with locals that much, but when we did, we tried to help them as much as we could. We probably like your friend, though, we didn't stay in one place long." I stop myself from saying more, surprised I shared that much.

"Yeah, he was in one place for 12-15 months, so he got to know people really well."

"I am glad that you have such a good friend." A cloud falls over her eyes when I say that.

"Yeah, he was a great person." I notice she used the word 'was'.

"I'm sorry." There's nothing else I can say.

"Thank you, he tried to go to those VA-sponsored meetings, but he hated it." I know the ones she is talking about.

"Well, we are here, I need to go anyway." Stacy flips on her flashers as she parks right next to my car.

"Can I call you?" It feels like there is a large canyon between us now, not just a gap, but something that seems impassible.

Her smile reaches her eyes, "Of course, oh, you think because of this? No, we both have things in our lives that are dark, and that doesn't mean we shouldn't or can't talk about them."

The ball of nerves in my stomach uncoils at her words. Outside of the people in the military I have to talk to, I never speak to anyone about what happened. They just wouldn't understand, I always thought. But here is a beautiful woman who knows what she wants, but she has a past, a darkness that may not match my own, but is still present.

Leaning across the middle console, she grabs my shirt and pulls me closer. "Look, Abel, I may be sad about my friend, I may be mad about how things have worked out, but whatever this is, it's just that. We are a culmination of our pasts." She pulls me closer and kisses me hard. I grab the back of her head and kiss her back. I finally pull back out of breath. Stacy smiles as she licks her lips.

"Now get to your meeting before you're late," I say as I open the door.

"Fine, I guess I will go." She laughs as I shut the door. Her aroma stays with me as she waves before entering traffic and driving off. As I stand next to my car, I feel I am being watched. Looking forward to the café, I notice nothing out of the ordinary, so I look around, trying to act casual. As I open the car door, I focus behind me. Getting in, I focus on the front. Still not seeing anything, I feel the sensation deep down. I start my car and look to the side, and that is when I see her.

Amanda, the woman whom I thought I loved. Sitting in a dark sedan, one surprisingly like the one I saw earlier on the way to the park. My awareness narrows on her as she sits. She's found me, but likely not as she expected.

Her eyes follow me, unblinking as I pull out. I can see her hands gripping the wheel, knuckles pale against the dark interior. She leans forward as I drive past, focus completely honed in on one thing: me.

I pretend not to notice, watching out of my peripheral vision. She can't hide what she is thinking, what she plans. Her face is a map of thin lines and willpower. As I drive past, I watch in the rear-view mirror. The sedan pulls away, steady. She will not let this sit, it isn't going to just go quickly, even though it is she who distanced herself. I see it in her narrowed eyes and thin lips. This is just the beginning, and it is a battle I do not want to fight, not now, not here.

As I watch the car disappear around the corner, I think the tension will disappear, but it doesn't. The streets hum, but it is nothing to the noise inside my head. I let the distance fall away; it is a risk for my heart, but my brain is telling me that every step away is a step for the better.

I need to prepare, because if I know anything, Amanda will not stop until something forces her to stop. Her perseverance is something to be admired, but her personality is not. Over the last week, I realized things about myself, and the truth comes down to not wanting Amanda anywhere in my life, ever again.

CHAPTER ELEVEN

Arriving home, I look around the house, deciding what I am going to do. I need to protect myself, especially now that Amanda knows I was back in the area. When I first came home, I considered reaching out, maybe even seeing if we were still compatible. Now, though, everything I knew about my romantic life was a lie. Relationships shouldn't be hard, they shouldn't make you want to hit your head against the wall because of the sheer stupidity of a conversation. There should be laughter, joy, and fantastic sex.

Making food, I look around the office to see if there is anything that may show a chink in my armor. One thing about being in the military was that I changed my passwords all the time, so there is nothing for her to log into legitimately. She never had the skills to hack, so I am not worried about that. She isn't overly intelligent, but she is conniving, as I recall.

I am turning myself into knots, worried about a woman I dated years ago. I don't even know if I have a photo of her still, especially with what happened during that one deployment. Shaking my head, I sink onto the futon, debating whether or not to turn on the TV. Looking at the remote on the coffee table, I wonder if it is worth reaching for it. Just as my brain is running the pros and cons, my phone rings. Not my cellphone, but Mongoose Security's phone.

Standing quickly, I rush into the office. "Mongoose Security, Abel Williams speaking." As if I have an entire staff of professionals ready to answer my phone.

"Mr. Williams, my name is Ruben Goldstein, and I find myself in urgent need of your assistance."

"What type of assistance are you looking for?"

"If possible, the kind that could start tonight, and come with technology." He answers. I look around. I have the technology and the time. It may be just the thing I need to get the past out of my head.

"Where are you located?" I look at the map I hung in the office, each suburb and town highlighted. I know my way around, mostly. But I have been gone for over a decade, and things have changed.

"I am in Kansas City proper. I have a parking lot with a space reserved for you."

"Would you like to talk about rates?"

"Abel, I will cut to the chase. I need you to come down to Goldstein's Fine Jewelry with all of your gadgets, and I will pay whatever you ask." He seems frantic, but still trying to maintain his composure.

"With the time and where I am coming from, I can be there in less than 30 minutes. Will that be acceptable?" The way he sounds, I know it would be, but this is my first actual client, and if by any indication of his words, a wealthy one. Looking around the office, I grab everything that I can think a jewelry store may need or want before making trips out to the car. After three trips, I survey the office, looking for anything I may have missed. I forward the work phone to my cell phone and lock up the house, not before turning on the state-of-the-art security system. It is a business expense after all, at least that is what I told myself when I bought everything.

The street stretches out like a half-forgotten thought, a plan set in motion but never finished. I turn away from the dark and toward the bright lights of Kansas City. Arriving early, I find the parking spot that Mr. Goldstein has reserved for me. Grabbing my laptop and go bag, I cross the otherwise empty parking lot to the front door of the store. The weight of the bag feels right, not as heavy as my service weapon, but enough to remind me why I am here.

Mr. Goldstein meets me at the door, gratitude written in the slump of his shoulders and the tremor of his hands as he shakes mine. His shop is bright and gleams with displays, carpet, and glass, displaying a lifetime's work. "Thank you for coming," his voice fragile, as if all is lost. I don't flinch as I respond.

"Glad to, Mr. Goldstein," the shop spread out in polished cases and lighting at exactly the right angles. Every facet of the stone is catching light. "We've had trouble with our system, and please call me Ruben." His wire-rimmed glasses flash with uncertainty as he glances between me and my small bag. "We had it professionally installed, but something is wrong."

I nod, already mapping the territory, knowing exactly where and what I am going to do. My feet go straight to the first point of attack, a tactical survey of his primary display. The exact thing I would go for first if I was planning on robbing him.

He follows closely, a nervous shadow, and I can't blame him. When I pause, the words gush out with the precision of an open wound, but I guess in some ways it is. Instead of blood, it is diamonds and gold.

"We've been here since 1939, three generations. Never had trouble like this." Looking over at him, his age is clear, as is the turmoil he is feeling.

I open my bag and pull out my laptop along with specialty tools. "We'll get you squared away tonight. Everything else is in the car, but first I want to get a good overview." I assure him, opening my laptop and logging in.

"I really appreciate you coming so soon." Hovering over the process, uncertain and hopeful. "There have been two attempts this month, and everyone is on edge."

The connection that drove me to start the company in the first place came slamming back. How our lives are interconnected, I think as I detail what I see.

"Let me get started. I have a lot, but don't worry, not all of it is going in." I wink as I move toward the door.

Every trip I make, I feel lighter, as if by helping him, I am healing a small part of my past. I know this is what I am meant to do, I feel it deep in my bones, and I smile.

Placing the first box near the main display case, I pull out a camera and a tangle of wires. As I uncoil the wire, each movement decisive and controlled, I feel Ruben's fear dissipate. "This camera here will cover your primary display; it is wide-angle, so the entire thing will be viewed at the same time."

Ruben exhales, a release of tension my body was building. Something is wrong with the security system; no one worth their salt would have installed it the way they did. His anxiety continues to circle the shop, bouncing and pinging off bare walls and glass cabinets. "Will it connect to my smartphone when I am not here?"

"Smartphone, tablet, anything you want." I keep my voice even, focused, the sound of expertise and unbroken faith. "It is completely wired and completely secure."

The wiring of the cameras is complex, but not as complex as Ruben's worry. He watches as I mount cameras and pull wires through the ceiling as if it might collapse. As I work, he continues on his flood of conversation, even if my responses are single words.

"You wouldn't believe how things have changed. Our father—" he pauses, correcting himself, each word slipping from memory's tight grip. "My father…he didn't have this kind of trouble. He knew everyone on the block and in this area. No matter where we went, he would know someone, and Mom hated going out with him."

His voice catches, but my hands don't as I finish up the wiring and lower myself to the store room floor.

"All of the cameras are placed. Next up are the motion sensors. I am going to put one at the front and one at the back." I watch to see if he has any issue with that, but he just nods.

His faith in security systems has failed, and I am trying to bring him back. I can see he is tentatively believing in their ability to work; it is small steps, and ones that I will take with him until his faith is restored. "The ones now aren't silent; the last attempt tripped the alarm, but because it was so loud, they got away before the police could arrive." His voice wavers. I put my hand on his shoulder and look down at him.

"They are silent, and not only will they alert the police, but also Mongoose Security, so no matter what, I will be here if something happens." It is a promise I shouldn't make, one that connects me to this store for the length of their business, but it is one that I feel needs to be said.

He looks up with his eyes wet, "It's just such a nightmare. You know how long it takes to rebuild a collection like this? Not to mention the more it happens, the less likely the insurance company is to believe you."

"Too long," I know a thing or two about rebuilding. "One positive aspect is that after I am done here, I will write up a full report that you will provide to your insurance company. Not only should it help with your premium, but it will give them a sense of security."

He falls silent, letting the sound of my words and progress carry the weight of his expectation. The remaining equipment is spread out before me, waiting to be connected to the system. The dustless counters reflect the harshness of the two men in the room. It is the intensity of never leaving a job unfinished; mine is with security systems, his jewelry. In a way, we are connected, even though we are very different.

I feel his anxiety relax, almost imperceptible but present as I attach the rear motion detector.

"Everything good so far?" he asks, his voice trying to be steady, but edged with unease. "This is also wireless, right?"

"It is." Securing the last connection, "they won't see it, and if they cut the power, these are all on backup batteries that will last over 24 hours." The sensors and wires lay complete, a field of protection that he likely never dreamed of.

"I have one more step, and then we will be done here, unless you want something specific?" I ask as I move toward the phone.

"While you were setting up this system, did you see what happened to the old one?" I had, but I am not about to tell Ruben what I found; it is best left in the crawl space, something for him not to worry about, and for Mongoose Security to focus on.

"It just looks like it is not robust enough for a shop of your size. It would have been great if you only had one exit and one display case." I lie easily, but I know he would believe me, and it is okay. I tie an extra connection from the old system to a receiver going directly to me, so if someone tries to interfere, I will know.

"That makes sense. It is a good company, but they took a long time, I mean, compared to you."

I smile as I crouch under the desk where the phone sits. I pull the cable until I find the end and attach a small box. Rewiring it back so it is out of the way, I stand up and brush myself off. Just as I am about to tell Ruben I am finished, my phone rings. Glancing at it, I see it is an unknown number that looks familiar. They can leave a message. Switching off the ringer, Ruben speaks, watching me.

"Our mother's wedding ring. Gone, probably melted down. We'll never find another." His pain is real and unguarded, the past haunting him with unfinished stories and lost loved ones.

"It has been rough, but it will get better." I allow, coiling up unused cable and pieces of equipment that will be used in a future job.

He draws in a shaky breath before moving around his store. I set three panic buttons, numerous cameras, and other security measures that I don't even know if Ruben knows. Everything is tight, unseen, and ready to watch and wait. "Can you show me?"

"Absolutely, let me get everything to my car, and then I will boot it up to my phone, and I can show you. I also have a packet of information on how to set it up. However, for now, there is a simple login that allows you to connect your phone, and it will display everything. Also, don't worry about it saving. The system I put in the back room will save automatically, and I have a space for saving as well, so if something was to happen to your back-ups, mine are available."

"Thank you, do you need help carrying stuff out?" He reaches for a box.

"No need, you stay in here and try to find all the cameras while I load this stuff up." I carry two boxes, much lighter than before, to the car before returning for the rest. Going back in, I open my phone and log in. Clicking on his business name, all the cameras pop up on the screen. There are two green lines as well, which indicate the motion detectors.

"As you can see, and you will have the same format, you can see every single camera and the motion detectors. If you want to make one big, all you have to do is double tap on it." I show him by double-tapping on the one screen. "To make it small again, you just double-tap again." I do it again, and the screen goes back to showing all the cameras. "You are in good shape now."

I survey the shop, but even with my trained eye, I cannot find all the cameras immediately. Mentally, I pat myself on the back. I create a virtual stronghold from glass and high hopes. The store is now part of a larger network, my network, my area to protect. The store feels lighter, feels as if it knows it is safe, and that helps. Ruben watches me with something akin to admiration, his worries no match for my abilities, and he knows it.

"If you have any issues or need anything, please call me," I say, offering my hand to him.

"I can't be happier," his words catching in his throat, overtaking him in their sudden simplicity. Looking around, he walks me to the door, and I feel his gratitude brush up against me. "We appreciate it so much, seriously, I can't tell you how much."

My hands find my sides, uncertain in their stillness, unfamiliar with standing still. "I am glad to help. Would you like the invoice now, or can I mail it?" I am in no immediate need for payment, and I feel like Ruben needs to sit with his new store for a day.

"Now is fine if you have it, but you can mail it too, I promise you, you will get paid."

"There isn't a doubt, Ruben. The invoice will be mailed in the next couple of days." Leaving him in the vastness of his new security system, an addition to his history. Crossing through the threshold, knowing that I didn't just add a security system, I gave him more than he hoped for. I gave him peace.

Getting home, I check the perimeter, making sure that nothing looks wrong. Since seeing Amanda near the café, there is a bit of a tingle running down my back. I know she will not stop, but I will not deal with her petty bullshit. Nothing seems off, so I open the front door to carry everything back to the office. I need to make a note that I need to buy more equipment and get accounting software. I close my eyes. If I bring on a couple of large clients, I'm going to have to hire someone, maybe a couple of people. I think about my savings and how much I can afford before needing to bring in large clients. As I am doing the math, I hear a crash outside.

Dropping the two boxes I am holding, I run outside to see equipment falling out of my car. It looks like one box has opened and fallen over. Reaching for the weapon I have in my thigh holster, I walk around the car looking for something, anything.

As I round the car, I see footprints near the box that has toppled. I live out in the middle of nowhere, so someone randomly coming onto my property isn't possible. No, this is intentional. *Do I call the cops, or do I move the stuff into the house first?* I think as I look between the door and the car. *Fuck it,* I put the equipment back in the box and carry two more boxes in the house, just inside the door, before going back for the last box and my laptop. Kicking the door closed, I return to the house to place the items before finding my key fob to lock the car's door. Closing the house door, I set the door's motion alarms before walking through the house, the pistol out as I clear every room. I check the back door and window locks before walking back to the front door.

Stepping outside, I close the door. I go back to the footsteps and follow them. Whoever it is walked around the garage, stopping by the door, but then continued on. Likely, they tried the lock but couldn't get in. The prints are large, roughly the size of my feet, so I know it isn't a woman, especially since the steps are confident and full-footed. When people try to use larger or smaller shoes to throw off a pursuer, the steps look different, and the pressure points differ from when you fit the shoe completely.

Either this is an amateur or someone who doesn't care if they are tracked. Either way, they will not get away with it. Continuing to follow the steps, they move through the little outbuildings that are empty before heading toward the train tracks on the far side of the property. There is nothing but trees and grass that way, and there is no need to track them if they are heading off the property. Returning to the house, I clear the rooms again before moving everything to the office.

Cataloging everything I used for the Goldstein Jewelry store and making sure nothing has been stolen when the box was dumped out on the driveway, I finally stand and stretch. Looking at the time, I see it is after 11. If I want to get up and listen to Stacy's morning show, I will need to wrap up what I am doing, and I can finish it in the morning. On initial inspection, nothing is missing, so I don't know if the crash was just a distraction or if I got out there before they could take anything. It is strange that the box only had cords in it, nothing of value like the motion detectors or the cameras. Shaking my head, I quickly push away from that task before logging into the security system to make sure the Goldstein Jewelry is up and running.

Good enough for tonight, I think, as I turn up the volume so that if anything trips, I will hear it. Falling into my bed, I think about the footsteps before Stacy's view takes over. I fall asleep with her on my mind and a smile on my face.

CHAPTER TWELVE

The next morning, I am up and in the gym an hour before Stacy is due to come on the air. 30 hard minutes in the gym, and I start oatmeal while I jump in the shower. Five minutes before her segment begins, I am sitting in my office thinking about who I can hire. My radio is already on, set to Stacy's station, before I focus on paperwork. Like I thought, everything is still there that wasn't used for Ruben's setup. Counting cables and cameras, I hear Stacy's voice come over the radio.

"Good Morning, Kansas City! This is Stacy Reynolds with KMBZ's Reynold's Reveals, a look at what is happening in Kansas City." Her voice brings a smile to my face. Her voice flows over me, and any remaining tension from the night before fades as she speaks. I pay half attention to what she is saying as I focus half on the paperwork. Until I hear the words "Ruben Goldstein" and "Mongoose Security." Putting down the inventory sheet I am looking at, I focus entirely on the radio.

"When we get back from our advertisement break, we will discuss how local businesses are helping local businesses." The station goes to a commercial, and I lean back in my chair. Before Stacy comes back, I check through the cameras of the jewelry store and the history to make sure nothing happened after he left last night. It is quiet until 7 AM when Ruben arrives through the back door and starts turning on the lights. I press fast forward on the machine and skim to see if anything strange occurs that may connect with the fact that Stacy is apparently talking to Ruben in the studio. At 7:45 AM, right before the store is due to open, I watch Stacy saunter into the store and hug Ruben. I don't bother turning on the sound because I already know essentially what they are talking about. I don't know if I can feel bothered by the fact that Stacy knows Ruben, or happy that Stacy feels sure enough in my skills to recommend me.

"Welcome Back, we are here with long-time business owner Ruben Goldstein, of Goldstein's Fine Jewelry. I am glad you were available to come in today. How long have you been in business?"

I can hear the slight nervousness in his voice, similar to last night. "My grandfather opened the store over 60 years ago in that very spot. When he retired, my father took over, and then I."

"So definitely a cornerstone of Downtown Kansas City then." Stacy's voice assures him that everything will be okay. I know it because she used the same voice on me.

"Absolutely, which is why I am so upset by what has happened lately."

"Can you expand on that comment, Mr. Goldstein?" I can envision her smiling at him, calming him.

"Yes, so in the last month, all of the businesses downtown have been broken into. We have been broken into twice. The first time, they stole mostly sentimental items that were on display. The second time they broke in, they tripped the alarm, but took a piece of jewelry we had planned on letting a celebrity wear for an upcoming event. They were gone by the time the police arrived."

"I am so sorry to hear that. So with those break-ins, what did you decide to do?"

"Well, a while ago I had the radio on, and usually I don't in the morning, but that morning I did, and I heard your segment with the young man who owns Mongoose security. I didn't think about it much, but after the second break-in, I called him up. Not only did he come the same day, but he set me up with something I never expected." While plausible, I don't believe him when he says he randomly remembered, no, I bet Stacy put the worm in his ear, maybe even during her 'meeting' she had last night after the park.

"So after Mongoose Security left, do you feel secure?"

He laughs, a sound full of relief. "More than secure," he clears his throat. "More secure than ever." His enthusiasm expands, and I can hear that I helped him reclaim a piece of his business, if not himself.

"So it is safe to say you are happy with the install?" I can almost see the glint in Stacy's eyes as she asks the question. That woman is occupying more and more of my brain with every passing day. I don't want to think about a relationship, or even a situationship. I have been through too many of those, and even though my heart is hardened, it isn't stone. Including the issues I have with flashbacks, I don't need anyone occupying my attention. I know what I am trying to tell myself, but both my brain and heart are laughing.

"More than happy, Abel knows what he is doing, and we trust him completely."

"Having obviously used other companies, what made his approach, in your opinion, different from your standard security companies?" The question is direct, and I can imagine her asking me that.

"His focus, he came in, looked around, and started working. There wasn't much small talk, and he did everything in a relatively short amount of time, at least in what I think was a short amount of time. His attention to detail was great; he picked up things that most wouldn't." He laughs, the gratitude coming from his voice.

"Thank you for your experience, Mr. Goldstein. Is there anything else you would like to say before we head to another commercial break?"

"No, well, actually yes. Many of you know me and my family. If you are looking for security, either remote or in person, I would definitely consider getting at least a walk-through by Mongoose Security. His professionalism blows most new companies away." My heart feels heavy, especially just after meeting me, he would speak so highly of me. I am not used to it. Even in the military, I kept my head down and just did my job.

"I hope everyone is hearing that, a glowing review by a local, well-known store owner. If you are interested, all of the contact information for Mongoose Security is on the station's website under my page; it will be there for the rest of the week, just as all companies I focus on are. I will be back with updates on the weather and traffic." Stacy's voice cuts off with a commercial for a car detailing company.

I want to have coffee with Stacy and ask her about her morning interview, but I need to attend to some business matters first. I absolutely need to hire someone if I ever want to actually do the work I want to do. Within ten minutes of the segment ending, my office phone rings.

"Mongoose Security, Abel speaking," I say, waiting for a response.

"I heard the segment on the radio, and I am hoping to have you come give me a quote on my house." The man's voice is tentative.

"I would be more than happy to. What day are you thinking of? Do you already have a security system?" I pull a notepad out of a drawer.

"I just moved here, was traded to the Chiefs, and am renting a place. It has a security system, but I would feel better if someone came and checked it out to ensure everything works correctly.

"I can absolutely do that. Let me get your name and address, and I can look at my calendar." My calendar is completely clear, but I want it to sound like I am busier.

"I have to start at the field in a week, so before then. My family isn't coming in until I have everything settled here, and I want the security system to be perfect." The man's voice softens slightly when talking about his family.

"I have a couple of hours tomorrow that I can do. Right now, I am the only one, so if there is an emergency at one of my other clients, I may have to leave."

"I understand completely. Hopefully, it shouldn't take long. The property management company said it was the best on the market, but you know how they can lie." The man laughs, a deep baritone.

"I understand, unfortunately. Well, let's get you set up for tomorrow at 2. I will only bring my laptop and the essentials. If you end up wanting more, then I can set that up later." I mentally run through what I want to bring.

"That sounds great, thanks, man. I will see you tomorrow." He hangs up after I get his contact information and his address. It is a wealthy part of town, so hopefully the security is good.

Now to see if I can get Stacy to admit that she got me at least one job.

Pulling my phone out, I see a text from the same unknown number Amanda had called me from before. Clicking on the text, I skim the sentences while rolling my eyes.

> *Abel, I know you don't really want to talk to me, but we must speak. Please call me back, we can go to dinner and have some drinks. I have my place, and I remember that thing you loved. Seriously, it is crucial.*

I laugh at the fact that she thinks anything she does physically would counter everything that she did while I was gone. I lost enough in my life outside of my control, I won't lose anything else in my life without making that decision. Ignoring the text, I pull up Stacy's number. Looking at the phone, I know she is on her break, so I call her instead of texting.

"Abel, I take it you heard the morning segment." Her joyful and slightly mocking voice comes over the line.

"I did, I would have called you earlier, but I had some business calls to take." Matching her tone.

"So why are you calling Mr. Popularity? I'm glad you called," I laugh.

"If you are free tonight, I would like to take you to dinner, if that is okay to be seen out in public with me."

"Oh, stop, it is you that needs to consider if being seen in public with me is warranted, I mean, the things you do with your—"

"Okay, that's enough, I know what you mean." This woman makes me tongue-tied and puts me in a good place.

"Okay, so dinner tonight? Where would you like to go? I will be done about 7 PM after the last segment, and then I have a quick station meeting. Do you want to pick me up or pick somewhere near the station?"

"Let's meet somewhere, just in case I have to leave for a client." I was initially going to pick her up, but I don't want her stranded somewhere if Mr. Goldstein calls.

"That makes sense. Text me where you want me to meet you?"

"Sounds great. See you tonight." The butterflies in my stomach do the Macarena. Yeah, we have been out together and fucked, but this is a date. At least I think it's a date. I need to have a conversation with Stacy. I enjoy spending time with her, I think she enjoys spending time with me, but are we just physical? It's not I would mind if we are, but I want to know.

Making a reservation at an Italian restaurant, I recheck the property before getting ready to go. Everything seems as it should be.

CHAPTER THIRTEEN

I arrive at 7 for our 7:15 reservation to make sure I am there when she arrives. I can also survey the location and ensure there are easy exits in case something happens. With the call, then thinking I saw a ghost from my past, and then having Amanda text me, I am not taking any chances. The night is brisk, but it feels good as I stand near the door watching the traffic pass. The cars edge forward as the traffic lights dictate just how many are allowed to leave the downtown center at a time. Nothing immediately jumps out at me, which I took as a good sign.

At 7:08, I see Stacy's jeep turn the corner and start toward the restaurant. Just seeing her car makes me smile. She pulls into the parking garage across the street, and I walk over so I can greet her when she steps out. Less than two minutes later, she gives me a little wave as she walks down the slope from the second floor. Her usual brightly colored pants are replaced by a muted knee-length skirt and a brightly colored shirt. Offering her my hand, she takes it as we walk across the street.

I hold open the door for her, but she doesn't need it as she gently pulls me in with her. As we wait for the hostess, I look around. The warm reds and greens of the tables and chairs contrast with the cooler colored walls. Instead of murals, the walls are filled with framed images of people and places. The restaurant pulls you in, not just with the aromas, but also with the atmosphere that speaks of home-cooked meals and great conversations.

As the hostess comes back to show us to our table, the quiet buzz of the restaurant fades away as Stacy looks at me, smiling. I hold her hand tighter as we walk toward the back, where I specifically requested a corner table. Even as the wait staff's energy spills into the room, causing my anxiety to spike, Stacy's down-to-earth, relaxed energy keeps me grounded. I focus on her hand and the connection we have, and take slow, steady breaths.

The hostess finally arrives at our table, a partial circle that sits against the back wall. It is perfect for people watching, as well as staying out of the main hustle and bustle of the restaurant. She slides in, and I slide in after her.

"The server will be with you soon with your menus and to take drink orders." The hostess slightly bows before leaving.

"Great pick." Stacy slides closer to me.

"It's not a café," I reply, my voice sharp because of the environment.

Stacy places her hand on my thigh, my brain telling my dick it is not the time. "We could have gone somewhere quieter, like the park." She smirks.

"No, I have to get out, and there is no one I would rather get out with than you. This may seem strange, but your energy comforts me, it grounds me a bit. Now, if we can pay and go out the back door right there." I point to the exit two tables away, "I wouldn't mind."

"I am sure they could accommodate that. So how was your day?" She flutters her eyelashes.

"Busy, I am sure, no thanks to you." I turn slightly to look at her, her hand raising slightly on my thigh.

"Whatever do you mean?"

"Don't play that, it was no coincidence that I was called by the same man that you interviewed this morning?"

"Oh, Mr. Goldstein, he is a friend of my father's, and I saw him recently, and we were talking about the break-ins and such. I may have suggested having someone look at his security system."

"So that wasn't the meeting you had after the park?"

"No, that was something to do with the radio station."

I felt dumb for assuming that she is getting people to hire me.

Her eyes get big, "Did you think I ran from the park to tell someone to hire you? I don't kiss and tell."

"I may have considered that, I am sorry." The sly smile on her face tells me she did something, but she isn't going to tell me.

"You are forgiven, especially if you are paying." Just then, the server comes over and hands us our menus.

"Do you want something to drink while reviewing the menus?" The young man asks.

"Can I get just a water with light ice?" I hear Stacy say as I quickly glance at the drink menu.

"Can I get the same? Since I am still technically at work." I smile.

The server nodded as he turned, "I will bring those shortly."

Once he is gone, I look at Stacy, "You look good. I am sorry I didn't tell you when I first saw you."

"Thank you, I decided to wear a skirt, you know better access and all." She grins.

"Not everything is about sex." I can't believe what I was saying as we sit in a restaurant. Especially since every time I look at her, I think about how she would look bent over my table, or car hood, or on the floor. I clear my throat before I need to readjust myself.

"I know, I am just giving you a hard time, because the red of your face is just." She kisses her fingers. "Chef's kiss."

"You do it to make me blush? Oh, let's see who is going to be blushing later."

"Is that a promise?" She gets close to my ear, "Because you know I am not wearing anything under this skirt."

I swallow just as the server brings the water.

"Have you decided on what you want for dinner?"

"Yes, I will take the shrimp scampi with the salad," Stacy says as she puts down her menu.

I look at her. How did she decide what she wanted so quickly? Gazing over the menu, I choose the risotto with chicken.

"Great choices, is there anything else you would like? I will bring out bread in a bit, it is currently cooling."

"Not that I can think of, thank you." I respond, and as he leaves, I ask Stacy, "How did you know what you wanted so fast? Have you been here before?"

"Once for a business buffet thing, but no, I just love shrimp scampi, and so I figured I should see if theirs is good, if it isn't, I will just eat your risotto."

"Oh no, you don't, who do you think you are?"

She leans closer, her chest sliding against my arm, "The person who is going to give you the best head you have ever received."

"Wow, someone thinks highly of themselves."

"Are you doubting my abilities?" She mock clutches her pearls.

"No, I am more of a seeing-is-believing," I smirk. "How was your day?"

"It was okay, the fan, or should I say fans, are becoming more insistent."

"What do you mean?" I perk up at her comment.

"I had someone call me last night and left a message about how I needed to watch out because, and I quote, 'your interviewee is mine', but I interview at least four people a week, if not a lot more.

"Weird, do you know who the person was talking about?"

"No, and it was a computer-generated voice, so I sent the message to my manager. Not that they will do anything, but they have a file for all the crazies who call or mail stuff in."

"That's good. Anything else?"

"Yeah, today during the evening show, I had someone call." Her hands move as she begins her story. "I was taking calls, but we screen them first during commercials for obvious reasons. Well, the caller claimed my microphone was bugged. He talked to my assistant for almost an hour about how I needed to be careful because the FBI was listening in and that every time there was static over the radio, it was them actively listening."

"Was it?" I ask, letting the humor ease into my voice.

"Not this time," she says, a lilt of laughter undercutting the words. "You can never be too sure, though."

"I feel like there is a much longer story to that, but I'll keep that in mind." I lean back, feeling the conversation like a full breath. My attention is split between the hand on my thigh and the conversation. The restaurant wraps itself around us, more intimate than I expect, unsure if I am ready for it.

"So what's been the hardest part?" Stacy asks, turning the focus without shifting her hand or the warmth of her presence.

"Of what?" I am surprised. She can mean many things, like sitting here not wanting to ravish her.

"Your transition," she says, knowing the exact time to ask me the more complex questions.

"I don't hesitate, even though it is nothing I haven't talked about before, nor really thought about; it is new and unplanned. "The silence," I say, feeling the weight of my past lighten a bit. I am startled by my honesty, the way it takes shape. "It gets loud sometimes."

She just nods, and I see that in her own way she understands.

The server brings dinner, and instead of talking, Stacy and I exchange glances as we eat. I pause after her second bite, "So, do you like your choice? Because mine's amazing."

Dropping her fork, she looks at me, "Oh, is it? Maybe you should let me try it." She takes the fork and tries to take a bit of my dinner.

"I will get stabby, eat your own food." I laugh as she pouts before focusing back on hers.

"It is fantastic. Can I have just a small taste, though, for research?"

The smile she gives me can melt ice, so I push my plate closer to her so she can taste it. She voices a small moan that goes straight to my dick. I need to stop thinking of sex every time I'm around her.

"Now, can I taste yours?" I pull my plate back in front of me.

"My what?"

"Your scampi, and you know what I am talking about." I laugh as she pushes her plate toward me.

"It's okay, nothing like mine," I say after I taste it.

"You are lying, I see it in your eyes." She teases as she reaches for her plate to continue eating.

"Okay, it is pretty good. I may consider getting that next time."

"Oh, next time? Are you saying there will be a next time?" She cocks her head slightly.

"I would like to, I mean, if you want to." I am at a loss for words and really hope that maybe the server will bring the bread, since it seems he has forgotten it.

"Of course, I really enjoy spending time with you, even if we are completely clothed." She winks. My gaze sweeps the restaurant, and it becomes emptier the later it gets. I think I see Amanda sitting at the front, near the doors, but I'm not sure from this angle.

"So now that you have clients, what's next?" Stacy asks, her voice bringing me back to the table, to where I am and where I want to be.

"Keep going, I am going to hire a couple of people, depending on where I see my gaps in knowledge. I already have someone on my short list, but I will have to go to Illinois to see him, at least if he is still there." I can't see the woman, I think it's Amanda, but I know she is still there. It makes me uneasy, not just for myself, but for Stacy as well.

Stacy catches my attention, holds it with the ease I've come to expect and desire. "And your radio plan?" she asks, a sly lift to her mouth, "giving it some thought?"

"Not much choice," I let her warmth spread through me, "I know a good station that provides some perks."

"All of Kansas City is going to know your story soon, and radio stations everywhere are going to want to interview you. I think my segment will be the only one with benefits, though." Her hand rises slightly higher on my thigh.

Acting nonchalantly, I counter, "I mean, most of them are old men, right? I am sure they know their way around a voice booth."

Her hand tightens on my thigh, "They may, but it wouldn't nearly be as much fun."

"You're probably right." Just then, the server arrives with the bread. Seeing our food mostly gone, he adjusts, "Would you like dessert? I could put the bread in a to-go container."

"That would be great, do you have a menu?" I don't want the dinner to end, even though I know both of us have early mornings.

"Yes, here is the dessert menu. The house specialty is the tiramisu; however, it is big enough for two people.

"Dinner and dessert, this is a perfect dinner." I hear Stacy say as I am thinking about dessert.

"How do you feel about sharing the tiramisu?" I ask. I am not normally a big dessert fan, but she seems to be interested, and I want to treat myself.

"That sounds great," She replies, leaning into me.

"Good, whatever we don't finish, you can take."

"Sounds good to me." She is already licking her lips in anticipation. I don't know if it is the dessert, or what she is hoping for a second dessert.

I see the server coming over with the dessert, much faster than the bread, and I catch eyes with the woman I had noticed earlier. It is definitely Amanda, and I don't want a scene. I know Stacy can hold her own, but it isn't something I want to bring down on her right now. Especially Amanda's face is contorted in rage.

"You okay?" She asks as the food is delivered, and she looks between it and me.

"Yeah, I thought I saw someone I knew." My pulse quickens.

"Well, you are from here, right? So I am sure that there will be people you know." She sounds confused by my behavior.

"This isn't someone I want to see." I can't focus on anything but Amanda's face, her eyes drilling into Stacy. I watch as she turns, and I take a breath.

"Do you want to leave?" Stacy looks concerned, but also questioning. Her hair slides over her shoulder, and I brush it back before kissing her.

"Absolutely not, I want to be here with you." I smile, but the smile doesn't reach my eyes as I monitor the front of the restaurant.

Stacy bites her lip, "Okay, we will stay because I want you to taste how amazing this cake is, but if you want to leave, we can."

I focus on her completely, pulling her chin so she faces me. "If I want to leave, I will tell you. What I want right now is a piece of that cake before you eat it all. Unless you want to take it and use it for something else." I wink as I pick up a fork. The indecision on her face as I go to take a piece.

"Me eat it all, how dare... No, you're right, this is great." Stacy smacks her lips.

Shaking my head as I take a bite, I must agree, it is great. A shadow passes over the table, at least to me, and when it does, every hair on the back of my neck rises. I am about to alert Stacy when her phone dings at the same time mine does. Dropping the forks, we both look at our phones.

I hear her gasp as she looks at her phone, before looking at mine. I focus on her. "What happened?"

"Someone broke into the news station and spray-painted the walls of my sound booth. The cops are there now." She looks through the messages.

I look at my phone and see a ping from the jewelry store; someone has attempted to break in through the back door. I bring up the camera, and the last person I think I would be looking at is standing there, unsure what to do now. Looking up, I see Amanda giving me a wave before she walks out the front doors.

"We need to go, NOW," I command as I stand up. The server is standing close, and I flag him down. "I need a box for the dessert, and I need to pay the check immediately."

He stutters before grabbing a box and putting the cake in it. He then hands me the box that I can pay directly with. Leaving him an okay tip, I grab Stacy's hand and pull her out of the booth.

"What's going on?"

"Someone is trying to break into the jewelry store, and I have a feeling you are in danger. Listen to me, we are going out the back door, then I will get you in your car. You need to go to this hotel and stay the night, tell them you need Abel's room. Do you understand?"

"Why can't I just go home?"

"Stacy, I will not argue with you. I need you to go there now. I have to go to Goldstein's, and I need to know you are safe. Please."

"Okay, will you call me?"

"Once I am done, I will come over, but not until I am done, so it may be late or really early, okay. We need to go."

Grabbing her by the waist, we walk toward the back door. I am already pulling my pistol from my hip when I open the door. Holding her back, I check both ways before stepping out.

"You stay behind me, and follow me, do you understand?"

She nods as I put her hand on the middle of my back.

"Keep it here no matter what." We quickly make it to the front of the restaurant. I see nothing off, but I will not be caught either. Dodging traffic, we get into the parking garage. Staying against the wall, we arrive on the second floor and see Stacy's jeep's flashers blinking.

"Where is your fob?" I ask as I inch along the wall toward her jeep.

"In my purse."

"Okay, I want you to lock it and see if it is still locked."

I feel the tension in her hand as she fumbles for her key fob. I continue to look around, making sure no one jumps out at me. Finally, she clicks it and it beeps, indicating that it was still locked.

"Okay, we are going to go to your jeep, you are going to unlock it, and get in, and then lock it again. Do you understand?" I say, turning my head slightly so my whisper voice carries over my shoulder.

"Yes, but what about you?"

"My car is on the first floor. Okay, are you ready?" I look at her and she nods slightly.

"Okay, go." I move toward the jeep, my head on a swivel. I hear nothing but the slight shuffle of our feet and our breathing. Reaching the jeep, I pull her around me to the driver's door.

"Get in and leave," I state, as I look around, my back to her. I hear the click of the jeep unlocking, and I step forward so she can get in. The jeep's deep rumble comes to life as I expect her to leave right away. Instead, I hear my name from behind me. Turning around, I see the window rolled down.

"What are you doing?" I almost yell, keeping my composure at the last minute. Every second I am keeping her safe is another second I am not at the store.

She reaches out and grabs my shirt before pulling me in for a deep, hungry kiss. "You be safe, do you understand?" She says as she lets me go and starts rolling the window up. All I do is nod, afraid my words will fail me.

I watch her drive down to the first floor before I run down the side stairs to get to my car. As I hit the first floor, I watch her turn out of the parking garage. *Damn it, I didn't think about warning her about someone following her.* I watch for a bit longer, and no one pulls out of the garage. Getting to my car, I chirp the alarm. Walking along the walls, I reach my car and get in. Locking it immediately, I look through the windshield to see if anyone is out there. I am starting to feel paranoid, but it cannot be a coincidence. Her office is damaged at a similar time to my known client.

The rev of the engine settles me slightly as I put it in gear and drive to the jewelry store. I have my phone to my ear the entire drive.

"Yes, this is Abel Williams. A taller brunette will be arriving in a red Jeep. She is to get the safe room. Yes, no one else but me is allowed. Yes, her name is Stacy Reynolds, and she is wearing a colorful shirt and a skirt. She will also have a bag of food with her. Thank you."

Hanging up with the hotel, I call Ruben, "Mr. Goldstein, this is Abel Williams from Mongoose Security. I detected a rear door break-in. I am going to be there in 2 minutes, and yes, the police have been alerted."

"Do you need me to come in?"

"Not at this time, I will go over what, if anything, is damaged and will contact you."

"Thank you for the call. You are already so much better than my previous security company." Mr. Goldstein hangs up, and it gets me thinking. Yes, there is money in the store, but it is mostly in physical items, which then have to be melted or pawned. It doesn't make sense that a break-in would happen so close to when I set the alarm. Unless that is the whole damn point. Fuck I slap my hand on the steering wheel.

Arriving at the store, I park in the front and key in my passcode. Locking it behind me, I hold my gun in front of me as I walk through the store. I go from case to case. I want to know everything before the police get there. All of the cases are in perfect condition, not a piece out of place. Looking at the glass with my flashlight, I don't even see any prints, which, now that I know Ruben better it doesn't surprise me. I walk toward the back office and the door. The office door is open and the overhead light is on. The back door is shut but unlocked. Upon returning to the office, I bring up the information regarding the break-in. The alarm tripped less than 20 minutes ago, which coincided with my alert. The little red light is still blinking, showing that whoever had broken in didn't know to turn it off in the office. Nothing seems out of place, and as I am about to rewind the footage, I hear knocking from the front.

Knowing it was likely the police, I put my gun away before walking out of the office. Walking to the front, it is in fact two police officers, both with expressions of aggravation. I don't know if it's me or just the fact that they have to do their job, but I walk straight to the door and unlock it before keying in the code.

"Evening, gentlemen," I say, offering my hand to shake. They both look at it like I have the plague.

"And who are you?" The heavyset cop with the name tag Timmons asks. I can still see the donut dust on his chin; at least I am hoping it is powdered sugar.

"Abel Williams, owner of Mongoose Security. Mr. Goldstein and Goldstein Fine Jewelry are one of my clients."

"So you do house calls? How did you get here so fast?" Timmons asks again while his partner scouts out the place.

"Yes, part of my contract is to be available during security events. As for how I got here so fast, it has been 20 minutes since the alarm went off. Usually, I would be here faster, but I was at dinner."

The younger officer turns. I cannot see his name tag immediately. "Could anyone vouch for your whereabouts when the alarm sounded?"

I know they are just doing their job, but my fingernails dig into my palms.

"Absolutely, I am sure the server whom I gave only a mediocre tip to because he was too busy trying to get the number of a server, would remember us since I demanded the check so we could leave."

"You said us, who were you with?"

"A female friend who doesn't need to be involved unless it is absolutely necessary." The two officers exchange a glance.

"I am sure it won't be," Timmons replies as he stands by the door, as if stepping into the store will cause him to actually have to work.

"Can you tell us what you found when you arrived?" The younger officer, now facing me so I can see his name is Smith asks.

"Absolutely, I could also show you."

"What do you mean?" Smith asks as he steps closer.

"The cameras record all the time, so even though I keyed in the code when I arrived so that you weren't called again by the motion alarm, you can watch everything I did."

"And you didn't tamper with the footage?"

"I haven't even watched it myself. I was about to watch it when you knocked on the door. Not to mention the system I have set up here, which you can't tamper with; creates a backup at my office. Neither of them can be tampered with the same way exactly, and if they are, it will take much longer than 20 minutes." There is no reason for me to lie; the system I have is almost tamper-proof. Yes, I know some men and a couple of women who could change things, but not in 20 minutes.

"Officer Timmons, do you want to stay out here while I go with Mr. Williams to the back to watch the footage?"

"Yes, I will check to see if anything is missing," He replies. I could have told him nothing was, but he wants to do it, so I let him. Security companies and police don't always get along, so for my first interaction, I want it to be positive.

"Follow me," I say as I walk back toward the office. "Oh, one thing, when I arrived, the red light you see blinking in the office was still blinking. That is the rear door's silent alarm. The door was shut but unlocked. Also, the office door was open and the light on, but nothing seemed to have been touched."

"Thank you for providing that information to me. So you just set this up?" Smith looks at the system.

"Yeah, last night, Mr. Goldstein was very anxious about the frequent break-ins and didn't want to lose more than he already had. I came in and completely redid the system."

"Didn't he already have a system?" I knew he was going to ask, so I am already prepared.

"Yes, but it was outdated, and many of the components were obsolete. It would be good for a local diner in a rural community, but for a jewelry store in downtown Kansas City." I smile. It isn't exactly the whole truth, I just gloss over some things.

"Many of the stores around here are similar. I am glad you were able to help him. He is a good guy. I bought my fiancé's ring from him less than three months ago."

"Congratulations." I feel that Smith and I can at least be acquaintances, while I don't know what Timmons and I will be in the future. Hopefully not adversaries.

"Thanks, okay, can you go back, let's say." He looks at his watch, "22 minutes."

Sitting down, with Smith standing behind me, I log in and open the portal on the monitor. That way, the cameras still record, but we will watch them. I explain the steps to him as I do them, so he thinks nothing suspicious is happening.

"So here is when the alarm was tripped, you can see the door open and someone walking through." I click on the camera in the office to show the person walking in and looking around before walking back out. Then I shift to the cameras in the main room of the store.

"They just looked around?"

"Apparently, I am seeing this for the first time as well." I know what the individual is doing and why they are doing it, but I do not feel the need to enlighten Smith.

"Okay, so they walk around, stick their head into some? Closets?" Smith points to doors that are opened and then shut.

"That one is the bathroom, that is the breakroom with a small fridge, and that is a closet." I shift to the cameras in the breakroom that shows the individual opening the door, standing silently, and then shutting it.

"Then about 5 minutes before I got here, the person turned on the office light, and walked out the back door, shutting it." I shift the cameras again so Smith can see what happened.

"So just a looky-loo? That doesn't seem right. Are you sure one of your cameras didn't miss anything?"

"No, and if you look at this one, the man made sure not to touch anything, even though he had gloves on. He kept his hands behind his back until he opened the doors." I point out how he is standing back from everything.

Smith has his notepad open and is watching, taking notes as the man walks around the room. "Wait, you said man, how do you know?"

Straightening up a bit, I put on my security voice, "As you can see from the way he moves, he has a limp on one leg, while that could be a woman, the height, shoe size in relation to the closet door, and how small pieces of hair are visible from the mask he is wearing indicates short hair. Also, the body build, even though the individual is wearing a jacket at least a size too big, shows that they know what they are doing."

"I agree with you, but if it is a professional, why didn't they take anything?" He taps his pen on the notepad.

"I don't know, but in my line of work and my past, there are a couple of reasons. Diversion, something is happening somewhere else in town, and he was sent here, knowing he wouldn't get caught, to make the police come here versus somewhere else."

"True, but we have a lot of police, so a simple breaking and entering may not bring enough police for a successful diversion." Smith thinks out loud. I like him; he is young, but I can tell that he is a critical thinker. I don't want him working for me; instead, I want him in the police force, hopefully training younger police officers in critical thinking.

"Good point, it could also be that a specific person is in danger, and you and I both know that police will focus on that, so if a couple of officers are pulled away for small things, then the person could be taken." I counter.

"True, we have had some off-the-wall calls tonight, but nothing I would guess that could cause major disruptions."

"When is the shift change?" I ask.

"About an hour ago."

"They were waiting for someone to come on duty, then possibly. Whatever the point of this and your other calls?" I shrug, not knowing how Smith would take my hunch.

"Interesting point, well obviously there is nothing here, and if there was, you would likely have it solved before we could. Mr. Williams, it is a pleasure working alongside you. I feel you may be able to help our city." He offers his hand to shake, and I shake it.

Walking back to the front, Timmons is in the same position as when we left him. There isn't even any change in the imprint on the carpet. At least no one got by him, I think.

"Officer Timmons, I got all of the information that I could from the videotape. Someone just walked in, hung out, and then left."

"Are you sure? That seems like a lot of energy." Timmons replies as he looks at me.

"Yeah, I showed him the recordings from all of the rooms, and nothing was touched, by that I mean literally nothing." Smith shrugs. Turning to me, he tips his hat, "Well, we will be going. If you need anything, please call dispatch and let them know what it is about, and we will call you."

"Thank you both." I stand there as they walk to their patrol car and get in. As they drive off, I lock the door behind me and go back to the office. I showed Smith everything I wanted him to see, but there are a couple of things that he doesn't need to know. Things like the fact that the guy walked in without his mask on, allowing me to see his face. Then, when he came into the office, he took off a glove and clicked buttons on the old security system's keyboard. *Got you,* I think as I try to figure out how to get the evidence removed from the scene without alerting Mr. Goldstein or the police.

I know who I need to call, but I don't know if he will work with me, or even consider it, after how we left things following our last deployment. We were both in bad headspaces, and things were said that shouldn't have been. There is no one that I would rather work with, though, so I make sure everything is as it was before grabbing the keyboard and walking out the back door, making sure it is locked behind me. I reset the motion detector from my phone and watch to make sure nothing moves in the store. Sometimes the criminals like to hide, but from what I could determine already, he wouldn't. No, he is long gone doing something else.

It is still early, so I decide to see if I can gain access to the radio station and assess the damage there. I want to see if they are connected. Part of my job in the military was to connect things that seemingly weren't connected. I did not feel I was the best in my unit, but we were all good at it. As I drive closer, I see there is only one police car still there, which bodes well with me. Parking down the street, I pretended to be just walking downtown, just another spectator. Both officers are in the same car, likely instructed to ensure no one breaks in until the glass can be repaired.

The front doors are shattered in, as if a bomb had hit them. Closing my eyes from the rush of memories, I rest against the wall for a minute. *The heat of the desert hit me as the sound of munitions going off all around me caused me to duck. My unit was on both sides of the door, weapons ready to engage. I wanted to yell "stop," but no sound came out when I tried. Seeing it all in slow motion: my guys, two by two, entering the building, the vehicle driving up the street. Turning to Tech, I yelled at him, hoping Tech would radio them to get behind something. Tech was looking the other way at another vehicle. Knowing there was nothing I could do, I took off running, shooting at the vehicle before they got to the open door. The shots were heard, and two guys looked out, saw the vehicle, and began yelling. In a blur, I was in the building, gasping for air as I saw my unit shooting from the broken windows. The vehicle didn't stop but tossed something near one of the windows. As the bomb exploded, I returned to the present.*

Taking a deep breath, I shake my head, still hearing the crunch of the tires on the hard pack. Slow swallow breaths, and I right myself, looking around to see if anyone saw me. No one is staring or running away, which is a good sign. Not a good sign for how I am dealing with the flashbacks, but good in that no one witnessed it. Looking at the police vehicle, they are both still playing on their phones, eating their dinner, so I duck under the police tape. As I get close, I take a deep breath, not smelling the acid scent of gun powder, and I know it wasn't a bomb. That helps, because if it were a bomb, I am looking for someone or a group that is more sophisticated than I want to deal with right now.

Looking down, I see the rubber marks of a car that has slammed to a stop. Looking around, I then notice the black paint on what remains of the door frame. Not seeing the marks from a tow truck, I figure that whatever they were driving wasn't damaged enough to be left. It has to be long enough to break in and have at least one door that could open, so the person or persons could get into the sound booth. Careful not to move anything that may be evidence or cause noise, I step through the reception area and move toward the sound studio. Other than the front destruction, everything looks the same as when I arrived for my interview.

I am not ready for what I see when I walk in the broken door of Stacy's sound booth. When Stacy said that someone had spray-painted on her walls, she did not elaborate, and I have a feeling that she knows exactly what is written.

FUCKING WHORE

HOUSEWRECKER

SLUT WITH A MICROPHONE

I step out of the room for a minute. It isn't just the words, but the meaning behind them. I know who did this with every being of my soul, and the rage I feel. But how? She was in the restaurant. *Fuck her,* I know she gathered her little minions to do the dirty work while she could claim plausible deniability, but not this time. Stepping back in, I am so focused on the words that I don't notice the rest of the sound booth. The chairs are cut, and the glass between the booth and the technicians is smashed, but not broken, likely thanks to the tinting Stacy had installed. I search under the desks, around her equipment, which is smashed, to see if the intruder has left anything. There is a single hair, and what could be a fingerprint, that I bag. It is better than nothing. Looking around the room, I close my eyes, remembering how it looked the last time I was here. Then I re-scan the room looking for anything out of place, well, more out of place than everything else. There is a box on a table that wasn't there before. It is small, about the shape of a necklace box, bagging that separately, I step out backwards, careful to make sure I didn't miss anything. Before leaving, I take photos of everything. Different angles, and of the box, to make sure it is well documented in case Stacy needs it in the future.

If I didn't know any better and I walked into this room, I would say that it is an angry ex-lover, a disgruntled former employee, or someone who is very much unhinged and a fan. I know the police will not look deeper than an unhinged fan, and since they know nothing about me, they will not look into my past.

The thoughts run through my brain, do I tell Stacy? Do I not, and go find Amanda and end this once and for all? Do I let the police know? It has been a long time since I interacted with the police before this evening, and if they are all similar to Timmons, I will not get anywhere. Gut feelings from a mentally unhealthy combat veteran don't go far, especially with whoever Amanda may have on her side. It is time to make the call, and I just hope he answers. Not knowing if the back door's alarm is still active, I step through the wreckage of the front again. I again took photos of the damage, making sure that the flash doesn't alert the officers. It doesn't, as they are still there, playing on their phones. I could have stolen whatever I wanted without them knowing. Yeah, not going to them with my suspicion that Amanda is at least part of this, if not directly involved.

Staying against the wall in the dark, I walk away from the building, looking back once to see if anyone has seen me or if the police have noticed that for the last 30 minutes someone has been investigating the crime they are supposed to be watching.

Pulling away from the building, I drive past the officers to see if they even notice a vehicle driving past. The driver looks up and gives me a small wave. I wave back, then shake my head. It is laughable how unimportant they feel this is, but then again, if they believe it is a solitary event not connected to anything else, why focus so much attention on it? I can't completely blame them, and then I realize I am looking at it the wrong way. Since I am invested, I have the skills to understand connections. I feel the pull, but they likely do not. But then maybe I am thinking too much about it, letting my brain run wild with possibilities when it is just a simple, unhinged fan. I know that Stacy's manager keeps records of everything. Maybe I can get my eye on them and see if there is someone who fits the bill that isn't involved in my bullshit.

All the way back to the hotel, I am hyper aware of any lights that appear behind me. Driving the dark streets, I worry if the headlights are someone trying to get to me or to Stacy. I think about what I am going to say. It will not be, "Hey, remember how I was a douche bag. Well, I need your help. Can you pick up and move to Kansas City?" *Shit*, I have that meeting with the NFL player tomorrow. If he will meet earlier, I can meet him, check out the place, and then do a quick trip to Chicago if my phone call goes well.

If it doesn't, then I will still go, and possibly have to beg, which my knees are not unused to when it comes to this person.

CHAPTER FOURTEEN

Pulling into the hotel, I take a deep breath before pulling out my phone. I see the valet running to the car. The hotel's lobby is inviting and looks warm, but I need to make this call alone. The valet is young, rolling down the window. I wait for him to approach.

"Hey, I will need a valet, but I first need to make a call. Is it okay if I sit here?" I don't want to impede his job.

Smiling, "Absolutely, this late at night, I have seen no one since a sedan about an hour ago."

Although my head is spinning, I smile back as if what he said meant nothing. "Great, I will let you know when I'm done." I roll the window back up. Using my thumb, I run it over the screen before entering my PIN. One thing I learned was never to use a thumbprint or a face scan; anyone can open it without a warrant, but a PIN? That takes a warrant. Checking quickly on the cameras, both at the house and at the jewelry store, I click on contacts. I didn't think it would be this hard calling someone that I lived next to for years.

Closing my eyes, I think about the last day that I saw Tech, it was on base, and he was just finishing up with a therapy appointment.

After just finishing another briefing about the deployment, I wasn't in a good mood. I turned the corner and ran into him, knocking him over.

"Here, let me help you," I said as I looked down on him.

"I don't need your help." He spit as he rolled over on his stomach and tried to stand up.

"Just let me help you; there is nothing wrong with needing help."

"Oh, like Kessler needed help, and you walked away." He glared as he used the wall for help.

"I didn't walk the fuck away, and you know that." At least I didn't think I did. Everything from that day was still fuzzy.

"Sure, you keep telling yourself that. Remember, I was there too, I saw everything, and from my perspective, you didn't save anyone but yourself."

"How did you see anything? You were under a fucking pylon, do you remember me helping you out from under it? Or did you mistakenly think it was someone else?" I should have controlled my anger. I know why Tech was mad; hell, if I was him, I would be mad too.

"Whatever, maybe you should quit where you can be alone, that way no one relies on you." He flipped me off before turning and walking past me, hitting his shoulder against mine.

What he didn't know, and I should have told him, was that I signed my paperwork that day. Even though the commander told me to stay, he dangled a promotion in front of my face. No, Tech was right, I didn't want anyone relying on me. I didn't see him again, even though we were in the same small area; we made sure not to interact with each other. The rest of the guys worried about us, knowing how close we were, but one death, and it was apparently enough to break that bond.

I focus back on my phone. I need him, not just for security, but for my own mental well-being. He knows more about me than I think I do, and I should have said bye. With tears forming in my eyes, I find his number, hoping that he kept it. Hitting connect, I wait; it is dead air, and then a ring, then a second one. I know he is likely asleep, so I wait. After the third ring, I hear Tech's voice.

"Abel? Are you okay?"

"I have been better, but hearing your voice helps. I need your help."

"Right now? It's what? 1 AM, I work tomorrow."

"Great, you are in Chicago, right? I can come see you in the afternoon, please, it is important."

"Yeah, I am working security at a mall, tomorrow I'm at Water Tower Place, and I will be there until 8. See you tomorrow." He hangs up. I collapse against my seat, the tears running down my face. He wasn't angry; he didn't hang up. He immediately asked if I was okay. All this time, I just knew he hated me, that he blamed me for everything, and I let that simmer. Wiping away the tears, I grab my duffel bag, which I keep in my car, and walk toward the valet.

"Hey, sorry that took so long." I pull the valet key off the ring and hand it to him.

"Sir, being able to drive this, you could have taken an hour." He grins as he accepts the key.

"Yeah, she is special. I don't want to hear her gunned down the road, do you hear me? At least wait until I am inside." I pat him on the shoulder. It is a fun car, and being a valet, he knows how to drive a stick, so I am not overly worried.

"Absolutely not, I would never, even if between you and me, I want to. I got to park a really nice Jeep earlier, and while the driver was older than me, she was FINE." He smirks.

"Glad you are getting to see some nice cars, well, I am going to sleep, long day tomorrow." I wave as I walk into the lobby. He isn't wrong, Stacy is fine, and she is older than him.

Laughing to myself, I wait for the automatic doors that open with a faint whooshing sound as I step into the bright and welcoming lobby. From the moment I stepped in four days ago, I knew this would be the perfect place for clients to stay if they needed to. The desk is positioned facing the door, so no one can enter without being seen. The elevators are only accessible from the lobby, and even the pool is enclosed with no external doors.

"Welcome, how can I be of assistance?" The young woman asks, her name tag reads Kyla. I see her briefly look me up and down, but the pleasant smile of someone trained in customer service stays on her face.

"My name is Abel Williams, and I need a key to the room that a client is currently in." I want to see what the staff will do.

She briefly frowns, "I'm sorry, Mr. Williams, but we don't have a room under your name currently. Would you like to rent one?"

I smile, she is trained. "No need, can I speak to your manager? You are not in trouble at all." I pull out my wallet and my ID as she pushes a button near her computer. I appreciate how they don't have to leave the desk to alert management. An older woman steps out of an unmarked door along with a large man.

"Hello, I am the manager. How can I help you?"

Giving her my ID, I notice no one else is in the lobby. Waiting a breath before speaking, "My name is Abel Williams with Mongoose Security. I have a client in a room; she came in earlier in a red Jeep. I would like the key to her room, please." The manager nods to the man who walks around the desk.

"This is Theo, he is going to escort you to the room. We do not provide key cards to your room unless you require one."

"I do not, thank you, and Ms.—" The manager hasn't introduced herself.

"Emily, it is nice to meet you, Mr. Williams."

"Ms. Emily, your employee here, did everything she was supposed to, thank you. Oh, one last question, did someone come in earlier asking about this room?"

Ms. Emily nods briefly to Kyla, who looks back at me. "Yes, a man came in roughly 45 minutes after your client did, requesting access to the room."

"Do you have footage of him?"

A shark smile spreads across Ms. Emily's face, "Oh dear, I already sent it to your formal email, and I have a thumb drive if you want to review it soon."

"Why, Ms. Emily, you are a special kind of manager."

She fluffs her hair slightly, "I do my best, especially for a wonderful person like you."

"Thank you, I should get up there. If someone comes in before we leave in the morning, please have Theo come up immediately."

"Will do," Theo says as he turns to the elevator. Every minute I am here is another minute I am happy with the service. Scanning his card, Theo pushes a single button. "I am sure they went over this with you when you came in, but you have to have a keycard to enter the elevator, as everything open to the public is on the first floor."

"I did not know that, thank you," I remember most of what they said, but I didn't recall the elevator process. Arriving on the 8th floor, high enough that no one can easily get into the room, but low enough from the roof that it wouldn't be simple to rappel, I follow Theo as he walks down the hall. Instead of watching his large back, I concentrate on the wall ornaments. Many of them are actually cameras, so no one staying automatically knows they are being watched. Even if the owner hasn't shown me, I can tell high-level security when I see it.

Stopping in front of room 812, he pauses. "This is the room. Would you like me to enter first?"

"No, that will be okay." I pull my pistol out and rest it on my side with my duffel in my other hand.

Theo looks at the pistol before nodding. "Okay, here you go." He scans the key card, and I hear the chime, but no green light. "We don't use green or red lights."

"Interesting, another security feature?"

"Yes, and no, it alerts us in the security room if someone scans a card and it doesn't work, but it also allows for higher-end key cards. The light is a gimmick."

"Good to know. Thank you." He cracks the door so I can push my back into it. Before I turn, he is already back toward the elevator. Dropping the bag, I clear the rooms. When I met with the owner, I told him I wanted a suite or at least a room with the bedroom separate from the rest of the room, so that I could work if I needed to, and the client would have the privacy they deserved.

Seeing the room for the first time, I am impressed, not only are there separate bedrooms, but a dining room and a living room that are separated by a wall. The small kitchen is part of the dining room. I check the empty bedroom with the bathroom first, then I move through the room toward the opposite side, where the other bedroom and bathroom are. Not knowing if Stacy is awake, I slowly open the door, my pistol down but ready if needed. Seeing the lump under the covers, I move to the bathroom quickly to make sure it is empty. Coming back out into the bedroom, I debate waking her, but decide against doing so, she needs her sleep, especially after the way today ended.

I set up my laptop in the kitchen so the light will not seep into the bedroom, and I pull up the images from the radio station. Clicking through them, I look for anything I may have missed while walking through. I wasn't in a rush, but coming down off the brief flashback and worried about Stacy, I may have missed it. Not seeing anything I missed, I stand and stretch before getting some water, checking the refrigerator, hoping against hope that Stacy hasn't eaten all of the bread. I say a silent prayer when I see the bread bag. Pulling out a tiny loaf, I sit back down to go over the jewelry store. Halfway through the pictures, I hear the bedroom door open and the soft patter of feet.

"Abel?" A small voice sounds from the living room.

"It's me." I stand and walk around the wall. Stacy, even with bed hair, is beautiful. She is wearing a long shirt that barely covers her lack of underwear. She rubs her eyes before looking at me again.

"When did you get here, and why didn't you wake me up?"

"About 45 minutes ago, and you were sleeping, little snores even, and I know you need your rest."

She pads closer and sniffs, "Is that bread?" She steps around me and looks at the table before going to the refrigerator. Bending over to grab the bag, her shirt rides up and her perfect ass is on full, unclothed display. I clear my throat as I stand there. Smirking over her shoulder, she rummages a bit more before coming out with a piece of bread.

"It does not take that long to get bread." I walk toward the table where my laptop is open.

"No, but if I were faster, you wouldn't have gotten such a good look at my ass. What are you doing? You need help?" She moves toward the table, nibbling on another tiny loaf.

"I want to go through the pictures of both the jewelry store and your station while everything is still fresh before I get some sleep."

The bread stops midway to her mouth, and she freezes. "What do you mean by my radio station? You went to the radio station?"

"Yes, and trust me, not only did no one see me, but I could have probably walked out with evidence without the police knowing, or wait, I may have."

"You may have what?" She moves to the front of the table across from me. "You may have what?"

"I found a fingerprint and a piece of hair, oh, and a box. I figured if they police hadn't thought it was important, then why shouldn't I make sure it wasn't?"

Brushing back her hair with her hand, she sighs, "You can't take evidence, what if it catches the person or persons?"

"If it is, then they should have grabbed it. I found it almost immediately, it wasn't like I did some serious sleuthing. On the other hand, the police, well, one of the two officers who showed up at Goldstein's was very good at his job."

"Don't tell me you walked out of there with evidence as well?"

"I mean, not really evidence per se." I grin as she lies her head on the table. "Look, I am allowing the police to do their job, but if I can assist them in finding out who it is, then it is a bonus, not to mention Smith likes me, so I don't think he would be that upset."

"Okay, so a former soldier, turned security company owner, is stealing things from crime scenes. I am sure that will look great in the newspaper."

"You and I are the only ones who know. That reminds me, are you super tired? I have one more thing to look at before I sleep. I have a consult in the morning, if I can change it, and then I have to go to Chicago."

"Why are you going to Chicago? I have work in the morning."

"You absolutely do not have work in the morning." I tense my jaw as I look at her.

"I absolutely have my job. I already talked to the manager, they are going to set me up in another sound booth, it will be fine, they are doubling security."

Taking a deep breath before I speak, knowing that if I didn't, it would push her away. "Stacy, it is not wise to go back to work until we find who we are looking for."

"And if we don't, then I won't be working, and they will have won. This isn't the first time..."

"What? It isn't the first time that this has happened?" I swing my laptop around and click on the pictures from her sound booth. Her mouth drops open right before she covers it with her hand. A soft sob escapes.

"You didn't know?" I should have thought about that before showing her. I figured her manager showed the damage.

"No." Her eyes fill with tears, and I stand and wrap my arms around her.

"I'm sorry, I thought you knew." I hold her as she cries.

"That has been my home, my refuge for a decade. Why would someone do that? The manager just said someone spray-painted it, not what it said. I don't even understand." She speaks between sobs.

"I don't either, but we will figure it out, but not right now, you need to sleep. I will go to sleep in the other room. If you want to go to work tomorrow, you can, but I want you to be careful. I can take you there, but I may have to meet someone." I figure he can meet me earlier, and the initial consult won't take that long, so if Stacy is in a booth the whole time with security, she will be okay.

"Will you sleep in the room with me?" She leans away from me a bit as she looks up. There is no plotting, no expectation, just Stacy drained and looking much younger than her years."

"Let me finish what I need to do, and then I will be in, okay?"

"Promise?" Her voice is so quiet I barely hear her, especially with my thoughts spinning.

"Promise, give me five and I will be there, but I expect you to be asleep." I grip her chin and force her to look at me.

"I will try, we are safe here, right?"

"Absolutely, we are probably safer here than at my house." As I say that, I realize it is true, I need to do some things to fortify my property, the first being probably to move the office out.

"Okay." She steps out of my reach and pads back to the bedroom. I wish there is more I can do to help her, but I have to be methodical about it, or else whoever did it will get away with it.

Sitting back down, I plug in the thumb drive. I keep my work email off the laptop so that if anyone steals it, it won't be compromised. Clicking on the icon, I bring up the file. There is only one file on the thumb drive. "Stranger Danger," and I have to laugh. Ms. Emily may look older, but she knows a lot more than one would think by looking at her.

Double clicking on the file, I watch the program open and a view of the front doors whoosh open. A man walks in, his head down so I can't see his face immediately, but the limp tells me it is the same guy who broke into the jewelry store. He takes two steps into the lobby before glancing around and walking out. *What the hell,* I let the footage play, and less than 30 seconds after he leaves, Amanda walks in with a briefcase. Watching, she walks to the desk and opens the briefcase. I can't see what it is from this view. Making a note to see if they have another view in the morning, I continue watching. She hands Kyla something and then taps her fingers on the desk. Whatever she gives Kyla, I see Kyla shake her head. Amanda reaches for the document, but Kyla pulls it back out of her reach. Amanda grows angry while Kyla places the document in what looks like a shredder. After some yelling, Kyla pushes a button, and another man steps into view, his back to the camera. After a minute, Amanda closes the briefcase and walks toward the door, glancing back at the end.

I am about to turn off the playback when the camera shifts. Instead of watching from the desk, I am now watching from the sliding glass door. *I am going to kiss Ms. Emily,* I think as I watch the entire event from a different angle. I watch as the man walks in, and as he walks out, he keeps his face down, but I can see he has blonde hair, which matches up with the man at the jewelry store. Then I watch Amanda walk in, so sure of herself. She approaches Kyla, who is already wary, I can see it in her body language, but I doubt Amanda does. The one thing I never learned was lip-reading, which right now would be very useful.

Opening the briefcase, I see what looks like a folder. The camera zooms in on the folder, which says 'Mongoose Security'. Amanda pulls a piece of paper from the folder and presents it to Kyla. Knowing what happens next, I fast-forwarded it. As Amanda is walking out, I see the rage in her face along with a gleeful smile. I am not changing my name, so I need to do some damage control. At least Kyla is smart enough not to allow her up.

Again, the hotel comes through. Once again, right as Amanda walks out, the camera shifts, this time to the piece of paper that Kyla supposedly shreds. I scan over it and hit the table with my fist. That fucking bitch has the nerve to try to forge my information. The paper has a random logo of a mongoose along with my home address. It is a letter allowing 'Ms. Amanda Reeves has all the rights and responsibilities afforded to her by Abel Wiliams.' As I skim the rest, it is all trash that won't hold up to a feather. She expected Kyla to be some young girl who didn't know what she was doing. Not to mention the logo is hideous and not something I would ever put on anything. Even my signature is horrible. Not surprising because I don't know if Amanda ever saw my signature, or if she did, she remembered it, but damn, the lengths this woman is going.

Tomorrow, I was going to give Amanda a call and see how stupid she really is. Shutting my laptop, I put it in the bag and walk to the bedroom, getting in, I debate again if I should tell Stacy. I need, or at least want to, handle it myself, and the more I keep her in the dark, the better, at least I hope so.

Pulling off my shirt and pants, I sit on the bed and pull off my socks. Sliding under the covers, I lie on my back, figuring out what I am going to do. I know Stacy needs comfort, but my mind is racing, and I am pissed. In fact, I am angrier than I think I have ever been at Amanda, and that is saying a lot considering what she did.

Thinking about the time I called her, and a guy answered, Amanda in the background. They both sounded fried out of their minds talking about random things until Amanda could wrestle the phone from the guy. The next ten minutes, she asked for money, told me the guy wasn't anything, to which the guy got mad at her, and then I heard them having sex after she dropped the phone. It was the last time I called her. After that, I sent her one last letter and cut ties.

As I am about to fall asleep, I feel Stacy wiggle over and put her arm across my chest. Her head rests on my shoulder. I put my arm around her and listen to her breathe. I slow my breathing to match hers, and before I know it, I am asleep. It is the fastest I have ever fallen asleep, and I know Stacy's presence helps.

CHAPTER FIFTEEN

Hearing an alarm break through my dreams, I open an eye and jump out of bed, forgetting where I am. The room looks different in the morning with the sun just coming through the curtains. After a second, my brain finally connects the room to what happened last night, and I sit back down. Stacy rolls over and smirks, "Not used to an alarm or waking up in weird places?"

"Both, mostly the alarm, weird places are a frequent occurrence until recently."

"Come back to bed, this is my early alarm." She raises the blankets, glancing at my phone, I see I have at least two hours before my client will take phone calls, so I lie back down.

"Your early alarm?"

"Yeah, in the mornings I have three alarms, I have my early alarm, which I wake up to if I want a full breakfast or I need to finish laundry and take a shower. My normal alarm is for when I eat my normal breakfast, and I can take a quick shower, and then my late alarm, for when I am going to grab a protein shake and my clothes are already out, ready for me."

"How do you know which one to choose?"

"However, I feel the night before or how I feel in the morning, but considering." She rolls toward me, resting her hand on my chest. "I'm much closer to the studio than normal, and I have extra clothes at the studio; I definitely don't need the early alarm; however, now that I'm up." Her hand trails across my chest and runs down my stomach.

"Oh, you think I am up? I have two hours to sleep." I roll over, smirking. Instead of huffing, she scoots closer to my back and continues running her hand along my stomach and down each thigh. There is absolutely no way I am going to go to sleep with her doing that, not that I mind.

Rolling completely over, I find myself on top of her, her giggling as she looks up at me. "So now that we are up, what are you expecting?"

"I have a question first." She lies there, running her hands up and down both sides of my torso. I close my eyes at the feeling, just enjoying the sensations.

"When was the last time you were checked for STDs?" Her question shocks me a bit, not because it is random, but because it isn't something that has come up before.

"The day after I got back from Iraq the last time," I answered without hesitation.

"Have you been with anyone since?"

"I was with this fucking bombshell named Annie at a bar, but I was protected." I wink as she blushes.

"So just me since you got back?" The realization hits me that, yes, she is the first person I have been with since returning from that final deployment. I usually go right outside the base and find someone, but this time I didn't.

"Yeah, what about you?" I hold myself up in a plank position as much as I want to be between her thighs, this conversation needs to happen, and right now is as good as any, I suppose.

"I was last tested 11 months ago, give or take a day." She runs her hands down to the waistband of my boxer briefs.

"And no one since."

A bit shocked, I look down at her, "Seriously? Are men around here that stupid?"

Laughing, she slides a finger into the waistband. I concentrate on the conversation. "It was a poor relationship all around, and I didn't feel the desire or need to be with anyone. I missed the companionship, well, I would have if it had been a good relationship, but physically I can handle myself."

"I am sure you can." Adjusting slightly, one leg going between her legs. "So why are you asking now?"

"I recently got back on birth control, and I like you, so I want to do more, be closer, experience more, damn, I sound like a… I don't know what, but not a 33-year-old woman."

"You could have told me, you don't have to be on birth control." I laugh as I kiss her, my tongue sliding between her lips. After I break the kiss, she looks confused.

"Why not?"

"I got a vasectomy on the military's dime when I was 23. It has been 9 years, and I was tested frequently to ensure there was nothing moving." I push her legs apart a bit more and rest both of my legs between her.

"You didn't want kids?"

"Not really, especially since I thought the military was going to be my career, and I didn't want to bring kids into all of that. Then I saw how relationships with kids were and no thank you. I froze my sperm in case at some point I got out or wanted kids, again on the military's dime."

"Wait, so you're saying we could have been fucking raw this whole time?" Her eyes widen.

"We have had sex once, I don't know what you mean by 'all this time'."

"Well, now that I know what I know, it could have been a lot more." She wiggles against my dick.

Resisting the urge to strip out of my boxer briefs, I pause, "Wait."

"Is this a wait and sit up conversation, or a wait while I tease you and we talk conversation?"

"It can be a wait and tease as long as you pay attention."

"Perfect." She says as her hands go straight for my waistband. This time, instead of barely going under, she slides her whole hand under, rubbing against my dick. Sucking in a hiss of breath, I focus.

"I don't normally fuck someone more than once, because I haven't wanted ties. Something about you pulls me in, and I don't want to fuck you, or continue spending time with you in this capacity, if you don't want something other than a good fuck."

She looks up at me before grinning, "You mean an amazing fuck."

"Focus, please. I am serious, I am already messed up in the head enough, I don't want to think something is going on when it isn't."

She stops moving her hand before speaking. "I want you, mind, body, and soul. You have treated me better since meeting you than any man in my life has. I know you have issues, I can see them in your eyes. I guess there is one more question before we decide if this is something we want, no matter the length."

"And what is that?" I think she will be sarcastic or witty, instead, she grows serious.

"The flashbacks you have, don't tell me you don't. Do you become violent with the ones you have? Will you hurt me in my sleep?"

I think about it. This is my escape, I can say yes and leave, not looking back, but I can't. I don't know if it is because I can't lie to her or because I want her in my life.

"No, they are always while I am awake, and always because of a sound, a smell, or something else that triggers them. I have never reached for my weapon, I have never fought back, and I will never hurt you."

"Well then, let's see where this takes us." Stacy reaches both hands to the waistband before pulling them down. I sit up and wiggle out of them, my dick ready and willing, but I know Stacy isn't. Sliding up to where my dick is barely touching her core, I kiss her hard while my hands roam her body. I move my whole body down so I can worship both breasts. I am going to be slow, or at least as slow as we can manage, given that we both have to be somewhere.

"How long do you have?"

"I have an hour before my normal alarm rings, and I have a feeling I will need a shower." She looks down at me as my tongue resumes flicking her nipple. I take her nipple in my teeth and bite on it slightly, watching her back arch and her head go back. I switch to her other breast and do the same thing, her nipples hard against my hands as I alternate between the two. Finally, I kiss down her torso, making swirl patterns with my tongue.

Her hand finds my head and tries to push me down. "Now now, we aren't rushing anything." I continue my lazy stroll down her body, feeling the goosebumps lift as my tongue flicks across her skin. As I get to her hips, I lick along where her leg joins her torso on both sides. I move further down and start on her inner thigh near her knee.

"Fuck, that feels so good." I hear her say as I kiss and lick up her thigh. As I get close to her core, I breathe hot air over her lips and clit before going back to her other knee.

"You keep teasing me, and I will do it myself." She says, looking down at me.

"No, you won't." I smugly smile as I continue up her thigh. I can feel her body vibrate slightly as if her nerves are expecting, just waiting for me to hit her clit. Once I get to it, I do the same thing before moving up to kiss her mound, my fingers running up and down her thighs.

"Please, just more." She cries, her hand deep in my hair.

"What did I say about good girls?" I smirk up at her as she lightens her grip on my head. I fun my tongue down both sides of her lips, enjoying her taste as she wiggles under me. Taking one hand, I put it on her mound and move slightly, bringing her clit out. As a finger from my other hand runs down her folds, I flick my tongue on her clit. She almost comes off the bed, my hand on her mound holding her down while I chuckle against her clit.

As I circle my tongue around it, alternating between flat tongue and flicking, I hear her pant.

"Already? I haven't even started." I say at the same time I insert a single finger into her wet, warm hole.

My mouth stays on her clit while my finger thrusts deep in and out before I insert two. I can feel her tensing up, but I am not ready. I want her on the verge. As her walls tighten on my fingers, I pull them out gently.

"So close, keep going."

"I know." Moving off her clit and sliding up her body, my dick sitting at exactly the right place.

"What? But I was so close." She huffs.

"Just wait." I slide deep into her until her hips meet mine. I sit up so my knees are under her butt as I grab her hips. Slowly sliding in and out, I wait for just the right moment before I take a finger and put it in my mouth. I pull my finger out, licking my lips before I press against her clit. Holding her with my other hand, I slowly speed up, rocking my hips into her with every stroke. My finger glides over her clit in circles, flicking it when I am at the deepest.

"Oh, that's oh." She says as she braces herself.

"Are you going to come for me? Come around my hard dick as I stroke deep in you." I press my finger hard against her clit and feel it throb. I pull out a bit and rub it hard. Just as she clinches hard and spasm, I thrust hard, grabbing her hips and holding her against me as she rides the orgasm out. After her clit stops trembling, I move my hand to her hip before I thrust again, two more thrusts, and her walls clench again.

"I'm coming again, oh fuck." She yells as she thrashes. This time, I do not pause; I move back and fuck her hard, my dick tight in her as she grabs my shoulders and puts her legs around my hips, allowing me slightly deeper access. I feel the tension in my balls start as I pound into her, the sweet feeling of an orgasm approaching.

"Do you want me to come in you?" I whisper in her ear as I thrust.

"Yes, fuck me." She screams as she arches against me, her body electric, her nerves firing everywhere.

"As you wish," I say as I brace myself above her while I thrust into her.

Just as I come, I kiss her, screaming her name into her mouth as I shudder twice.

Moving her head to the side, she whispers in my ear, "Yeah, I'm not letting you go anywhere." I laugh as we lie there, just basking in the rising sun through the curtains and the feeling of satisfaction.

Rolling to my side, I rest my hand on her stomach. She laughs, "What's funny?"

"I hate birth control, and before you, every single partner required that I be on it even if they wore a condom. It messes with my hormones and such. It is just funny that the one time I willingly go on birth control, is the one time I don't need it."

"That is pretty ironic," I say, lying my head on the pillow.

She raises herself, resting her head on her hand, "Do you want me to go with you to Chicago?"

I haven't really thought about it, between everything else. "You probably should, but on the way there, I need to brief you on some things."

"Cryptic but okay."

"It is just the person who we are going to see; we didn't leave on the best of terms, and when I called him, he answered, which is good, but I don't know how the reception will be."

"Okay, yeah, let me know, I can even stay in the car." Stacy smiles as she stands up. "I am going to jump in the shower. You want to join me?" The smile she gives me is if I get into the shower with her, we are having sex again. As much as I want to, my body is not ready for it.

"I want to so bad, but I am on three hours of sleep, and I just spent every ounce of that sleep on what we just did."

"Spoilsport, but I understand, okay, I will be out soon." She hums as she walks into the bathroom, leaving the door open as she turns on the water. I watch her get into the shower before my eyes close. The next thing I know, she is dressed and doing her hair.

"Shit, what time is it?" I ask, trying to grab my phone.

"I have 30 minutes to get to the station, so if you want to escort me, you should probably get up." She smirks as she adjusts the necklace she is wearing.

"Why didn't you wake me up earlier?"

"Because you were snoring and looked adorable, and I figured, former military, you could take quick showers." She doesn't look at me, instead concentrating on her hair.

"You're not wrong, give me ten." I jump up and quickly take a shower, the hot water feels great on my skin. I wash and I am out in less than 10 minutes. Getting dressed, Stacy is in the dining room eating cake.

"That's your breakfast?" I try to grab it, not to keep her from eating it, but so I can have some of it.

"You made me leave last night, so I am going to enjoy it. Here you can have a bite." She takes a piece on a fork and hands it to me.

"Thank you. I need to call my client and see if he can see me earlier. If he can, I will follow you in and go do the consult and be back before your segment is done."

"Sounds good, you ready?" Stacy grabs her keys and purse. I open the door and look down the hall before we walk to the elevator. Pushing the down button, the elevator opens almost immediately as if it had been sent.

I hold her waist as the elevator descends. I know it is likely to get worse before it gets better, but I wish it wouldn't. Reaching the bottom floor, I release her, and we walk alongside each other. I stop at the desk and let them know to tell Ms. Emily thank you. Leaving through the front door, I have her walk behind me until I am sure we are alone. It is still early, and the only one there is the valet, different from last night, but eager and happy.

"Two cars, get the Jeep first, please," I say as I hand over the two tickets. He nods as he jogs toward the valet parking.

"Why me first?" Stacy asks.

"Because then you can be in your locked car in case anything happens, versus you standing out in the open."

"Oh, that makes sense. Thank you."

The valet arrives with her Jeep, and after I do a quick walk around, I open the door for her. "Drive forward and wait, okay?"

She nods as she puts the Jeep in gear and drives to the end of the overhang. The valet is already leaving to retrieve my car. I lean against the building and watch the city come to life. The air is fresh before the thousands of cars hit the roadways to get to work, or in some cases, leave work. I always liked the morning hours before everyone is awake; it is peaceful. It gives me time to think, to have a coffee, and relax before everything hits at once. I am brought out of my thoughts by the sound of my car pulling up. Handing the valet a 50, I slide into my car and bring out my phone. Finding the note regarding the client, I call him.

"Reggie here." A deep voice greets me.

"Hey, this is Abel from Mongoose Security. I had something come up, and I am wondering if I can meet with you in about 90 minutes."

"Heck yeah, brother, I just finished my morning workout. I am planning on watching some tape, so you are welcome anytime, just call me when you get to the gate, okay?" His voice is cheerful, with a hint of gratitude mixed in.

"Great, will be there as soon as I can." I put the car into drive and move it up to Stacy's Jeep.

"We are ready. I rescheduled my appointment, so I can follow you in."

"Sounds good, you don't think there will be any issues, do you?"

"No, but I am always on the side of caution." I tap her door before walking back to my car. She waits before pulling out. I follow her out of the parking lot and into the flow of traffic. It is easy to keep track of her, even when I drop a couple of cars behind. I want to know if anyone is following, and being right behind her will not be useful. Turning on the street, the radio station is on, and I sharpen my focus and catalog everything. No sedans, no black vehicles that could have run into the station the night before. It is quiet, and while I enjoy the quiet, it is almost as if the city is holding its breath waiting for something to happen.

Pulling into the lot designated for radio staff, I park on the street and walk over to her. Upon seeing me outside her door, she rolls her eyes.

"Seriously?"

"Yes, seriously, now let's go." I help her out of her Jeep as we walk toward the front of the building. The crime scene tape is gone, but the doors are covered with plywood. Opening the door, Stacy walks in first. The receptionist sees us and picks up the phone. In less than a minute, a short, stocky man flanked by four security guards walks toward us.

"Stacy, I am so glad you are okay. I am so sorry about what happened to your studio. I have technicians coming in to fix everything, and then painters will come to cover the spray paint. Um, who is this?" The short man asks. The four other men just stand there, glaring down at me and Stacy.

"This is…"

"Hi, I'm Kevin." I reach my hand out to shake his. He looks at it with disgust. I see Stacy look at me sideways, but she keeps her composure. "I am a friend of hers from way back, thought I would help her come in today."

"Yes, sorry, Kevin, this is my manager, Todd."

The man looks me up and down, "How did you know what happened?" One of the security guards step forward. I dismiss him; he is just a paid lackey.

"Oh, Stacy called me up last night. See, I live in Independence, and our girl here was just so worried that she wanted me to bring her to work today. I told my old lady that I had to do it, I mean, you do things for friends, right?" I keep it short and to the point. Not that I don't trust him; I don't know him.

"Well, your services are not needed anymore. We hired additional security." The man puffs out his chest.

"I mean, it may sound dumb, but can I see some credentials? There is this guy running around Branson who is pretending to be a cop, or at least that is what my cousin told me." I ask the four men.

Todd steps forward as if to stop them from doing it, but I glare at him. "Why is your dumb hick friend asking for credentials? I have four for your safety."

Stacy smiles, "I have known him my entire life, since we were young. If he wants to see the credentials, then show them to him. Can you please allow him to ensure they are legitimate?"

Todd huffs but nods to the four men. Three immediately come forward and hands me their security licenses, along with information on where they work.

"Thank you, and you back there, with the blonde hair?" I ask the man who steps back when the other three come forward.

"You don't need to see my license." He crosses his arms in front of his body.

"Well, since it is one of my besties' lives on the line, I will call the company, or maybe I should take my jacked-up pickup down there, it only has a bit of rust. We'll get it figured out." I pull out my phone, and the man takes off running.

"Now, what is that about? I haven't seen a man run like that since old Billy lit his pants on fire." I ask Todd and the three men.

"No idea, he is new, started yesterday, I think. I am surprised the boss put him on this job. He has a limp when I watched him earlier." One of the two that has been there before answers.

"Left or right leg?" I ask.

"Right, right?" The guy looks at the other two, who both nod.

"Oh well, maybe that's for the best then, since someone who has a limp may not be the best at security. Which room will our girl be in now?" Todd stands there sputtering while one of the original guards speaks up.

"I can show you." He smiles as he passes Todd and begins walking down the hall. Getting to the sound booth, I check the room before Stacy walks in.

"Lock the door, and don't let anyone but me or what's your name?" I look at the guard.

"Kyle, but I go by K because Kyle is for a douchey man-boy." He smiles. I snort before turning back to Stacy.

"Unless K here or I tell you whatever special word you want, do not even let us in, do you understand?" Stacy nods.

"What is your special word?" I ask, figuring that she will need to think about it.

"Artichoke." She says with finality as if that word is the best word ever. I purse my lips before turning to K.

"You heard her." All I could do is shake my head.

"Yes, I won't tell the other guards. I thought something was fishy about that one, but I am just paid to be here, you know? Aren't you Abel Williams?" K shrugs.

"Yes, thanks for playing along. I appreciate you not telling the other guards. I need to talk to Stacy for a minute alone, if that is okay?"

"Absolutely, you do what you do." K tips his head slightly before walking back to the reception area.

"If it isn't too much, and please tell me if it is, can you please address the fact that there are people out there with fraudulent documents, and not let anyone do anything unless they know the person directly. But you know finesse it up."

"Why?"

"Someone tried to get into your room last night with a fake logo of Mongoose and a poorly worded permission slip."

"Do you know who it was?"

"That doesn't matter right now, please don't mention me exactly." I kiss her on her forehead as she narrows her eyes at me.

"Okay, I will definitely finesse it up, because whatever." She motions to me, "That will not fly."

"Thanks, I appreciate the vote of confidence. I am going to go see Reggie and be back. Remember, me or K, no techs, no other guards, if the building is on fire, K or me, do you understand?"

"Reggie as in the Chief's new…" I put my finger on her lips. "Shush, just shush." I smile as I release her lips.

"Okay, so a random stranger that you are going to see. Got it." She winks as she steps into the room and shuts the door. I wait to hear the lock engage before leaving.

"Who do you…" Stepping into the reception area, Todd gets into my face while the three security guards watch him.

"I told you, I am a friend of Stacy's. Name's Kevin. Now I need to get back home, the old lady is about to pop, and she doesn't want to see any damn doctor. Blahblahblah midwife. If my truck gets me back home, that is. Speaking of which, you know who has a motor shop around here? I need my catalytic converter replaced, it was stolen. Anyway, can I get out of here before she calls me?" I hear at least one, if not two, of the guards chuckle before coughing. He turns on them, "And you just let him parade in? What am I paying you for?"

"To protect your business interests, and if someone is dedicating their time to protect one of your employees, that leaves us more time to protect other things. It is a win-win, and you aren't even paying him."

Todd grumbles, "But he forced one guard to run away."

"Well, in my mind, if he went running because of needing to show an ID, he shouldn't be protecting anything," I tell the guards, who all just nod as I walk to the front door. Pushing it open, I expect Todd to say something, instead I hear him storm back down the hall.

After entering the coordinates for Reggie's place, I have about 15 minutes to stop by the security firm and have a chat. Pulling away from the curb, I check my surroundings to make sure there isn't anything suspicious. Not seeing anything, I drive to their security firm, a four-story building with a large parking lot that is more than half empty. I begin turning into the parking lot, but on second thought, I continue down the street. Looping back, I park near a diner half a block from the building.

I walk up to the building, admiring the architecture, "Must be nice." I tell myself as I push open the front door. As I step into the lobby, a young man stands up from the control desk. "How can we help you at Ares Security?"

"Yes, I would like to speak to someone about their hiring practices," I say as I look around.

"Hiring practices?" He asks, unsure how to proceed.

"Yes, I was just at one of your sites, and a person of interest in many thefts was there as an employee."

His eyes widen before he looks down at the desk. "Um, I don't know, probably HR, but maybe not, how do you know?"

I almost feel bad for him; he is probably a year or two out of high school, making close to minimum wage, and have to sit and tell people to leave. "Oh, forgive me, I own a small business, and one of your guards that I saw this morning has the same gait as a person who recently broke into a business I manage." I didn't even know if this man knew what a gait is, but I am not getting anywhere with him.

"Can you please have someone meet me? I am on a limited time, and I need to make sure that someone in power knows they are hiring criminals, unless that is the intention?" I add, letting it float in the air.

"Oh no, let me get you the VP of human resources, she should be able to help, or at least take a note."

"Thank you, and like I said, I only have a short amount of time, so if she isn't down here soon, I will go talk to my friends at the police station." I don't want to pull the police into it, but if it makes them move faster, then not my problem.

"Oh, of course, yes, we wouldn't want you to waste your time." The man says as he picks up the phone. I step away toward a wall with their distinguished client list on it, far enough away that he assumes I cannot hear him, but close enough that I can.

"Yes, Ms. Shrader, there is a man, no, I know you said not to call, I understand that, but I really think you should come down here, he is threatening to" his voice lowers, "go to the police. Yes, I know, yes, he is here, okay, see you soon."

I don't turn around when he hangs up to further push his assumption that I didn't hear him. I pull out my cell phone as if I am checking texts and take pictures of their client board. How egotistical does one have to be to have a list of all your big-time clients? Shaking my head, I pretend to text someone before putting my phone back in my pocket.

Less than a minute later, I hear the ding of the elevator and the click clack of high heels against the tile floor. I wait as the sound gets closer. "Where is this man who demanded to speak to me?" I hear a shrill voice ask. Planting a smile on my face, I turn and walk toward her.

"Hello, I'm Tony, and the reason I came down to your office, beautiful by the way, was to let you know you hired a criminal."

"No, we didn't. What proof do you have?" She argues, but her eyes shifts to the man at the desk.

"I own a small security company out in Independence, two business clients, and a handful of residences. Well, it just so happens that one of my clients had a break-in, all the way out in Independence, and the suspect had a very distinctive limp. Well, if it wasn't fate, I was down here talking to a friend of mine, your company are the guards for. I ask to speak to one of them to make sure my friend is being taken care of, and they had the same limp. When I asked him for some more information, he ran."

"You think you can tell the difference between people because of a limp?" She laughs and circles to the guy behind the desk. "Please remove him."

"Ms. Shrader, is it right? If you don't believe me, that's well and good, but I have some friends who work in the independence police department who may be interested in my theories." I shrug as I walk out of the building.

"Now, Tony, let's not get hasty. Why don't you come up to my office, and we can talk about it? Did you see the man's face?"

"Sure did, but I can't, I have a client I have to meet with in Branson, and I am sure you know how much of a drive that is."

"I do, well, thank you, Tony, for bringing this to our attention. I will relay it to the right people." Her smile tells me otherwise, but I let the lie stand.

"Well, just trying to do my civic duty. Have a good day." Walking through the front door. I do not go straight to my car, instead, I walk around the side of the building as if I had parked a street away in the opposite direction. I double-back and see that the man at the desk is out front looking for me. He is on his radio, probably telling whoever he is talking to that I can't be found. Inexperienced and young, a double whammy for someone expected to be the face of a security business. After a bit, he walks back inside, and so I continue to my car and leave.

Entering Reggie's address, I drive straight there, making sure to mentally note Ares Security and have Tech look into them, provided he agrees to work for me. *Damn it, I need a new office.* I keep forgetting that I need to scope out another place, but something always takes precedence.

CHAPTER SIXTEEN

The road up to Reggie's gated community takes winding turns, revealing the lush landscape of the southwestern Kansas City metro area. It is beautiful, and I love driving this road, even if I could never afford property here. Every aspect of the landscaping, from the flowers to the smallest details, is carefully arranged to provide the best view from any angle. At least my car matches the area, I laugh as I arrive at the gate. It takes longer than I want, especially with Stacy at the radio station, but it is something I need to do for my business.

Dialing Reggie, he answers on the first ring.

"Yo, Abel, you at the gate?"

"I am."

"Perfect, I have a clicker somewhere." I hear him rummaging through things, "Here it is, I haven't used it from this distance, so let me know if it works."

"Will do." I put the phone on speaker and watch as the gates open inward. "It worked, see you in a minute."

"Sounds good." Reggie hangs up as I drive up the road, watching the road signs that are all indigenous tribe names by letter. Finding the road, I turn down it, and shortly, at the end of the road, I see a ranch-style, single-story house in front of me. For a gated community with some houses I passed, I expected more.

Pulling into the driveway, I walk up to the front door with my laptop. As I get to the door, it opens, and a large man steps out.

"You must be Abel." He smiles, offering me his hand. I shake it, "and you must be Reggie."

"Yup, welcome to my home, for at least the next two years."

"It's definitely different from what I was expecting." As I walk in, I notice the outside and the entrance. A simple 1980s-style ranch, with at least one remodel and definitely upgrades, but other than that, it feels like a home. It isn't sterile like other places, screaming money. I am impressed.

"Oh, yeah, you expected one of those mansions or something?" He laughs as we walk into the living room.

"Not expected, but this area is known for them."

"Nah, I am from Alabama, I graduated from there, and growing up, we shared rooms. I didn't want to waste all of my money on a nice house, so the neighbors could ooo and ahh. Nah, that isn't me. We had lived in Cleveland before this, spending a year there and living in the city. I hated it, so when I got traded to the Chiefs, I wanted somewhere that was out of the way from the major cities. The schools are good here too, I mean, of course, they are with how much money there is."

"That's true. So married and how many kids?" I ask as I inspect the room.

"Yup, married to Janice, married her in college, she has a degree in Business Administration, I definitely married up." He laughs, and I laugh with him. It is nice to see a husband talking positively about his wife, especially coming from the military. "We have three kids, Tina, Kaden, and Jaden, they are, and I may be wrong, 10, 8, and 5."

"Oh, so they are all in school this year?"

"Yeah, which is great, because between games and moving and everything, it is hard, and it has been even harder on Janice."

"I understand that, so let's see the system, and thank you for meeting me earlier. The last two days have been something."

"Absolutely, so there is this door panel, and then each room, except for the bedrooms and bathrooms, have cameras. The basement isn't finished, but there is supposedly a camera in there as well."

"Okay, so standard, now let me ask you, do you want motion on all windows, especially the kids' windows?"

"Yes and can I get cameras in their rooms. Before you say anything, at least Tina and Kaden sleepwalk, they got it from me, and I really don't want anything to happen to them." I feel his hesitancy in asking. I understand; having cameras in certain places can get tricky.

"Reggie, this is your house, at least for the time being. We can put cameras everywhere. I would suggest not in bathrooms, but if you feel safe having your kids with cameras, I can make it so I can't see them unless the window's motion detector goes off. You can watch them all the time."

"Seriously, that is great. I just worry, especially with how much I travel." I feel his relief radiate off of it.

"Do you know who the company that manages the security system is now?"

"I think the property manager said Ares, but they said I could change, and I called them to get a consult, and I didn't really feel the vibe. You know how it is."

My jaw tightens involuntarily when he says Ares, but I keep my calm, "Absolutely, I do. Let me dig into it a bit, and then we will see if and what you need upgraded, okay?"

"Sounds good, my house is open to you, I found the crawl space in the ceiling, and if you need that, you may be able to fit, this lineman's body ain't going up there."

"I would never make a client or even a prospective client climb into crawl spaces." I laugh.

"Okay, well, I am going to get something to drink and watch a tape. Let me know if you need anything. I will be right through that door." He points to a large room that doubled as a gym and a movie room.

"Sounds good, give me 10 minutes and I should be able to give you a good estimate."

"Professional and quick, thank you." He grabs a Gatorade and walks back to the gym. I put my laptop down on the table and go to the front keypad. Easily I locate all the cameras and enter the crawl space. While I am concerned about what I might find up there, and as I expect, it is the same thing that I saw at Goldstein.

Pulling myself down, I brush off and go see Reggie. Walking in, I see him going over the same bit of tape repeatedly, as if trying to memorize it. I respect that, a man similar to me.

"You done already?" He stands up after pausing the screen.

"Yeah, so I have some good news and some bad news."

"Hit me with the bad."

"This is not top-of-the-line anything." I put it bluntly, he doesn't need to know the details unless he specifically asks.

"I figured, it looked, I don't know, flimsy."

"That's a good word for it."

"So what's the good?" He glances at the screen before turning his attention back to me.

"Because you live in a single-story house, and the basement is unfinished, it won't be hard or expensive to put a new system in. Also, because you may decide to move, especially once you fall in love with the team, I can easily yank it out, keep the existing system in, and move it to your new residence."

"Seriously? You would do that?"

"Yeah, your family seems like the most precious thing to you, so why wouldn't I help you protect it?" Reggie comes closer and for a minute I think he is going to hug me, which, I mean, larger men have. Instead, he grabs my shoulder.

"You don't know how much this means to me. So what do I need to do?"

"When I get back from Chicago tomorrow, I will call you, and we can set up when you want the install. Then once it is installed, all you have to do is call your property manager since you pay the subscription as part of your rent, right?"

"Yeah, 1000 a month."

I choke back a gasp when he says that. "Yeah, so when I get all up and running, you call your property manager and let them know you found another company and that you will pay out of pocket."

"So how much? I figure that 1000 is high, but I don't know."

"Yes, that is absolutely too high, especially for what you have. Our package will run significantly less, be more robust, and if an alarm trips, we will be here in under 30 minutes. It also alerts the police, so we can meet them here, talk to them about our system, etc."

"No way you are significantly less with all of that?" Reggie is side-eyeing me as if I am going to pounce with a higher number.

"You pay the install and the equipment. Depending on the total cameras and such, it runs from 200-400 a month."

This time, he hugs me, wrapping his arms around me. "Thank you so much, people see the NFL and automatically think we have all this money, and while Janice is a whiz with money, we have three growing kids."

Stepping back, I just smile, "I get it, and we are here to help, not to price you out. I need to go, but I will call you either tonight, depending on when we get back from Chicago, or tomorrow, okay?"

"Great, thank you so much. Talk to you soon." He turns back to the screen and hits play while sitting down.

I gather my things and let myself out. Another project for Tech, if he agrees to come back, or at least come down to work. Now, to get back to the station. I turn on the radio, and Stacy is just starting her segment. If I drive straight through, I may be able to run to the café and get her a coffee, I think as I pull out of Reggie's driveway. While in a hurry to get back to the city, I don't miss the black SUV that is parked right outside the gate when I turn to head into town. Because of the way it is sitting, I can't tell if there is damage to its sides, but I suspect there is.

Turning onto the main road, I watch as the SUV slowly inches forward. *Amateurs,* I think, as I speed up and hit the freeway, losing them easily in the traffic.

CHAPTER SEVENTEEN

Arriving at the station, I still have 45 minutes before she is due to be off the air, so I park and walk down to the café, grabbing us coffee and a muffin for her. As I wait, the warm sun, along with the noise, settles me. After losing the SUV on the freeway, I didn't see them again. I stand by the windows, ignoring the other customers waiting for my name to be called, when I see her.

She hasn't seen me yet, but it is only a matter of time. I want to run out there and demand an explanation, a reason for her doing what she is doing. Pushing through the customers, I open the door. "AMANDA," I yell. Instead of turning to face me, she turns away, moving her bag onto her shoulder and picking up her pace. Just as I am about to move to catch up with her, the barista calls my name. I feel a push-pull in my brain. Do I follow her and demand answers, or do I bring Stacy her coffee and protect her? My heart wins out and I go back in to retrieve the coffees and muffin.

As I walk back to the station, the sun doesn't feel as warm and is less bright, as I try to figure out how the pieces fit together. It isn't just Amanda and the strange man who looks like a ghost from my past, but now another security firm is involved, one that either intentionally hires criminals or is simply a terrible company. I focus on walking, trying not to think too much about what I see. Maybe it isn't actually Amanda at all, maybe it is some other woman that I scared when I screamed the name.

Standing by the door trying to figure out how to juggle the coffees and the muffin bag, the door opens, K standing there smirking.

"I figured you would be back."

"You figured right, anything strange?"

"Not strange per se, but weird," K says, scratching his chin.

"How so?"

"Right before you got here, a woman walked by, and she had a bag on her shoulder. She paused as if considering coming in, but then looked behind her and almost ran down the street."

"She is about 5 feet 2 inches with blonde hair. Blue bag?"

"Yeah, that's exactly right, how did you know?"

"I saw her out the window at the café and noticed she was walking this way."

"Yeah, she didn't seem suspicious, but the way she paused and then hurried on was weird."

"Yeah, I don't know, but if you see her again, let me know, and I will go track her down." *Boy, will I.* I think as I walk back toward the studio, Stacy is in. Turning around at the last minute, "Hey, Todd isn't around, right? I hate having to fake being dumb."

K snorts, "No, he already left, he doesn't enjoy being here during the day, says it ruins his love of radio."

"Good to know. Is she due for a commercial soon?"

"Yeah, should be, if not I can let the techs know to push one, she is by herself and will take calls after the mid program updates."

The tension that had been released earlier is back; she is taking calls on a day like today. Of all days, of all times.

"Thanks." I nod as I stride to her door. Waiting for K to give me the thumbs up down the hall, I knock. Nothing, and then I knock again.

"Who is it?" I hear Stacy's voice sound tinny and small from the other side of the door.

"It's me, Abel, let me in."

"Not without the special word." I smile at her comment. I decide to test her a bit more, though.

"The coffee is burning my hands, and I have a muffin." Either I will be very proud or slightly disappointed.

"Nope, burn then, not without the magic word."

"Fine, it is artichoke." The door swings open, and she stands there with both hands on her hips.

"Testing me, really?"

I kiss her forehead as I walk in, "What? It needed to be done."

"Whatever, anyway, you have perfect timing, I am about to take calls."

"Yeah, I heard from K, why?" I shut the door behind her after she takes the coffee and muffin bag.

"It is what I do when I don't have a guest, and as you can see, I don't have a guest."

"Fine, but I can stay in here, right?" I am not planning on leaving, but I figure I can ask her.

"Absolutely, I still have a bit. This is a longer commercial break, followed by an update on the weather and other news, and then a shorter break and calls. It gives the technicians time to sort them."

"Sounds good, well, you enjoy your snack." Just as I say that, there is a knock on the door. I walk up to it, my hand reaching for my pistol, which is in my bag in the trunk of my car. "Yes?"

"It's K, Artichoke. I need you to come here now." I tell Stacy to stay behind me as I open the door. K is standing there, his eyes wide, shifting from foot to foot.

"You stay here. If I am not back, make an excuse and postpone the calls." I tell her as I shut the door in her face before she can respond.

"What's going on?"

"Someone in a black SUV delivered flowers," K stares as we walk back to the reception area.

"Okay, how is that weird?"

"First, the SUV was damaged on the sides, like it had gone through something too small for the vehicle."

"Oh, like a door?" I counter, seeing where K is going.

"Exactly, and then they gave me the flowers, and just said, 'We heard about Stacy's traumatic evening and wanted to give flowers.' But we have told no one, and we kept most of it out of the paper. The damage to the door is there, but nothing about her studio."

"Okay, so still following you."

"Then I look to see if there is a card and nothing, but I can hear ticking."

Instantly, my alarm bells ring in my head. "Ticking, from the flowers?"

"Yeah, should we call the police? Todd? Get everything out of here?"

My training kicks in, and I take a breath. "No, you won't do any of that. What I want you to do is leave the reception area and get me a big, like five-gallon bucket of water, can you do that?"

"Yes, we did the ice bucket challenge last year. I am sure we have some."

"Perfect, you find that and fill it with cold water, I am going to look at it and tell everyone that something happened to the plywood and to stay back. I don't know, make something up."

"Okay, will do." K quickly leaves the room. I hear a door down the hall open and then close. Carefully, I pick up the vase and look at it. It is a small vase, approximately four inches tall, with a bouquet of flowers arranged neatly, which makes the whole thing about eight inches tall. The vase is covered with shiny paper and a ribbon. Looking through the flowers, I don't see anything, but they are so tightly packed, it makes it almost impossible.

The ribbon is a simple package ribbon with a single bow tie, so I untie it and pull it away from the paper. Then I check the paper and pull it away. At the bottom of the vase is a small device blinking with a countdown. It is due to go off right as Stacy's show is ending, give or take a couple of minutes. On top of the device is a small white cube that has a blasting cap attached. It is rudimentary, which usually means effective, but I don't think the would-be attackers factored in my presence.

I hear K huffing back as he carries not one but two five-gallon buckets of water.

"I didn't know, so I figured if one was good, why not bring two." He shrugs as I motion to the two.

"Is that a——"

"Yes, it is. Now it is simple and has a timer, so what I am going to do is take out the flowers that are stuck in the RDX, then I will put it under water and dismantle it."

"Oh yeah, easy peasy." K steps back so he is standing near the hall.

I carry the vase with the flowers over to one bucket and start pulling out the flowers. Slowly, I can see inside the vase better. It looks like they have used an adhesive to create the cube. After all the flowers are removed, I place the vase completely underwater in the second bucket. Pulling the blasting cap away from the RDX, I close my eyes on reflex. The water should neutralize the RDX, since I don't know what compound they mixed with it, I am not sure how it will react.

Opening my eyes, my hands are still there, and the vase slowly bubbles. I pull out the timer and RDX and remove the batteries from the timer. *Rudimentary but effective.* Leaving the RDX in the water, I make sure the vase is empty and toss it in with the flowers.

"Okay, it's fine, but here is what I want you to do. I need you to call the police after Stacy and I leave, and ask for Officer Smith.

His partner is Timmons if they ask. When he arrives, explain to him what happened, using my name, and he has my number. Okay?”

K nods, looking at the two buckets. “Are they safe?”

“Yeah, well, that bucket is completely safe; it could be thrown in a sink, but you should keep both just for the police. Also, place them behind the desk or something similar so that someone doesn’t accidentally trip over them. Here I will help you.” I reach for one, but he pushes me away.

“She is about to take callers; you should be in there with her.”

“Thank you, you saved a lot of lives today.” I pat him on the shoulder as I walk by. People need to know when they’ve done something good, as it helps ease the boredom of life.

Reaching the door, I knock.

“Who is it?” Stacy’s voice is still small but less timid.

“Abel Artichoke.” The door swings open, and she flies into my arms.

“Settle down just a smidge. You still have work to do, and we need to go to Chicago.” I laugh as I put her down.

“Grab your headphones, you are looped into the calls, but you can’t speak.”

“Works for me.”

Over the next 15 minutes, Stacy takes calls from listeners who have driven by and want to ensure she is okay. She has a call asking who the next guest will be, and some ask if she can host the night spot once a week because they work at night. Mostly mundane listeners who just want a piece of Stacy’s time.

Her voice flows strongly through the microphone, assuring her listeners she is okay, and that no, she is a morning person, not an evening person. I listen as she wraps the listeners in blankets of comfort, answering their questions and reassuring them.

"Well, that is about the end of my time here. I won't be here tonight as I have a trip I have to make, but Tabetha will be spinning the music and providing updates. We have time for one more caller."

She nods to the window behind me before clicking a button, "You have Stacy Reynolds with Reynolds Reveals, you are on the air."

Static surges in, then drops away. Replaced by a clear and sudden voice. I see Stacy set up straighter, and I focus on the voice. I know exactly who it is. My focus tightens with every single syllable. I can't do anything other than cut my hand across my throat, but Stacy is focused and ignores me.

"Been listening to you for a while," the caller says, her tone as smooth and confident as Stacy's. "Always wondered how far you could push it."

I can tell she is curious, but she is also tense. She knows something is wrong, but can't pinpoint what it is. I catch her eye and make the throat cut motion. She just shakes her head.

"Glad to hear I've got your attention. What's on your mind?" Stacy's voice comes across the headset clear and authoritarian, but I can tell she is wondering what is going on.

The caller pauses, just long enough for the quiet to feel deliberate or for them to be confused by Stacy's response. "You think you know your audience, but you don't know who's really listening."

It is a feeble excuse for an accusation. I wonder how far she will push it. The warning is there, and Stacy places both hands on her desk. She laughs into the microphone. I can tell the laugh is rehearsed; there is no mirth in her face. "Well, that's what makes it so interesting, right? Never know who might tune in. Thanks for the call." She looks up at me with a glint in her eye.

Moving her finger to disconnect, the voice breaks in, quick and sure.

"Some voices deserve to be silenced." The words snap, and the line goes dead. I look at Stacy to see if she disconnected or if the caller did. She shakes her head, which means the caller did. She sits back and collects herself.

"Well, audience, that caller is right, not all voices deserve to be heard all the time. I, for one, know that, which is why I am only on the air twice a day and only during the week. That is it for today, like I said, Tabetha will be here for the evening's updates. Until more is revealed, Stacy Reynolds is off the air." She clicks the button and drops her headphones on the desk.

Her fingers find the edge of the desk and she holds on as she breaths, her face lowers. I stand up and walk around to her. Placing a hand on both shoulders, I just stand there, not moving. She doesn't need me to say anything, she needs me to be her rock, at least until she finds her inner confidence.

Finally, I see her look up, her eyes sweeping the studio, focusing on the glass and shadows. I can see the uncertainty in her eyes, but I just stand there, a silent sentry against the outside. Standing up as if in a daze, she turns to me and puts her arms around me. I hold her as she cries, time becomes immaterial as we stand there. I am her shield against the storm. The storm that I brought down upon her.

"We need to leave for Chicago." I step back to allow her to look up at me.

"Do I need to go? It's not that I don't want to, I just am worried."

"I am more worried about you being here without me. So yes, you are coming with me."

"Fine, are we taking your car or mine?"

"Mine, I have a trunk of gear. Let's go." I grab her hand and we walk toward the front.

K is standing near the reception area. He nods as he sees us walking toward the front.

"I did what you said to do. Do you want to look at the buckets before you leave?" He is nervous, and I can't blame him.

"What does he want you to look at?" Stacy stops and walks toward the reception desk.

"You don't need to worry about that, Ms. Reynolds, just something Abel helped me with." He tries to block her path, but she isn't having it.

"Why are there flowers and a vase in a bucket and something in another?" Stacy directs her glance between us.

"I will tell you in the car, we need to go." I am getting impatient, and I know she is curious, but I want to know if Marcus will help; if not, then I need to take action.

"Sure, you can also tell me all about how you knew the voice that called in last." Stacy pointedly tells me as she walks out of the building.

"Have fun," K smirks.

"Yeah, Chicago is what? Eight hours? Maybe I have something to knock her out in the trunk." I ponder as I leave the radio station, K's laughter follows me out.

CHAPTER EIGHTEEN

Stacy is already standing by the car when I get out there, her arms cross and tapping on the ground.

My senses sharpen, each detail standing out with precise clarity. Scanning the area, to make sure everything is in order to address my concern for her safety. I see Stacy standing up straighter as she notices my heightened awareness.

"Sorry, I shouldn't have run out like that, but no, you know what, I am not sorry."

"Whiplash," I say.

"One thing I expect from you is the truth. Especially if it is connected."

"And I am planning on telling you, but you huff out of the station like you want to be kidnapped."

"No, I fucking didn't, I pay attention to my surroundings. I want to know everything or else." She leans against the car.

"No, we aren't going to do that. I will hogtie you and put duct tape on your mouth if you think we are going to spend the next eight hours in a car with that attitude." I motion to her.

"Try it," is all she says as she turns to open the door.

"Wait, do you need anything from the Jeep?" I notice it sitting at the back of the lot, alone and exposed. Something is slightly different about it. "Stay here."

"Why? What do you see? It's my Jeep." I hear her jogging to catch up.

"Fuck." All four tires are slashed, a betrayal more complete than she expects. Stacy's expression transforms, the lines of fatigue deepen into something more immediate, more consuming.

"This isn't fucking random, and how dare someone fucking touch my car?" Her voice is thin with the realization that something bigger is at play.

I look at the tires, and they are cut multiple times to ensure complete replacement. "No, it isn't random at all."

"You sure? I mean, it could be right?"

"A bomb, your studio vandalized, a caller, and now this?"

"A bomb? What the fuck are you talking about? Oh, we are so fucking talking on the way to Chicago."

I grimace. *Maybe I should just fly.* I think, but no, I want to drive, I need to know the area, and apparently, I'm a masochist since I decided to bring her along.

"Don't have secrets from me, and you won't have this attitude." I can feel the fear coming off of her, though, even as she tried to talk a big game.

"I will always keep some secrets from you, I have to in my and your line of work."

"You know that isn't what I mean." She turns in her seat to look at me. I haven't started the car yet, so I take a deep breath before facing her.

"Look, I will tell you everything you need to know on the drive, and if by the end you don't want to be with me or part of this, then I will fly you home."

She narrows her eyes at me, "You would fly me home even though I am safer with you?"

"Well, after you know everything, you may not want to be associated with me, which could possibly save your life."

"Okay, but can we stop to get something to eat in Springfield? There is a great diner I go to if I drive that way."

"Absolutely, we need to stop at your place and get you a change of clothes because we will likely be staying there overnight, especially if the meeting goes well."

"Sure, it says it takes eight hours to get there, so we should be there around seven if we go straight through. He works nights, so I can drop you off at a hotel and then meet him." I am trying to do what is best for both of us, all while figuring out how to tell her about Amanda and the bomb.

"Okay, then let's go to my house. Then we can talk before dinner." Stacy turns and stares out the front window.

"You going to tell me where you live, oh Passenger Princess?" I try to calm myself down, but so much is coming at me so fast that I don't know if I can keep my composure.

"Oh, you don't have that in a file somewhere?"

"That's it." I reach into the bag I had open in the back seat and pull out a roll of duct tape.

"What do you plan on doing with that?"

"If you can't keep your smart ass, wise-cracking comments to a minimum, I will tape you quiet." I am serious; I need space to think, and she is over the top. I know she is scared, and that her life is in a spin as well, but that doesn't give her the right to be snappy at me.

"No, I'm sorry, I won't be as lippy, now let me put my address in your phone and we can get my stuff."

"Okay. Thank you." I pull out of the parking lot and follow my GPS.

CHAPTER NINETEEN

The city blurs past, the roads are not as busy since it is in the middle of a workday. The drive carries the unease of the day, the sharp edge of uncertainty that comes with it. Stacy alternates between nervous chatter about everything and nothing and an anxious silence. Her presence is as bright to me as normal, but there is a dark sense about it. I watch her from the corner of my eyes, feeling the pull of worry and of emotional attachment. I see her fingers alternate between tense fists and more relaxed ones as she speaks.

Climbing the hill, I drive through a small corpse of trees before it opens up to three Victorian houses at the end of a cul-de-sac. The middle one is large, three stories tall, and imposing, while the other two are only two stories tall and don't have the same presence as the middle one. All three are set back slightly from the road with large swaths of natural flora and fauna between them.

"It's the middle one." Stacy points to the white three-story with a wrap-around porch.

When we arrive at the house, I am out of the car, and I ask, "Is this all yours?" I am already aware of the vulnerabilities. The building is older and less fortified than it should be. My assessment is quick and professional, but I'm sure that Stacy sees the lines on my face. I see a small glint of an alarm sign push back inside the bushes. Its promises are weak and unreliable. Stepping closer, I recognize the company and frown.

"Why are you getting out? And no, it is multiple residences, I am at the top. The owner owns all three houses and about 50 acres, give or take." She walks up the steps.

"Um, because I need to make sure it is safe. Let's go." I reach for her key, and she grumbles as she hands it over.

Pulling out my pistol, I enter the main foyer and clear the small area. Hitting the elevator button, I survey the place. It is a Victorian-era home that is retrofitted into an apartment complex. At least the owners kept many of the architectural qualities of a Victorian. The elevator dings, and I step back with Stacy behind me. No one came out, so I check before getting in.

"Seriously? That paranoid?"

I put my finger in her face, touching her nose. "You never know who or what may be around every corner, especially with what happened to your radio station, so calm down and let me protect you."

"I will bite that finger if you don't get it out of my face."

"And I will bite you," I say as the elevator starts moving.

"Try it." Even with her attitude, she is the hottest thing I have ever seen, and my dick is hard just thinking about all of the places I can bite her.

Stacy glances down before smirking, "Seems like your brain is the only thing that is mad at me." She grabs me, and I let out a cross between a yelp and a moan.

"We don't have time." I struggle to say as the elevator comes to a stop.

"That's a pity, I have a toy that I would love for you to use on me." She struts out of the elevator before I can stop her. Looking around, I realize that the entire top floor is her residence, and the elevator opens into an open concept penthouse. The view showcases the large piece of property that spreads to all sides of the house. In the distance, the view of the city only highlights how exposed I feel she is. The air is warm and familiar, like her. It comforts me even as I am on high alert.

"You sure it is only 50 acres? This property looks massive. Also, you said top one, not 'I live on the entire top floor.' Anyway, stay here and I will clear it."

Stacy rolls her eyes but leans against the wall.

"Not much for décor?" I ask, gesturing to the sparsely furnished room. I am trying to break the awkward silence that hangs in the air between us.

"Minimalist Chic. I don't bother with the property, so I do not know how much they own." Stacy says as she walks into the foyer.

"I am checking out the rest of the place. Please stay here."

"That's fine, I have zero places to be until you tell me it is safe in my OWN home."

"Stacy, I am warning you."

"Oo whips and chains." She mocks, but she stays in the foyer.

I go from room to room. As I approach the bedroom, I admire the canopy bed for a moment before I hear a crash coming from the en-suite bathroom. Raising my gun, I walk toward the half-opened door. Pushing it open with my foot, I have my weapon ready.

A black ball of fur hisses from the floor of the bathroom. A shampoo bottle next to it.

"STACY!" I stand there, unsure of what to do. Finally, I put my gun away and wait.

"Oh, Sir Fur, what did that mean man do to you?" She pushes past me and goes into the bathroom, picking up the cat and cradling him like a baby. I swear I see the cat smirk at me as she scratches its chin.

"I did nothing, I heard a crash, then walked in here and this thing hissed at me."

"He doesn't like strangers. Are we done?"

"Um, what are you going to do with that?"

"We are only going to be gone a day, right? Stacy carries the purring cat into the living room.

"Yes. We will be back tomorrow."

"Then he is fine, I have an automatic water dish and feed bowl, let me clean out his litter box, and then I will grab what I need and we can leave."

"Okay. Make it snappy." I am worried that the longer we are here, the more likely someone is to find us.

She shoots me a death glare as she walks into her room, continuing to carry the black cat.

I stand in the room so I can see the bedroom and the elevator. I have a feeling that something is going to happen if we don't leave soon. Walking over to the windows, I watch the sporadic traffic pass by the building. Nothing seems out of the ordinary, but that doesn't relax the tension building in my shoulders and neck.

"We need to go."

Stacy's muffled voice comes through the bedroom. "They won't hurt Sir Fur, will they?"

"No, but if you are worried, do you have somewhere for him to go?" I don't think they will, because it is really me they are after, but who knows when people become this unhinged.

"Yeah, I can take him down a floor. Here." She drops a bag at my feet while carrying the car.

"This all? I will follow you down." I pick up the bag, and it is heavier than I thought it would be. "What do you have in here? A shoe collection."

Turning right as she gets to the elevator. "For your information, I only own like 5 pairs of shoes, no, my pistol and ammo are in there." She turns and steps into the open elevator.

Standing there shell-shocked, I follow her into the elevator. When the elevator dings, I step out and look both ways, nodding to Stacy. She steps out. Walking up to the closest door, she holds Sir Fur with one arm while knocking with the other.

After a pause, the door opens, and an elderly woman peeks out before opening. "Stacy, I haven't seen you in a while. Is everything okay?" She focuses on me while glaring, "Who is this?"

"Ethel, this is Abel. He is helping me with some things. I have to go out of town tonight. Will you watch Sir Fur?"

"Of course, dear, I still have his food here from last time. Are you sure you're safe?" Ethel eyes me up and down.

"Yes, I am safe, I just have to leave, and I didn't want him alone."

"Ms. Ethel?" I step forward.

"What do you want?"

"If anyone comes looking for Stacy here, can you just tell them she is staying with a friend in town?"

Ethel snorts before answering. "Yeah, or like normal, I act like a woman who has dementia, and they leave me alone."

"Have people asked for me before?" Stacy pauses from walking in with Sir Fur.

"Yeah, some blond guy trying to act all tough and mighty. Please, he was a pushover. I fumbled some words and dropped this hideous teacup that my son's ex-wife gave me, and he left faster than I could say hello."

I look at Stacy and then at Ethel, who are both laughing.

"Thank you, I may have stirred some feathers during one of my shows, and you know how people can be." Stacy walks inside, and I wait out in the hall because I have a feeling Ethel might stab me.

Less than two minutes later, Stacy walks back out holding something that is not her cat.

"What's that?"

"Pumpkin bread for the road. Isn't she the best?"

"Yeah, that is something that she can be called." I walk back to the elevator and hit the button.

"Her kids live somewhere west, and so I spend as much time with her as I can. She is feisty."

"Yup, that is another word I could use to describe her." I wait for her to get in before pushing the button.

"You don't think they will hurt her?"

"No, I really don't. Especially if someone already came by and left. They won't come back unless they have a reason. So we don't give them one." I place my hand on her lower back and direct her to the car.

"Okay, I just, you know." I feel the worry and fear for others in her voice and tension in her lower back.

"Well then, let's get to Chicago, do what we need to do, and get back and get this finished for good." I smile, even though I feel the same amount of tension. I don't have much other than my house here, but I still worry about the possibility that innocent people can get hurt because of me.

Briefly, my eyes didn't see my car, but the desert, the building that held the school of children that we were assigned to evacuate. It was only a matter of time before they realized the teachers had been helping us, and we needed to move them.

Tech yelled they were ready, and we moved the truck in. The clank of the tailgate coming down sounded so loud, and I worried that its echo would draw someone closer. Posed and ready to take out any enemy that approached, I was ready. What I wasn't ready for was the stream of young girls jumping into the truck bed. I nodded to Cam, and we both walked away from the truck slightly to ensure we were vigilant. Jackson and Kessler were on the ridge watching while Bradyn was with Tech in the building.

My radio sparked to life, and I heard Jackson yell we had incoming. I caught Cam's attention, and we moved back to the building to load everyone.

"Tech, we have incoming, we have to go."

"Last group now," Tech said as I heard a woman's cry.

"Tech, what is going on? We have less than 30." I called out to Bradyn and Cam to get out and secure the truck.

"She is saying that they are missing a kid; she can't find her."

"We have to go Tech, we can't protect them and neutralize the enemy."

"I know, but just wait." Tech turned to the woman and began speaking to her quickly.

"She won't leave without the child."

"Sir, we have incoming and fast; we have to leave." Jackson's voice came over the radio.

"Tech, I am pulling you out of here in 10 seconds, so do something." I turned and headed out front to join the other two.

I counted to eight in my head and then went back in. Tech was trying to pull the woman back away from the staircase, but wasn't having any luck.

"She won't leave without the girl."

"Then we have to leave her, GET IN THE TRUCK," I yelled as I could hear the rumbling of the incoming vehicles.

I grabbed Tech and pulled him out, just as Cam and Bradyn drove the truck away. We ran to catch it and got in right as they sped up to get out of town. I watched as the building was bombed by the incoming group.

"It's gone." Jackson came over the radio, "The entire thing is gone. Did you get everyone?"

I looked at Tech, who just shook his head. "No, a teacher and a student, we couldn't locate. You two stay and go back to check once it is clear."

"Copy that." I heard as I looked around the truck. We were able to save four teachers and over 20 girls. But it was the innocents that we couldn't see that bothered me.

"Abel, Earth to Abel." I hear Stacy's voice come through my flashback.

Shaking my head, I realize we are still standing next to my car.

"Are you okay?"

"Yeah, sorry, I had a flashback. Here, get in so we can go." I unlock the car and we both got in.

"Bad one?"

"Not bad, but sad," is all I say as I get the car on the road to Chicago.

"When we get back, we need to make your place safer, okay?" I don't look over as I watch her from my peripheral vision unwrap the bread.

"That's fine, the system is old anyway, and I don't know if it even works."

"You know what is funny?" Stacy says as she pauses, unwrapping the bread.

"What?"

"My entire life, I wanted a life like this, Fast-paced. Unpredictable."

"And now?" I ask, aware of the complexity behind the simple question.

"Guess I got my wish." Taking a bit of bread, "Just didn't think it would come with this much excitement or danger."

"Yeah, it is nice when the adrenaline is pumping, but the aftereffects aren't always good." I go silent, knowing just how bad the aftereffects can be. I don't wish those on anyone.

"Okay, I will not tiptoe around this. I want to know what is going on." Stacy says, wrapping the bread back up and putting it in the backseat.

"You want me to tell you everything, and I don't get a piece of bread?" I try to lighten the mood, but I can tell she isn't in the right headspace.

"Oh, did you want some?"

"No, it is okay. So where do you want to start? Remember, anything I tell you is between us because it may involve people or things you know about."

"Just because I am a radio host doesn't mean I run my mouth every minute of the day. Who do you think I am?"

"Sorry, it is a force of habit."

"So start talking." She leans against the door so she can look at me.

"I dated a woman by the name of Amanda when I was younger, off and on, but once I started deploying, it went more off than on. Finally, on my second or third-to-last deployment, I called her, and she was with another man. I found out later that it wasn't the first nor the last."

"I'm sorry, but what does that have to do with this?"

"I'm getting there. So I mailed her a letter saying we were done, I never wanted to see her, speak to her, interact with her ever again."

"Rightfully so."

"Then I moved to Kansas City. I am originally from outside the metro area, and so was she, so I expected not to see her. If we did, then we would say hello and go our own way. Well, she found me, and not only did she find me, but she saw us together."

"Wait, like together together?" Stacy's eyebrows shoot up.

"No, I don't think so. The day that we were at the Café, she was there, I think. I also saw her at the restaurant when we had dinner."

"Oh, okay, so you have a stalking ex, should have told me that before."

"I didn't have one before; it wasn't until you started getting stalked that I realized it may be her. But there's more."

"So crazy ex, what else? There is a man that I saw at the park, or thought I saw, who has a limp, is blond, and is about 6 feet 1 inch tall. His name is Nick, and he is not a good guy. However, he shouldn't be here, he should either be in California or dead."

"Are you sure he is here?"

"I thought initially it was just a flashback or an image from the past, but I have seen him twice more, well, on camera twice more."

"The break-ins?" Stacy is smarter than I give her credit for.

"Yes, and I believe they are working together, I don't know why, since they never knew each other, but the timing of things is just to set to be random."

"Okay, but why me?"

"Because Amanda is using his skills of a former special forces soldier to try to either intimidate you at the beginning, but now maybe kill you because you are between me and her."

"Well, I don't want to be on this ride. How do I get off? And what do you mean by kill?"

"Remember how I said Nick wasn't a good guy? He would have no qualms killing you if whatever fantasy he has requires it."

"Fantastic, so one quick fuck behind a bar, and now I am marked for murder. You know what, let me sit on this for a while, okay?" I can't tell how she is feeling as she won't look at me. I reach over and try to put my hand on her shoulder, but she brushes it off.

Once again, I am putting someone I care about in danger, and I can't stop it.

"I didn't want this, I'm sorry," I say as I concentrate on the road. The silence is affecting my ability to focus on the road, so I turn on the radio and tune it to a rock station. I don't know what to say. I want to say something to ease her mind, but the rest of what I have planned to tell her will not ease her mind.

After almost two hours on the road, I hear Stacy clear her throat. "Okay, so this could be an ex-girlfriend trying to get back with you and using someone who may be messed up from his time in service to exact that?"

"Yeah, that pretty much sums it up, but there's more."

"Of course, there is, first, what was at my office?"

"The vehicle that ran into the radio station was a black SUV. I know that because they left paint when they scratched the sides of the vehicle. That same SUV showed up when you were on the air to give you flowers for what you have endured. K noticed right away those flowers were ticking, so that is why he got me."

"And you are a bomb dismantler?"

I take a deep breath before answering her. "My job comprised many things; one of those things was creating and dismantling bombs."

"How long were you in special forces?" It is as if a lightbulb goes off in Stacy's head.

"Since I was 18, they pulled me from basic training to specialized training."

She pauses as she does the math, "So how many deployments did you do?"

"Officially right around 15."

"And unofficially?" I can tell that she is getting worried, or maybe just curious, with a hint of fear.

"A lot more, let's just leave it at that."

"I thought we would not lie to each other." Stacy crosses her arms across her body.

Seeing an exit coming up, I take it and pull into the back parking lot of a gas station. Turning to Stacy, I grab her hand. "It isn't lying, first, I don't know, I was gone all the damn time. Second, we aren't supposed to talk about it, then, now, in the future. I did bad things, and I have flashbacks about some of those things. I don't want you to carry any more of my weight than you already do, do you understand?"

She doesn't answer but slowly nods.

"My unit was created to do certain things; we were very good at those things, but we all didn't come back whole. Do you understand?"

"Yes, I'm sorry for asking."

"Don't be sorry, just know that there may be times when I can't tell you everything, no matter how much I want to."

"So there was a bomb in my office, you and K took it apart, wait, did you put him in danger?"

"No, he went and got buckets of water; he was never in danger." I hear her let out a huge sigh of relief.

"That's good, I like him."

"Yeah, that brings me to the next issue: your manager hired people from a company. That company hired two additional people for the radio station, one of them was a blond man with a limp." I let the accusation hang in the air, hoping I don't have to spell it out.

"So the company could have possibly hired a known criminal to work security in a place where they may have been the vandal? Am I understanding that right?"

"Yes, and it goes deeper." I grimace because I don't want to pull her in more than I need to.

"Oh, now you have to tell me, even if it puts me in more danger, now I am just interested." Stacy perks up, sitting straighter.

"The company, Ares Security, I went and talked to them. Wait—" She starts to say something, but I stop her.

"I pretended to be someone else, didn't mention Mongoose at all, and just was very noncommittal to calling the police. A couple of things, they are shady, I don't know how shady, but I know shady. Second, they have a list of top clients on a wall."

"Wouldn't that cause a security concern?"

"Yes, it should, but as I was standing there waiting for HR to grace me with her presence, I noticed Goldstein was there."

"Ruban was?" I could see the gears clicking.

"Yes, and your radio station, and then when I went to my unnamed football player's home, he also had Ares technology. I found some evidence from the radio station and Goldstein's that I need to double-check, but something is weird."

"This could be huge. Ares is well known for being the largest security firm in the Midwest."

"Which is why I need to get a bigger office, because I have a feeling I may start getting a lot more clients."

Now Stacy is almost vibrating in the chair. "Oh, can I help? I know people, and I have the perfect place for you to have an office. Wait, why don't you want to keep your office at your house?"

Pondering the question, I haven't answered it myself, but I just know that I need to move it.

"It's a feeling that I need to move it. Not to mention if this meeting goes well, there would be too many people in that small office slash spare bedroom.

"Yes, I definitely can help you, especially if you are in the market to do some bartering." She claps her hands together as if the darker elements of our conversation are but dust in the wind. It is one thing I like about her, she can switch topics. I am sure she files them away for later, she doesn't let past words bring her down. Reflecting on the upcoming meeting, I hope to do the same.

"I wouldn't be opposed to it depending on what their needs were or what the bartering was for." I can't imagine anything more than setting up security for a place to exchange for partial lease payment.

"Perfect." Stacy is already texting people on her phone.

"Seriously?"

"What? You need a place, and you may need it sooner than later, and it gives me something to do."

"Okay, then carry on. Can I turn on the music again?"

"Absolutely," Stacy says as she types away. I just shake my head and turn the music up. This is going to be a long drive.

CHAPTER TWENTY

I slowly shake Stacy's arm as we approach Springfield. Either from the adrenaline leaving her body or the energy she spent texting people, she crashed soon after she started messaging.

"Where are we?" Stacy asks as she wakes up.

"Almost to Springfield, do you know where the place is?"

"Yes, second exit, small airstream-looking place." She puts her head back against the door.

Rolling my eyes at the fact that she is back asleep, I follow her directions and end up at a little diner. It gives off a neon and '50s vibe, and I already like it. There is something about it that is familiar, but I can't pinpoint what that is. Pulling up to the only space left, I shake her again.

"We are there, do you still want to eat?"

"Absolutely, let's go." She is out of the car before I can turn the key.

After locking the car, I catch up with her just as she walks into the building. The inside is much larger than it appears on the outside, which is nice because I notice a corner booth away from most of the patrons.

"Can we get that corner booth if it is not too much to ask?" Stacy asks..

"Absolutely doll, now our special tonight is chicken fried steak, but I wouldn't suggest it, Fred's cooking tonight, and while he is good, that is not his specialty."

"Thank you, Doris, for the suggestion. Everything else good?" It is as if Stacy and Doris have known each other for a long time; they are chatting like old friends.

"Oh yeah, the pot roast is delicious and comes with your choice of potato. You also can't go wrong with the grilled cheese and tomato soup."

"Thank you, Doris, I think I know what I am having," I say as she shows us to our table with the menus.

"Well then, I will be back soon." She winks at Stacy and walks away.

"Do you know her?" I ask before opening the menu.

"Not like know know, but she is the owner, and I have talked to her multiple times."

"Okay, now the pieces are coming together."

"What?"

"Just she acted like she knew you, and I didn't know how."

"Oh yeah, she is a great person. I did a special on her when she owned a restaurant in the Kansas City Metro area a long time ago, then her kid got sick and Springfield has the doctors they needed, so she essentially picked it up and moved it."

"Wait, was it like this? Outside of Kansas City?"

"Yeah, her dad owned it before her, and then when he got sick, he retired so he could travel before he died."

"That's why it is familiar, I used to go to it when I was in High School."

"Small world, huh?" Stacy says as she looks through the menu.

Doris comes back a couple of minutes later, and I order the pot roast. It has been a long time since I'd had a good pot roast, and the way Stacy talks about this restaurant, I know it will be worth trying.

Stacy orders the grilled cheese with tomato soup and an order of fries. I respect the fact that, unlike some women, she doesn't bother hiding the fact that she eats. After handing the menus to Doris, she steeples her hands on the table.

"So who are we going to see? You have said nothing, and while I guess it really doesn't matter, I am curious."

"His name is Marcus Chen, but we all call him Tech. He was our tech guy in the unit and was my best friend." I look down at my hands, and I can see the sand and blood, and I try to wipe them off.

"Was? That sounds like a story." She isn't prying, but is pushing, and maybe it is time I talk about it. No one knows what happened outside of our unit. It isn't a secret about Kesseler, but the events weren't publicized.

"Yeah, after our last deployment, no, let me back up, during our last deployment, something happened, and because of that, when we came home, Tech and I had a falling out. In the matter of a day, we went from the closest thing you can get to hating each other. Well, I never hated him, but he hated me, I could see it in his eyes." The hurt from that day rages through me again.

"Do you want to talk about it? Talking about it with my friends who served can actually be helpful. I am not a therapist, but I am a good listener." Stacy moves closer to me, resting her hand on my trembling ones.

"It was fast." My throat catches on the words, on the memory I relive and can't escape. "It feels like everything happened at once, but also everything slowed down. Does that make sense?" Looking up at her, she just nods.

I can't see the restaurant, can't see the light through the windows, or the indistinct murmur of nearby voices. Taking a deep breath, I feel her, knowing it is going to get worse before it gets better.

The past starts to slowly creep back in, an ambush I am expecting, but not the intensity. "He was there, right there, and then he wasn't." I feel the panic spread through my chest, the tightness like old scars. My fingers curl around the table, bloodless and certain, as Stacy's fingers tighten around mine, keeping me grounded while an anchor from another time tries to pull me under.

"Go on, we can stop anytime you need, but I'm here."

I take a breath, and the air is the sand of the past and her perfume of the present. My eyes stay on the small world around me, her face and her eyes. If I look away, I know I will be back there. Her gaze is steady, unwavering support flowing from her to me.

"It's hard to explain." The words struggle out, raw and wounded. "You get in this zone, where nothing but the objective matters. It is all noise and adrenaline and completing the mission."

I see it as I speak, the entire scene stretching out as vivid as the moments it left behind. Gunfire like fireworks, chaos in every direction. Kessler's eyes just before he fell.

It floods me, and I can't stop. Cannot contain it. "We thought it would be safe, a simple grab and go, like we had done multiple times before." The memory grips me with its suddenness, the violence as real as the table beneath my hands. "Should have been safe."

"My eyes stay open, but my thoughts narrow, closed to a small point of vision. I can't hear my voice over the sharp sound of it all, the pulse of panic and explosions. Stacy's hand, not on my hands, moves up my arm, helping me to stay focused.

I can't stop. The entire scene spills out, loud and uncertain. I am glad that Doris put us away from others, because my story is not something people want to hear while they are eating.

"One of our unit's specialties was to save people. Translators, students, teachers, and any opposition to the enemy we would go in, get, and leave. Usually, no one even knew we were there. We had a school with over 20 students, all girls, and their teachers. Everything was going well until the enemy found us. We were able to save everyone but a teacher and a girl. Well, we know the teacher for sure because Jackson found her body when he assessed the scene after the enemy bombed it."

"Oh, I am so sorry, that must have been hard." Stacy's calm voice carries through.

"It was, but let's be honest, it wasn't the first or last. That happened, I don't know, four or five missions before the last one. What we didn't know at the time was that the teacher had been in a relationship with a soldier, not one of mine, but another."

"Oh, how did he take it?"

"I will get there, so in the time between that mission and the last deployment, a special forces soldier was found to be going out by himself and killing women, children, and anyone who helped us. At the beginning, we thought it was the enemy, but it turned out to be a fellow soldier. They found him, and he was dishonorably discharged and sent back to the United States. We thought it was done."

"But it wasn't?"

"No, in his madness at seeking revenge, he was able to turn a couple of other soldiers against their own military. So on that last mission, we set out on a safe assignment. We were to go to this burned-out building in the middle of a vacant town that had been that way for quite a long time to rescue a group of supporters who had taken up in a building for safety. There had been no enemy activity anywhere near the town for months."

"Okay." Her hand runs up and down my arm. It is as if she can feel the tension build.

"We got there, and it was clear. I sent four to the door, two on each side. They kicked in the door, and everything went silent. Tech was with me, spotting from the roof of a nearby building that was mostly intact, when I saw a truck full of the enemy heading straight for us. I tried to get Tech's attention, but he was focusing on another truck heading from the opposite direction. I couldn't reach anyone on the radio, but I could see them in the doorway; they were sitting ducks. So I yelled at Tech and ran there. I got to the building in time to have them get down. That is when I turned and saw the bodies. Someone had slaughtered every single person we had been there to help. It wasn't just a coincidence, it was deliberate."

"Oh no, that sounds terrible."

"It was, but what is worse was that I thought the trucks would drive by; we were below the windows and not in the door, and there was absolutely no reason they would stop. But they did, and we engaged, all five of us shot through the windows at the enemy. Tech was up on another building, and he should have stayed there, but he didn't. Instead, he came down to assist, which would normally have been okay, given the two pickup trucks of men; that was nothing. But what we didn't know was that they had attached a bomb to the inside of the building. One truck left with no one in it, and then as the other truck pulled away, the bomb went off."

My voice falters, and my heart doesn't. I can see the scene, "It threw the three of us on our side of the building back against the wall, and I watched as the wall crumbled down around the two on the other side. What I didn't know was that Tech had been close enough to be hit with the blast on the outside. The minute my vision cleared, I ran over, pulling debris off. I couldn't find Kessler, I couldn't find Cam, and I didn't know where Tech was. Jackson went outside and found Tech, then called in medical and support in case they returned. Finally, I found Kessler, he had been right next to the wall. All I heard was Tech screaming for Kessler outside. I knew he was gone, but I still tried, I tried everything."

The room narrows again, and I can barely breathe as my heart pounds in my chest. Closing my, I see Kessler, see that I can't do anything but still tried. "Turning to Bradyn and told him what happened. After ordering him to look for Cam; we had to find Cam. I pulled Kessler out of the debris and outside. I met Jackson's eyes and shook my head. Tech was in shock; he could barely focus, but he saw me with Kessler, he saw the senior NCO standing over the dead body of our youngest soldier."

The last moments played out, too vivid to look at, too real to ignore. My heart pounds a brutal rhythm, drowning out the words, the light, everything.

"I was their leader, I was the person they looked up to, and I couldn't save him, I couldn't bring him home, and it was my fault. I should have known, it was my job to know that something was wrong. Why didn't I know something was wrong? Why couldn't it have been me?" The table shook from the impact of my hand slapping it. I drop my head, not wanting Stacy to see me crying.

Finally, I look up, tears blurring the world, Stacy, my future. She holds my arm steady, the softness of her touch, the certainty of her being there. My words hit, and I can finally let them go; the walls fell.

I look up, my voice all but gone, my defenses the same, I am but a shell at the moment.

"I'm here, and I am not going anywhere," Stacy says as she holds my hand. In that moment, I know I am here, in the restaurant. I am not in the sand, unsure what to do, but I am safe.

It is as if Doris knows exactly when to deliver the food, as I take a deep breath and look around, she arrives with our food. I can only nod, but I hear Stacy talking to her briefly. As I breath, I find the strength to see her, not the feisty radio personality, but the woman who helps to pull me out. Inch by inch, ghost by ghost, she is pulling me out of the past since I met her.

Even while we eat, she stays close, keeping me close, with a hand on my knee the entire time. We eat in silence. Not the uneasy absence of not talking, but the fullness of not needing to talk. As we finish, she shifts slightly as if uncomfortable.

"I have a question, and I don't want to bring anything back, but who was the soldier whose lover died?"

"Nick Reeves, the one with the limp."

"How did he get that limp?"

"I gave it to him. Right before he was discharged and sent back to the United States, I got to spend some time with him while he waited under military police custody. Everyone knew what he did; everyone, or so I thought, was disgusted by what he did. I knew the commander fairly well, and he allowed me to have a chat with him. Tried to find out information and get him to tell us if he knew anything. He stood up, and I kicked him on the side of the knee hard enough to shatter his knee. Maybe not my proudest moment, but to this day, I don't feel regret. There was a time when I worried that me breaking his knee caused him to set in motion an attack, but it wasn't. It was one of his lackies who didn't even know he had been injured or who did it."

"Well, I guess fuck around and find out, right?"

"I just worry that all of what is going on now is because of him."

"Why do you say that?"

"Well, he is the man that the security company hired, he is the one who broke into Goldstein's, yes, Amanda is helping him, but who is the ringleader?" I ponder that question as I consider the options. Doris brings the check, and she and Stacy go to talk for a bit while I sit and drink my water.

Words spoken earlier are lingering, memories aren't fading as fast as I would like. It could be because I am hoping to convince

Tech to come back to Kansas City, or if something else is bothering me.

Looking up, I see Stacy walking back with a to-go bag.

"What's that?"

"Oh, just dessert for later, are you ready to go?"

"Yeah, let me pay." Stacy puts her hand up.

"We don't pay here, well, I paid for the dessert, but we didn't have to pay for dinner, and I got you a lead on a place to have your office."

I hug her. "You are pretty amazing, you know that, right?"

"Of course I know that." She flips her hair as she turns to leave the restaurant. Seeing Doris, I wave as I walk out the door, catching Stacy near the car. I push her against the car and kiss her hard, my tongue slipping between her lips. I hear a small moan as I grind my leg between hers. Finally breaking the kiss, I unlocked the door.

"See, I know how to get rid of that attitude," I smirk as I walk around to get in the driver's seat.

I pull out of the parking lot. "Do you have everything you need? I want to get to Chicago and get you into the hotel before I go meet Tech."

"You don't want me to come with you?"

"If you want, but I need to warn you, he isn't whole."

"What do you mean?" Stacy cocks her head.

"He lost both legs in the explosion."

"Oh," Stacy grows quiet as I pull on the freeway. I turn on the radio and drive, not expecting us to have a conversation, especially after everything I dropped on her. As I listen to music, I wonder if I broke something, whatever fragile and new thing Stacy and I have, I wonder if I shattered it beyond repair. Only time will tell, and I have more pressing issues.

CHAPTER TWENTY-ONE

Arriving in Chicago just as dusk hits, I marvel at the lights. It is a city, but it also feels comforting. Finally, putting in the directions to the hotel, I look over, only to find Stacy fast asleep, which doesn't surprise me. Not everyone can stay up for days like men and women in Special Forces, and even though I can, I don't like to.

"Stacy, we are at the hotel," I tell her after returning from checking in. Groggy, she sits up and looks around.

"I thought we were going to see Tech." She stretches slightly before stepping out.

"If you want to come along, you can, but I wanted to put most of the stuff in the room before we went over there." I grab her bag and mine.

"Is that all you have?" Stacy asks, looking down at the two bags.

"No, I have a case in the back that I need to bring in."

"I can grab the bags if you want to carry it." Stacy holds out her hands, and I put both bags in them, then go around to the back of the car and lift out the case.

"You bring your entire security system?"

"Most of it, just because I am out of town doesn't mean I don't need to watch my client's places." I shrug as we walk into the hotel. "We are on the 6th floor." I motion to the elevator with my shoulder.

Getting to the room, I look around, making sure it is what I want. Near the stairs, away from the outside windows, exactly. Not that I think Nick or Amanda would come to Chicago, I don't want to assume anything.

"Okay, I am ready to go if you are." Stacy stands in the bathroom's doorway, pulling her hair back.

"Great, let's go." I hold open the door for her as she walks out into the hall. Checking to ensure my pistol is in my holster, I shut the door, and we walk to the elevator.

"Do you really think you are going to need to use your gun?" Her eyebrow shoots up as she sees me check.

"You never know, I may have to shoot Tech." I'm mostly joking.

"Probably not something to joke about," she says, elbowing me.

"Okay, but seriously, it is part of me and has been for a long time. I feel naked without it, even though I am more than capable of defending myself without it."

Stacy looks me up and down before whistling, "Yeah, you are."

Rolling my eyes, I unlock the car door for her, and then I get into the driver's side. "Can you put in Water Tower Place? That is where Tech is on duty tonight."

"I'm not just along for the ride, pretty passenger princess and all." She bats her eyelashes as she pulls up the GPS for it.

"No, because you didn't stay in the hotel, you get to work, sort of." I chuckle as I follow the directions. I intentionally found a hotel close to where he was. Less than 20 minutes later, we are looking at the mall in front of us. Instead of pulling into the parking garage, I park a block away on the street.

"Why not park in the garage?"

"Force of habit, especially if we have to leave soon."

"Okay, whatever, I can walk a block." She unplugs her phone and gets out of the car.

Taking a deep breath, I hold my hand out to her. Taking it, we walk across the street and into one of the mall's main entrances.

"Wow, this is much larger than I thought it was from the outside." Stacy is standing near the stairs, looking up the seven floors. "How are you going to find Tech?"

"I am going to go to the first security guard I see or the first customer service representative and ask them." Shrugging, I hadn't really thought about it. "Do you want to shop or?"

"I will stay with you until you find Tech, and then I will wander around if that is okay?"

"Absolutely, well, let's go find someone to help us." We walk through the crowd; every once in a while, Stacy sees a store or restaurant she likes and ooh and ahhs over it until we pass. I am sure that she is making a mental list of where she wants to go once she leaves my side.

Seeing a security guard in front of Claire's on the fourth floor, we walk over to him. The first thing he notices is my weapon, which causes him to stand straighter.

"I'm private security, I have my license if you need to see it."

"Yeah, just for protocol."

"I totally get it, here." I fish out my security license for the state of Illinois and show him my Missouri one as well.

"Thank you, how can I help you, Mr. Williams, since you seem dead set on talking to me?" He smiles, but it's tense.

"If possible, I need you to radio for Marcus Chen. I know he's working tonight."

He side-eyes me, "What do you want with Chen? He's a good guy, stays here all night when the rest of us are home."

"I know him from when we served, he knows I am coming. I just didn't want to find him in this maze." While still hesitant, when I say served, he nods slightly before pulling out his radio.

"Todd to Chen, Todd to Chen."

"Todd, I told you, you don't have to do that, it is a closed frequency." I can hear the annoyance in Tech's voice. Maybe it will be easier to get him to move to Kansas City than I thought.

"Chen, there's a man here, his name is Williams, who says he knows you. He has a gun. Do you want me to kick him out?" *As if he could in any world kick me out.*

"No, it is okay, please show him how to get to security." I can see him rubbing his eyes, the way he does every time someone does or says something stupid.

"Roger that, I will be heading there 10-4." The guard says as he clicks off. Stacy tries not to smile, even though I can tell she thinks it's hysterical.

"Okay, I am going with him, you go do whatever you want to, okay?"

"How long do you think it will be?" Stacy is already eyeing the guide in front of the store.

"Give us 30 minutes, and if you haven't heard from me, call me?" I figure 30 will be enough, but it can also be two if he kicks me out immediately.

"Great, bye." She scampers off.

"Your woman?" The guard asks as we walk toward the first floor.

"Not really, a client sort of, it is complicated." I don't want to have a conversation about my life with a stranger.

"Well, she is a looker, so when you're done with her—" his sentence is cut short by Tech standing outside the door.

"Thank you, Todd. I can handle it from here." He looks good, not happy, but healthy.

"You sure? I can stay around if you need anything, you know, because…"

"Todd, please return to your post at Claire's. I said I would handle this, and trust me, you don't want to mess with him if you don't have to." The corner of Tech's mouth creeps up slightly.

"Okay, you know I wrestled in High School." Todd puffs out his chest a bit.

"I do, which is why I need you at Claire's." Tech takes a big breath.

"Okay, well, I am just a radio call away if you need help." Todd uses two fingers to point to his eyes and then to me. I pretend to look a bit frightened when I am really just annoyed.

As we watch Todd walk away, Tech waits and then shows me into the security office. It is less an office and more a room of monitors. We stand just inside the doorway, not really sure what to say. I figure I should be the first one to say something.

"Cream of the crop, I see."

"Look, not many people want to police a bunch of teenagers trying to steal earrings and bubblegum." Tech shrugs.

"It is good to see you." I don't know what else to say, but it's the truth.

He steps forward and hugs me, hard. I don't know what to do before hugging him back. We stand there for seconds, but it feels like minutes as we just hug each other.

Pulling back, it looks like Tech has tears in his eyes.

"So you don't hate me?"

"Oh, I am still beyond mad at you, but I never hated you. I thought you hated me because you didn't call, you didn't write, you just disappeared."

"That is what I thought you wanted, you were so angry."

"I know, and I am still angry, but I have been trying to work through it."

"Oh, you're going to therapy?"

Tech chuckles as he sits behind his monitors, "Fuck that, the VA therapists are a bunch of whiny ass kids who don't know shit, and some of the other veterans are just as bad."

"Tell me about it."

"Wait, you went to therapy? Has hell frozen over?" Tech spins around in his chair from the monitor he was looking at.

"Once, the VA told me about this group therapy in the basement of a building, but I lasted half the time. Some of them were Glory seekers, and just nah." I pick up the one other chair in the room and move it so I can at least see what Tech is watching.

"Yeah, that sounds about right, so why are you here, and who's the woman with you?" Tech doesn't look at me, but I envision his smug smile.

"That is Stacy, she is a radio host, I am protecting her, I guess you could say."

"Oh, I am sure you are doing a lot of protecting." Tech snorts.

"No, actually, that is why I am here. So I started a security business in Kansas City, Missouri, and I need you to come help me run it."

"What do you mean you need me to help you run it? You are smart most of the time unless it comes to women."

"Yeah, so that's the problem. Long story short, remember that bitch I was with, Amanda?"

"Yeah, the one who cheated on you on a daily basis and you just let it go." Tech's fingers run over the keyboard as he brings up different screens and information.

"Yeah, well, she is stalking and threatening to kill Stacy. And she has some help."

He spins around. "That ditzy bitch is trying to kill someone? Wait, who is helping her?"

"Well, remember Nick Reeves?" I grimace a bit because we are getting into the past quickly.

"Oh yeah, that grade A douche canoe who killed all those innocents, isn't he in Leavenworth?"

"Apparently not, he is in Kansas City, working for a security firm that two of my clients had been with before they came to me."

Tech narrows his eyes, "You have been out what? Six months and you already have two clients, both of which were with a former company that hired someone who hates you with the heat of a thousand suns, I assume at least, and now your ex is attacking your current 'girlfriend'?"

"Yeah, that pretty much sums it up, so I need you to be my tech person." I lift my shoulders slightly.

"Okay, when do you need me?"

"That's it? Just okay? What's the catch?"

His smile scares me. I usually only saw it right before he took all of someone's money at the poker table. "A place to stay, pay that is comparable to what I make here, and a vehicle that is specially outfitted for me, you know." He motions to his legs.

"Done, when can you come down?"

"I can leave tonight. I have been living on the couch at my cousin's, he works days, I work nights, and I don't even have to pay rent."

"How do you get around Chicago?"

"An Uber brings me here for work, and then one back to the place. I leave money for him, and his girlfriend buys food and stuff. Don't get me wrong, it is a nice setup, but I want my own room."

"What do you get paid here?" I don't care, but I am curious.

"Why, you're already trying to back out of the deal, you said done."

"Call it recon, I want to know everything."

"I make 62k a year."

"That's it?" I pick my jaw off the floor.

"Yeah, it is like five more than Todd out there is making."

"Todd is making 25 an hour, the Todd I met?"

"Again, it is hard to find security."

"Oh, I can absolutely pay you what you are making here, but seriously, you aren't paying a dime?"

"Nope, and I don't expect to be in Kansas City, at least until I find a place I want."

"Oh, so we are at the emotional blackmail stage of forgiveness? Yeah, absolutely, I need you, so come work for me."

"Great, can I ride down with you?"

"Are you okay with living in the security office until I get a better place? Apparently, Stacy has a contact who will show us a place tomorrow."

"As long as I don't have to hear you and Stacy fuck, I'm fine. Do you remember that redhead?" Tech makes gagging noises.

"Look, I've made mistakes, I was young."

"Dude, you were 30, calm down on the young." We both laugh, and it feels like a weight that I didn't know was weighing me down is being lifted off. I feel better than I have in a long time.

"Do you need to finish tonight's shift?"

"Why do you expect me to need a security job with zero mobility in Chicago soon?"

"Absolutely not, okay, well, I have a hotel near here, pick you up in the morning from your cousin's place?"

"No, we are going to have a good breakfast before we leave. Place called Wildberry Pancakes. It is so good, and then we can head down."

"I'm glad you want to partner with me. I was scared, like terrified coming up here."

"Why? Wait, partner?" Tech hit a button before looking at me again.

"Yes, I don't want you as an employee; I want you as a partner. Because I was worried you were going to kick me out, or not want to see me, or yell at me."

"That may all be coming later, after I get a better place than a couch."

"Fair." I nod my head. "See you tomorrow at what? 8?"

"They open at 7, and if you aren't there before 6:45, you aren't getting a table, so be there at 6:30, now get out so I can quit."

I stand and clap him on the back. "See you tomorrow."

Now, to tell Stacy that we need to be at a restaurant to stand in line at 6:30 in the morning.

Walking out of the security office, I pull out my phone and call Stacy.

"Hey, you already done? How did it go? Do you want pretzels or yogurt?"

"No, where are you? I will explain everything when we meet up."

"I just so happen to be standing near your friend Todd, but don't worry, far enough away that he can't hear me over his attempts at flirting with high schoolers."

"Fantastic, well, I will be up there soon, don't move."

"Sounds good, see you soon." She hangs up. I jog up the stairs. I could have taken the elevator, but since I haven't worked out as much as I should, a good four-flight staircase is a great warm-up.

Seeing Stacy standing there leaning against a pillar, watching Todd, I walk up to her.

"Hey," I say as I step next to her.

"FUCK, I almost dropped my yogurt, why are you scaring me like that?"

"I walked up to you, after I told you I was coming up, no scaring."

"Sorry, I am just captivated by the attempted courting dance of a security officer."

"Yeah, that's not great. Anyway, are you ready to go?"

"Yes, but how did it go?"

"Well, we have breakfast tomorrow morning, and then we have a passenger riding back with us. Oh, and your contact with the place? Is it too late to call them tonight?"

"It isn't, but I have other plans, well, after I finish my yogurt." She smiles as she walks toward the stairs.

"Did you buy anything? I see nothing other than your yogurt." Catching up with her. I figure she would have purchased something, especially given how wide-eyed she was when we arrived.

"What? No, I am a window shopper, well, I go in, but I rarely buy anything. I like my money and I live a minimalist life, what more do I need?"

"Good for you, okay, let's get back to the hotel, I need to set up the security monitors and make sure both places are okay."

"Sounds good."

"What are you planning on doing with your yogurt?" I ask as we get to the car.

"Eat it, I spent good money on this, and I will not throw it away." She purses her lips at me.

"Fine, but if there is one single speck of yogurt in my car, you will be cleaning it with a toothbrush. Do I make myself clear?"

She sticks her tongue out and leisurely licks her lips with it. "Not my tongue, no imagination. Don't worry, I won't get any of my frozen yogurt in your precious car."

"Thank you." I open the doors and get in. She slides in, her yogurt on her lap. I side-eye her but drive to the hotel. I will have her on her hands and knees if she gets sugary crap on my seats.

"You seem happier. Well, maybe not happier, but lighter." She looks at me as she eats a spoonful of yogurt.

"I think I was more worried about the meeting with Tech than I thought. He said that he would come down to join me. That did something to me. I don't know how to explain it, but it really helped."

"So is he mad at you?"

"Absolutely, but we are best friends, and while he can be mad, he still loves me."

"Interesting, guys' relationships are different."

"No, they aren't, Tech and I, and by extension the rest of the unit saw things that no one should, we became close. Tech and I were older than them, just slightly, and so we bonded."

"That makes sense, well, I am glad that he is supporting you."

"Oh, I will also support him, beyond normal salary." I laugh. I would have honestly almost given him anything to get him to join me. What he asked for was nowhere close.

"What do you mean?"

"I told him I would set him up in a place, pay his salary, and buy him a car that was specially outfitted for him."

"That seems like a lot."

"Not at all, I would do more if he asked. He knows it too, which may come back to bite me, but for right now, he is going to be living with me until I can get that new office, hopefully, it will be big enough for living quarters."

Stacy's sly smile sets off warning bells. "What did you do?"

"I have done nothing, but my contact owns a high-rise. Well, let's just say he is in the market for new security, and I told him that if you were amicable, you could trade security at his building for half of a floor in that building."

"Half a floor in a building the size of yours? Or half a building in a large building?"

"Large building, he built it, I don't know, five years ago, and while he hasn't had issues with it, his tenants seem to come and go, and he wants a tenant there that will stay there, and I figured you need an office, he needs security."

"Can we look at it tomorrow afternoon?" I am getting excited, but I don't want to get too excited.

"Yup, I am just supposed to call him when we get into town. You three can now talk about all the logistics and requirements, and all of that is beyond me, I just connect people." She grins as she goes back to her yogurt.

"You really are special," I say as she does a happy dance with her yogurt.

Pulling into the hotel, I stop by the front door. "Here you get out and get into the room, and I will park and be up there."

"Sounds good, don't be long." She steps out with her yogurt and walks toward the main door. She is putting extra sway into her steps, and her ass is calling my name.

Parking, I check my phone quickly before getting out. Nothing of top priority, so I lock my car and jog to the main door. I hadn't realized how sticky the outside air was until I got into the hotel's lobby. The cool, crisp air hits me and sends goosebumps across my arms. I waste no time getting up to the room. As I step in, I call for Stacy and hear no response. Her yogurt is on the table, so she is in the room.

"Stacy?"

"I'm in the bathroom, you need to set up the cameras, so get with that." Her muffled voice comes from the bathroom off the bedroom. Breathing a sigh of relief, I get to putting out the three monitors and hooking them up to my Wi-Fi. You can never be too careful when it comes to logging in, especially as a security firm.

"Shit." I slap my forehead with my hand.

"Everything okay?"

"Yeah, I didn't tell Tech what the company's name was." I can't believe I didn't tell him; it can ruin everything. I might as well tell him tomorrow at breakfast. With everything loaded, I watch the screens to make sure everything looks right. While scanning through Goldstein's, I see that one of the display cases was in a different spot. I make a note to go back and ensure that it is an employee who moved it. Clicking over to Reggie's house, I see him working out. The outside scans reveal some wildlife, but nothing concerning. Setting up the alerts to alert both my phone and this mobile system, I stand up.

"Are you coming to bed?" Stacy asks from the doorway to the bedroom. She is wearing a blue nightie that both hides and shows everything.

"I am now." I walk toward her and pick her up.

"Wait, my yogurt." She pats my shoulder so I can lower her to the floor. She runs over, puts it in the freezer, and then walks back.

"Where were we?" She asks. Picking her up again, she wraps her legs around my waist, my dick is hard and rubbing against her core.

"Is this why you took so long getting packed?" I ask as I nibble on her neck.

"No, it really was my gun, I had to remember my code to my small lock box, this was easy to find." I laugh as I get to the side of the bed, lowering her to it.

She lies there looking up at me as I pull my shirt off. I reach for my pants, and she sits up.

"No, it's my turn." She reaches out and unbuttons my pants, then pulls them along with my boxers down. My dick is at full attention as I look down at her. She looks up before sticking out her tongue and running it the full length of one side of my dick before starting at the other side. I moan as she flicks her tongue across the tip. Her hand is gently cupping my balls as her tongue continues to run up and down, playing with and flicking the veins and head.

Grabbing her hair, I pull her closer.

"Absolutely not, at least not yet, this is my turn to tease." She smugly smiles as she goes back to licking. One hand wraps around my dick as she licks and kisses my upper thighs and hip bones. The hand slowly strokes the entire length, including the head, as she continues to barrage the rest of my lower torso with light kisses.

It feels so good I am panting, needing more but wanting the same. Looking up, she winks as she deep-throats me, her entire hot mouth enveloping my dick. All the while, her hand is still cupping my balls, slowly running her fingers over them. I grab her hair, and this time she doesn't complain as I hold on as she begins slowly, agonizingly slowly bobbing her head on my dick. Her lips are tight but not too tight, and her tongue continues to move separately from her mouth, doing things that I have never felt before. She pulls back with my dick, making a popping sound as it leaves her mouth, as she moves to take a ball in her mouth. The moan that leaves my mouth is likely heard by the entire floor as she gently sucks on one, then the other.

Before I can focus on that, she is already back sucking my dick. She places her hand on the hand I have in her hair and pushes it slightly, showing she wants me to control some of the speed. I gladly oblige, wrapping her hair in my hand as I pull it back slightly before pushing forward. Knowing she likes things rough, I tighten my hold on her hair. She moans on my dick, a sound that goes straight to my balls. I can feel them tighten as the orgasm approaches, but I'm not done. I pull her hair back so she is looking at me.

"That's enough of that."

"But why? I want you to come in my mouth." She pouts up at me.

"Because I want to fuck you until your voice is hoarse."

"Oh, well, that works too." She moves back from the edge of the bed.

"Where do you think you're going?" I ask as she lies down, "Follow me, or I will pull you there." Her eyes light up, and she scrambles to get off the bed.

Grabbing her hair, I whisper in her ear, "Do you want rug burns or bruises on your hips?" It was the only decision I'm going to let her make for the rest of the night.

"Decisions. Decisions." She puts her finger to her mouth like she is thinking.

"You don't decide soon, you won't get to," I growl in her ear.

"Bruises, please."

"Great, you go into the bathroom, I will be there soon." I push her toward the bathroom gently. She looks at me, confused, before walking in.

I go to the table and grab a chair. On second thought, I grab two chairs. Carrying them into the bathroom, I set them down. Placing them with their backs against the counter, I pull off her nightie before telling her to put a knee on each and lean on the counter. It takes a brief second for her to realize what is going on, but she eagerly gets on the chairs.

I am very glad I decided to get a bigger hotel room, most of the bathrooms are too small for what I am about to do.

"Perfect, now come stand back up here." I direct, and she stands up and moves next to me. I sit down in the middle of the chairs. Then, thinking, I pull a towel out of the pile and put it against the chair, not against the wall. Then I sit down again.

"Now come, do the same thing but stand."

"Absolutely," she says as she stands on the chairs. Her wet pussy is right in front of my face, and I use my fingers to open the lips so I can lick her clit. Holding her ass with one hand, I bring her pussy against my face, licking and sucking on her clit. She braces herself against the glass as I lap at her clit.

I feel her shake, and so I tell her to step down, she does with a sad look as if I was planning on stopping. I tell her to get back on the chairs but lean against the counter. As she does, her ass and clit are on display. I bite her ass as I slide a finger into her. My goal is for her to come least once before I fuck her.

Inserting two fingers while my thumb is working her clit, she gasps. I run my other hand around and cup her breast, tweaking her nipple hard enough for her to squeak. I can feel her walls tighten against my fingers. Pulling them out, I lick them, making sure she watches me in the mirror. I slide them back in and slowly thrust as I work her clit. Her walls tighten and I pull my fingers out and bend over to taste her, my thumb still circling.

"I'm close, I want you in me."

"No," Is all I say as I continue to use my tongue to thrust in and out of her. She tastes so good, I want to lap up every drop as she shudders. I use one arm to hold her in position while I continue to use my tongue and thumb. She freezes slightly before she convulses, her entire body shaking as she comes. I continue licking after removing my thumb from her clit as each spasm lessens.

Standing up quickly, I slam into her, grabbing her hips with my hands as I feel her continue to spasm around me, much less than before, but still going. I watch her in the mirror as I see the whites of her eyes as she rolls them back.

"Watch me or I'm done," I demand. Her eyes open, and she watches as I pin her against the chair back as I pound into her. I lift my leg and place my foot on one chair, allowing me to gain deeper leverage. Every time I thrust in, I can feel her hitting the chair backs as they hit the counter. If I break them, it will be a price worth paying.

Pulling out, I pull her back so she is standing. I sit down with my back to the mirror and pull her onto my dick. She moans as she slides down. "Watch yourself as you come." I rock in her, so her clit hits every time she rocks forward. Her walls feel so good as they rub against my dick on every stroke. If I could live in her if I would, it feels like nothing I have ever had before.

Feeling her tense up under my hands as I hold her hips. I continue rocking her as she braces herself against my shoulders. "Fuck, this feels so good, I don't want to come yet." She says as she looks at me.

"Why not?" I ask as I speed up.

"Because it feels so good, and when we get back, you have your business, and I have radio, and FUCK." Her walls tighten so hard I have to slow down.

"How about you worry about the future later?" I kiss her hard, holding her against me, my arms around her lower back as I rock. I pull her lip in between my teeth and gently bite down. As I do that, I feel her speed up on her own. Holding her tight, I feel her freeze. I slam up into her as she comes, her head back. "ABEL, HARDER," I pull her off and turn her around. I brace her against the chair backs with my hand between her and the chairs as I fuck her. Her screams continue as her whole body flexes. I feel my balls tighten and know I am about to come.

"I'm about to come, are you ready?"

"HARDER." She pushes back into me. So I do, with every bit of energy and strength I have, I fucking rail into her. I grab her hips as I come, my fingers digging into her hips as I hold her against me, my come deep in her. I hold her tight as I catch my breath. Finally, I slide out and help her stand.

"Shower?" I ask as she wobbles a bit.

"Yes, please." I turn on the shower and wait for it to warm up. Once it is warm, I help her in the shower. Wetting her hair, I apply enough shampoo to wash it and start massaging it in. She braces against the wall as I go from her hair to her shoulders. Once her hair is properly lathered, I rinse it off as she moans.

"You like that?" I step closer and bring my arms around her.

"You are the first man to ever wash my hair, and it feels so good. You're hired." Stacy says as she leans back into me.

"Wait until I wash you." I smile as I kiss her neck. I run conditioner through her hair and then get the washcloth and begin washing her. It is methodical, and I enjoy it, making sure every part of her is washed. She leans against the wall as I wash her front, her eyes closed, and her head tilts back. After making sure she is washed and rinsed, I quickly wash myself. Turning off the water, I grab a towel and wrap it around Stacy first before getting one for myself.

"You look like you are about to fall asleep…again," I tell her as I help her to the bedroom.

"Wait, not before I eat the rest of my yogurt." She is suddenly awake, walking to the kitchen to pull open the freezer. Shaking my head, I pull the covers back and put on a pair of boxers. As much as I enjoy sleeping naked, I never like to in a hotel room.

I check the monitors as Stacy happily leans against the table in her towel, eating the rest of the yogurt.

"Hey, we have to be there at 6:30, so we should probably leave here at 6, just to be careful," I absently say as I make sure everything is still good. Looking up to see how much she has left, I considered watching the video of the day to see who moved the display, but she is already finished, and I don't want to make her wait, especially since I am tired as well.

"Ready?" She asks as she throws away the container and walks up next to me.

"Yeah, I was just checking some things out. How well do you know Ruben?" The display case is bothering me, and I don't know why.

"Well, we didn't have holiday dinners together or anything, but I knew him and his father."

"Look at this." I point to the display case. "Have you ever known him to move stuff?"

"Infrequently, have you watched through to see if he or one of his staff did it?"

"Not yet because I didn't want to make you wait to go to sleep."

"Absolutely not, you watch that, and I will go to sleep unless you want me to stay up with you in case you don't catch something." Stacy grins, her hand resting on my shoulder.

"Me? Miss something? No, go to sleep, I will be in there soon." I pull her hand off my shoulder and kiss it.

"Don't need to tell me twice." She finger-waves as she drops her towel and walks into the bedroom.

Watching her walk out, her ass sways as she leaves the room. Taking a breath, I turn back to the screen. Bringing up the day's entire video, I start at the beginning to see if the display case is already moved. It didn't look like it, so I fast-forward to see when it was moved. At 2, I pause it to see its location, and it was in the same place. Fast forwarding to 6, when Ruben cleans the display case is still in its original location. Now I am confused, because when I check around 8, it is already moved. Slowing down the tape, I watch as Ruben finishes cleaning and locks up. Checking the time of the video to when he engages the alarm system, they match up.

"What happened?" I ask myself. At 7:15, I notice a flicker of the screen and a figure dressed completely in black come in from the front. They walk over to the display case and push it. Bending down, they pick something up before walking back toward the front door. They may have been in the store for less than 10 minutes. I check the front motion sensor to see if anything has been tripped. Nothing looks out of the ordinary. Going to the other screens, I try to see if any of the other cameras pick something up, but they show nothing.

"That is so strange," I tell myself as I check everything twice. I go back and pull up the camera again that shows the display case being moved. Zooming in on the floor before the case was moved. Watching, I slow the replay down when the figure moves it and then kneels down. I can see something glittering but can't tell what it is. Taking a still shot of the item, I put it in a folder and close the video. Tech's first job will be to see how someone walks into the store with nothing tripping.

Making sure the alarms will wake me if anything happens, I set my phone alarm for 5:45 and walk into the bedroom. Looking down at Stacy, she is star fishing across the bed, so I carefully and slowly slide in beside her. Half of my body feels like it is off the bed, but it doesn't bother me. Sleep happens no matter where I am or what I am sleeping on, and a soft bed is better than a cot in the desert.

CHAPTER TWENTY-TWO

Morning comes too early, or at least too early after the night I had. Waking up, I am instantly thrown back into the desert. I think I have a scorpion or something on me, and I just jump, brushing myself off.

"You done?" Stacy asks as she continues to lie in bed.

"I thought it was a spider or scorpion or something." I look down to see nothing on me.

"It was my hand." Stacy muffles a laugh as she shows me her hand.

"Oh, sorry, I am not used to sleeping in a bed with someone."

"I get it. Anyway, we have about 18 minutes before we have to leave to get to the restaurant. Do you want to check the monitors while I get dressed?" She pauses, getting out of bed, "Did you see anything on the camera to explain the display case?"

"Yeah, I am going to have Tech look at it because something is odd."

"Odd how?" Pulling out a pair of capris and a tank top, she puts them on.

"A figure walks in, moves the case, takes something from the floor, and then leaves, but nothing trips, no alert sounds, and they should have."

"Unless they had the code and turned it off?" She looks over her shoulder.

"I thought of that, but the alarm wasn't touched after Ruben left that evening."

"Maybe it was a ghost." She smirks as she passes me on the way to the bathroom.

"Unlikely, we deal in facts around here." I counter, even though briefly, the thought had crossed my mind.

"I know, there are times when things go bump in the night and we don't have explanations, but if someone or something physically moved a display case, then took something, then it is likely a flesh and blood individual." She shrugs from the bathroom as she pulls her hair back in a ponytail.

Pulling on a shirt and a pair of pants, I walk out to the monitors and check them. Reggie's is quiet, which I expect, and nothing seems odd in the overnight log. Switching to the jewelry store, I scan through all of the cameras, and nothing else seems out of place, other than the display case.

"It makes no sense." I rack my brain trying to figure out who moved the display case.

"Still trying to solve the mystery of the moved display case?" Stacy asks as she comes up beside me.

"Yeah, but I am sure that Tech will figure it out. Ready? I just need to pack up."

"Yup, do you need help?"

"No, my bag is in the bedroom already packed, and as soon as I close this all down, we can leave."

"Great, I will get the bags." Stacy leaves as I return everything to the case. I am almost done when she walks back in, so I finish up and we leave the room.

Stowing everything in the car, I type the directions into the GPS and we drive there. Not that I don't believe Tech, but when we get close, I realize he hasn't exaggerated the popularity of the pancake house. The line was already starting, and it was only 6:15.

"Why don't you get out and get in line, and then I can meet you after I park?" I suggest as Stacy stares wide-eyed at the line.

"This is for breakfast, right? Not like drugs?"

"Yup, apparently one of the best breakfast places in the city. Now get out and hold our place, because we need to get back to Kansas City, and I don't want to be in the back."

"Fine, but you're buying." She pulls her purse onto her shoulders and steps out. I drive down the street, watching her walk across and get in line. Finding a parking spot two blocks away, I parallel park and lock up. The air is chilly, but it feels good. It is early enough that the humidity isn't thick, and I can see the flowers just opening for the day. The city is just starting to wake up, and it still smells clean before the roads are full of cars and horns.

Reaching the restaurant, I notice the line is almost double the length from dropping Stacy off. She is standing there playing on her phone as I walk up. There are a couple of grumbles as I stand next to her, but after kissing her forehead, most of them quiet down. *Just wait until Tech gets here,* I think as I grin.

As we stand there, I see the town speed up, it went from a quiet, chilly morning to the normal morning chaos with cars, people, and mass transit all jockeying for the best position at the light.

"Tech was right," I tell Stacy.

"I was right about what?" A voice behind me says. I turn to see Tech walking up to us, his gait just off normal. If one didn't know any better, they may think this is how his gait is normally. He is carrying a green duffel, the same kind we were issued during our service.

"Oh, just wait," I whisper to Stacy, who puts her phone away.

Tech reaches us, and the same grumble from people further back in the line starts. I reach out and pull him in for a hug, kissing his forehead.

"What was that for?" Tech tries to wipe the kiss off.

"People were mad when I got here after Stacy, so I figured they would be angrier when you showed up, so for right now, I am with both of you."

"So I get kissed, will this happen every morning, because I could accept that." Tech grins as he steps in front of us.

"So, since you are now a partner, I already have a task for you."

"Oh, what's going on?"

"Shit, first. Stacy, this is Marcus. Marcus, this is Stacy. Tech, do you want me to take your bag to the car?" Stacy smiles and shakes Tech's hand.

"No, I will put it under the table. Way to read the room, dude. Stacy, it is nice to meet you. You seem to have taken the edge off this." He motions to all of me.

Pursing my lips, I just look at him, "Can we now get back to what we were talking about?"

Stacy whispers, "Sorry, he burned off all his calories from last night, he is hangry."

Before I can say anything, Tech laughs, and then continues to laugh until tears run down his face. Rubbing my eyes with my thumb and forefinger, I just stand there.

"Are you two done?"

"Oh, we are just getting started. I like her already," Tech says, beaming with gleeful enjoyment.

"Well, someone has to run a business here, and apparently that's me."

"Has he always been like this?" Stacy asks as she steps closer to Tech.

"Absolutely, he gets even worse." Tech chuckles. "Okay, we are done, for the time being. What is going on?"

"So I set up a system, let's just call it F. Well, I did everything I was supposed to, but at some point last night, someone broke in, moved an item, and then took something from under it, and left without a ping on the motion sensor."

"Strange, I assume you checked to see if someone logged in."

"Second thing, after checking to see if the owner logged out."

Rubbing his chin, he thinks about it. "It is rare, but they could have come through under the sensor or above it?"

"Unlikely, but maybe, but I have the tape, so if you want, you can watch it on the way to Kansas City."

"No, thank you, I will be sleeping, dreaming of my own space with my own bed and soon to be in my own car."

I roll my eyes, "That's fine, we are meeting with the owner of the building that we will likely have an office in. There is a small catch, but it isn't big."

"What's the catch?" Tech turns as the line moves.

"I'll wait until after we order." Now it is his turn to feel a bit of pressure.

"Fine, but you're paying, right?" Tech asks.

"He absolutely is." Stacy takes Tech's arm, and they walk in together.

"Tough break, dude," someone behind me says as I climb the steps to the front door.

If only they knew, I laugh to myself.

During breakfast, Tech almost forgets about the catch, instead talking to Stacy as if I wasn't there. After ordering, they discuss Stacy, Tech, and Jackson, who I later find out is working in hospital security. It makes me realize that while I am standing still, the rest of the unit moved on, got out, got jobs, and started lives. Well, Tech didn't, but other than him.

The food is fast, considering the large number of people sitting around us. They must have multiple chefs, as we are able to start eating within 20 minutes of sitting. We are quiet as we eat, which sets my mind racing about what I may need to do with it, if it is Nick. As I think about potential outcomes, I miss Tech asking me a question.

"Earth to Abel." He waves his hand in front of my face.

"Sorry, I was thinking about the issues back in Kansas City."

"No worries, I was just asking what the catch was with the building?"

"So if we decide to agree to the lease, it is in exchange for providing security at the building."

"So cameras, motion, that kind of thing?"

"Likely someone at the front desk as well," Stacy offers.

"Okay, so what is the place?" Tech asks.

"It is a high-rise in downtown, your office will be half a floor," Stacy answers.

"That sounds good. I think we could definitely spring for someone to sit at the front desk." Tech nods mostly to himself.

"Oh, can we?"

"I mean, does the office have rooms? Or just one big room?"

"From what he told me, it has separate rooms that could easily be turned into bedrooms or other small rooms. There is also a bigger conference room, and internet and phone lines are already running through it."

"Sounds good to me, let's make the deal," Tech says as he pushes his plate away.

"You have been a partner for less than 12 hours, and you are already making decisions."

"I mean, you're the one bankrolling it, so why not?" Tech grins.

"Let's see the place. I have a budget for equipment until we get more clients, you need to stick to."

"Whoa, you did not tell me I had to budget myself with gadgets. I may have to rethink this partnership." Tech mock clutches his chest.

"Yeah, okay, go back to the mall." The server places the check and tells us we can pay at the front.

"On second thought, I will just make sure we get more clients." Tech stands up and helps Stacy up before I can.

"Let's get on the road. Oh, Stacy, were you able to contact someone about your Jeep?" I forgot to ask her earlier.

"Yeah, K knows a guy who came and towed it to his shop and got four new tires on it. It should be back at the studio under essentially armed guard when we get back."

"Sounds good. I think we should definitely hire K if he ever wants to leave the station."

"He may, as long as it isn't as exciting as someone driving through the doors."

"Wait, who drove what? Who is K? Fill me in?" Tech asks from behind us as we walk to the car.

"Stacy will fill you in on the drive back, if you don't just go to sleep immediately, and by you, I am talking to both of you." I point a finger at both of them.

"Probably not," Stacy says as she fist bumps Tech.

Shaking my head, I unlock the doors, and Tech gets into the back seat while Stacy takes the front.

"You sure you want the back? I am more than happy to sit in the back." Stacy says as she opens the front door.

"Yeah, this back seat is big enough for me to sleep on if I take off my legs." Tech laughs as he slides into the seat.

Groaning, I look between him and her. "I'm sorry, Stacy, he is like this."

"Oh, he's great, I can see why you two are best friends."

"He said we are best friends? Tell me more." Tech put both hands under his chin as he put his head between the two seats.

"That I would stab you if you don't sit back and relax. It is an 8-hour drive, and I want to see the property."

Pouting Tech sits back and pulls out his phone.

***

The drive back is uneventful, both Stacy and Tech fell asleep within 30 minutes, long enough for her to give him the truncated version of what has been happening, and for him to tell her some not-so-great stories about me. The downside of knowing someone since you were 18, I guess.

"Okay, sleeping beauties, we are back in Kansas City. Stacy, I will drop you off at your Jeep, along with Tech. Tech, don't get handsy, please." Tech raises both hands with a look of pure innocence.

"Stacy, can you send me the directions for the building? I want you and Tech to go there first and check it out. I want to get back to the house and get the equipment out of the car. No use in me carrying it to the building just now."

236

"I like that idea. How long will it take for you to get to your house and back?"

"40 minutes give or take. Stacy, don't forget your bag when I drop you off. I will take Tech's back to the house."

"Works for me," Tech says as he sits up straighter, watching the city.

"Have you been here before?" I ask, looking in the mirror.

"No, I heard about it all the time from you but never saw it. It is a pretty city."

"It is, but there is crime, which I guess is helpful for us."

"All cities have crime, it is just a matter of how it is reacted to," Tech says, continuing to watch out the window.

Pulling up to the radio station, I see Stacy's car sitting in the parking lot with K sitting next to it.

"Why are you out here?" I pull up and roll down my window.

"Inside has been quiet since Ms. Stacy left, and her car needed to be watched." K shrugs as if it makes perfect sense.

Stacy and Tech both get out. I open the trunk and pull out her bag before shutting the trunk.

"Thank you."

"K, this is Marcus, Marcus, this is K he was really helpful when I defused the bomb."

"Stacy failed to mention you defused a bomb."

"Long story, but it's because of K that I was able to do it."

"Mr. Williams, all I did was carry water." He blushes.

"True, but that helped. Did you tell Officer Smith about it?"

"Yes, and he would like you to call him at your earliest convenience." K pulls out a business card from his chest pocket and gives it to me.

"Thank you, okay, I am going to run home, and then I will be at the meeting. See you soon." I pull out onto the street and start toward home.

I know Stacy will be safe with Tech, he may be missing legs, but he can still put up a fight, and I notice he has a gun on him anyway. Old habits die hard.

Driving, I am focusing on the road in front of me. I turn on the music and sing along. For once in the last couple of months, everything seems on the right path. I am quasi-dating an amazing woman, and my best friend doesn't hate me. I own a business that is so far successful. Yes, there are some small speed bumps, but so far, everything is going well. I am excited about the office space, and hopefully it will work for us. Thinking that I will call Officer Smith once I am on my way back to the city, I turn onto my driveway.

Getting back to the house, I pull onto the circular driveway without looking around. I am in such a rush to get into the house, get everything unloaded, and get back for the meeting, I don't survey like I always do. I park right in front of the house, leaving my car door open as I grab my and Tech's bags and jog to the front door. Unlocking it, I open it and instinctively put in my code to disarm the system. Without looking, I toss both of our bags onto the futon and jog back outside. Opening the trunk, I pull out the big box and walk into the house. My phone beeps, notifying me of a security alert. I drop the box just inside the door. I pull my phone out and notice it is alerting me to my house.

Looking up at the alarm system, I see it blinking. Before I can turn around to go to my car, something hits me on the back of my head, knocking me to the floor. The last thing I remember seeing is a pair of combat boots before one of them stomps down on my head, and everything goes black.

CHAPTER TWENTY-THREE

I come to with a pounding headache. My eyes open slightly and then slam shut as the light blinds me. Taking a deep breath, I take inventory of my body. I can move my fingers and toes, and I can rotate my neck. So far, this is promising. I try to move my arms and legs, but they are attached to something, allowing me only minimal movement. I can feel my arms behind me, and I am sitting on something hard. It has to be a chair.

I try to remember the last thing before the world went black, but I can't. Am I in training? Have I been taken prisoner overseas during a deployment? My brain is frantically trying to recall anything at all. Small snippets of a woman laughing, Tech talking, and music. Okay, so wherever I am, Tech may be nearby, but who is the woman?

I try to open my eyes again, and while it is still searingly bright, I push through it to look around. Chair, floor, light in my face, window with curtains. It doesn't look like any buildings in the desert. So, training, but I can't remember what the training is for. I hear the door open, and I close my eyes, pretending to still be asleep.

"He looks like he is still out." Why is Amanda here? None of this makes sense. It isn't training, bits and pieces start coming back. I see Stacy's face but can't remember her name. See the radio station, her Jeep. *Come on, brain, get with it.* I know I have a concussion, but I don't know how bad.

"I bet he is faking. It was a technique we learned." The male voice comes up close and kicks my foot. I keep quiet.

"I don't know Nick, he seems out of it. How hard did you hit him?" Amanda asks as she also steps closer.

"Not hard enough, go get me some water, and I will wake him up," Nick demands. I hear soft footsteps leaving the room before the door shuts.

"Listen, you motherfucker, I know you are faking it, and when she gets back, I am going to fucking waterboard you and then torture you so the only thing that that piece of pussy sees before I fuck her is your dead body."

I open up my eyes and spit in his face.

"See, I knew you were up I had to get Amanda out of the room before we had a chat, she wants me to let you go as soon as you admit your feelings for her, so you two can carry on."

"That won't happen, not now, not soon, not ever."

"That is what I have been trying to tell her since she was young, and I saw the real you. But females, right? They never fucking listen."

"Nick, I don't know what is going on, but why am I tied up? Where are we?"

"I must have hit you better than I thought, for you to forget everything, that's a pity, you'll still scream though." Nick laughs as the door opens. Amanda walks in with a bowl of water.

"Abel, you're awake, good, now we can talk."

"What do you want to talk about, Amanda? You could have called me instead of having me tied up and kidnapped."

"You wouldn't have listened, so I needed to do it the hard way. Let me get a chair." She rushes to the side of the room and pulls a chair over. Sitting in front of me, she crosses her legs.

"I didn't want it to come to this. I just wanted you to come back to me, instead, you started dating that slut. She isn't good for you." Amanda pleads.

"Amanda, I cared about you, but you cheated on me, multiple times, when I was deployed. I couldn't be with someone like that long term."

"I'm better, I am not doing drugs anymore, and I need to show you something."

"What?" I am instantly suspicious when she leaves the room again.

Coming back, she is holding the hand of a toddler, bright-eyed with blond hair.

"Abel, meet your son Abel Junior."

I can't control myself, I laugh, deep laughs that strain my shoulders.

"What's so funny? You would know if you ever contacted me." Amanda pouts slightly.

"Please go put the boy back in his room or wherever you had him. He isn't mine."

"How dare you call Amanda a slut?" Nick slaps me.

"Absolutely, he doesn't need to see or hear what is about to happen." I plead with her. The boy is innocent, and I worry about his safety when I tell Amanda and Nick how I know he isn't my son.

"Amanda, go put Abel away, then come back, and we will talk, okay?"

I see her looking up at Nick before nodding and walking out with the toddler. He is no more than three, if that, and I know he isn't mine. What game are they playing, and why are they together?

Nick approaches me, "You better have a fucking good answer for her when she gets back, because I know you were fucking her."

"Why do you care? Seriously, why does my former relationship with Amanda affect you so much? We have our issues because you're a sociopath who killed for fun, but it didn't involve Amanda. Also, why are you even here?"

Before Nick can answer, Amanda comes back, all smiles, before sitting down in the chair. "Abel, you hurt me. Why did you say that Junior isn't your son? Of course, he is."

"For a couple of reasons, one, you cheated on me, at least once, when I was on the fucking phone with you from Afghanistan, so I know you were cheating."

"No, I didn't, that wasn't me."

"Amanda, you were so stoned that you didn't know what was going on. I listened to you getting fucked, and I had people tell me you were seen making out and leaving bars with people."

"No, they are wrong, they just don't want us together." Amanda tries to dodge the issue. I look over at Nick, and he just stands there watching our conversation.

"Okay, even if they are wrong, he can't be my kid."

"Why?"

"Because I had a vasectomy when I was 23, I was deployed, and the military clinic there was doing a week-long campaign, and you already cheated on me twice at least, and I didn't want kids, so I had it done. They then tested me every time I came back to the states to make sure I was still sperm free."

She stands up so fast that the chair falls backwards.

"You're lying, you would have told me!" she says as she steps closer. I see Nick smirking from the corner of my eye.

"No, you were chasing anything with a dick, you didn't care about me, you wanted what you wanted, and not what I wanted, so I did something I wanted to. You never even bothered to care about me, so why should I have told you I did something?" I shake my head, finally seeing Amanda for who she really is.

"We were going to be together and have a family. You fucking lied to me, you told me we would be together forever." She slaps me again. My head is clearing slightly, and I remember the meeting for the office.

"No, I told you I loved you and that if we made it through the deployments, I would marry you because I didn't want you to be a widow, especially when we were so young. My missions were dangerous, and I could have died at any time. I didn't want you to go through that."

"NO! You promised, you told me that when you got back, we would get pregnant, and then you never wrote, you never called, you did nothing." Amanda is screeching as she stands in front of me.

"When? When did I tell you that?"

She looks confused by my question. "What do you mean?"

"When did I tell you we would get pregnant? What year? What deployment? How old were we?"

Still confused, she steps back. "It wasn't long ago, maybe three years, that is why when I found out I was pregnant with Abel Jr., I knew it was yours."

"How old is Abel Jr.?" I cringe at the name because he isn't mine, and now he is going to be raised by this woman standing in front of me.

"He just turned three a month ago."

"So three years ago, which would have made it three years and 10 months ago when you got pregnant?"

"Yeah, that sounds right." Amanda is counting on her fingers.

"Nick, tell her where we were 44 to 48 months ago?"

"Why would Nick kn—"

"Amanda, please let Nick speak." I turn my head to Nick, who does the math, and his eyes widen.

"Amanda, Abel Jr. couldn't be his, even if he is lying to you about the vasectomy."

"Why not? Why are you lying for him?"

"Amanda, dear. Listen to me, when you said you got pregnant, Abel and I were in Iraq, we had been there at the same base. As much as I hate him, he couldn't be his father." He places his hand on her shoulder, and that is when I notice it. I dated Amanda and knew Nick for a long time, and never put it together.

"You're related?" I ask as I look at them.

Neither of them answers as they walk out the door, Amanda sobbing into Nick's shirt.

Rocking the chair slightly to see how sturdy it is, it feels as if it is attached to the floor. I can tell that it is getting dark, but I don't know what day it is or how long I have been out. I close my eyes and take slow breaths, trying to visualize how I am tied up and how I might get free. My wrists are bound, and I have no movement. They may be tied to the chair, but I can touch one palm with the other hand's fingers. My legs are tied to the chair, separately.

With my inability to move my hands or feet, I know that Nick likely secured both. There is no way that Amanda could tighten them enough. Trying to slide my hands around to find the clasp of the zip tie, I barely move before I can feel it cutting into my wrist. There is no way I am going to get out of these, at least not in my current position.

An unknown while later, Amanda walks in with a plate of food. Sitting in front of me, she lays the plate on her lap.

"I don't know why you and Nick are lying to me, but I don't want you to starve."

"Amanda, how long have I been here?" I don't feel hungry, but this will not be the first time I have to go without food, and something about pancakes is sitting just on the edge of my memory.

She shrugs, looking subdued. "I don't know, two or three days, I think."

"How do you not know? Were you here when I arrived?"

"I was, but with taking care of Abel Junior, and making sure no one finds this place, I lost track of time."

"Amanda, look at me," I try a different technique, "do you think holding me captive will make me want to be with you?"

"Nick said that we could change your brain pattern or waves or something, and you would forget all about Stacy and you would want me again."

"Amanda, honey, it doesn't work like that, you can't just remove memories or thoughts." I feel uncomfortable calling her 'honey,' but I think being nice might help in the long run.

She perks up at my comment, "You called me honey, see I knew you would want to be with me again."

"Amanda, our time was in the past. I loved you, and yes…" I swallow hard, "A small piece of me still loves you, but you did some really mean things to Stacy, who is just a friend."

"If she is just a friend, why did she go to Chicago with you?"

"Because I had to keep her safe, she hired me, you know, my security firm? I was hired to take care of her because people were trying to hurt her."

"Oh, so you don't like her?" I don't know what happened, but Amanda was no longer the 30-something raging woman who had been standing in front of me, now she seems like she is a kid again, just wanting affection.

"She is a friend, but that's it. I am not dating anyone," technically true, "but I can't be with you, especially since Abel Jr. isn't mine."

"Oh, here, let me feed you so you get some food."

I smile, not because I want to, but because I feel I need to. Amanda is broken, and even though I didn't cause it directly, I still feel bad. She feeds me chicken noodle soup and a piece of bread. Between sips of water, I ask her what has been on my mind the entire time.

"Thank you, what do you plan on doing with me? There are people waiting for me, I have a business to run."

"I don't know, Nick offered to bring you here, and said that he would help me get you back."

"Amanda, where are we?"

"Don't say another word, Amanda. He is trying to get information out of you. We were trained to do this."

"We are talking, he called me Honey." Amanda smiles as she stands up.

"Okay, go back to the living room. I will be there soon." Nick hugs her as she walks out of the room. As soon as the door shuts, Nick turns toward me, his soft expression shifting to one of pure hatred.

"Now that we know the kid she has isn't yours, I get to do what I want with you."

"What the fuck is your problem? So I broke your knee, you killed innocent people."

"It wasn't the knee that I could live with, it was the fact that you left Shara to die."

"Who the fuck is Shara?"

"My wife, the only woman I ever loved, you and your unit left her to die like a dog."

"Nick, you are going to have to give me more information. We saw a lot of death."

"The teacher, the student, you didn't take her, you let her run back in to save that worthless brat, and because of that she died."

"Wait, are you talking about the school that we evacuated before they came and flattened it?" I was remembering it now, the woman who screamed at Tech to let her go save the kid.

"Yeah, you left her there."

"No, the fuck we did not. We waited, we waited until it was almost too late. Tech didn't want to leave her, fuck I didn't want to leave her, but she wouldn't leave without the kid. She kept screaming she had to find her, that she couldn't let her die."

"Yeah, well, we could have had another, but no, I lost her." Nick sits in the chair across from me. It makes sense now, everything.

"You weren't there, ask Tech, he is here in town, we didn't just leave her, she fought against Tech, screamed and yelled. We waited until the truck was pulling around the corner when we left. We saved everyone else."

"But not my Shara and my daughter, you left them to be crushed by a building." He sniffs.

"So what? You are going to kill me because I made sure my unit and many of the students and teachers were saved, to what? Save Shara? We would have all died, and you know that."

"It doesn't matter, she died, so you are going to die. At least her death was likely quick." He grins as he stands up.

"It was," I know there was nothing else I could say. I, at least, wanted him to know that.

For the next two days, all I remember is pain. I try to think of Stacy as he tortured me, but the pain even clouds her face. I just hope that she doesn't see me when he is done, because it isn't going to be pretty.

At night, or what I perceive as night through the small curtain, I don't fall asleep, instead pass out from the pain. I can feel the blood dripping from my fingers. The point of trying to get out is long past. I don't want to die, but I don't know how much longer my brain and body can endure the pain. It isn't just him beating me or breaking my leg, he also cut pieces of skin off, waterboarded me, and cut off my oxygen until I passed out. I can't bring Shara back, and since I can't reason with Amanda, there is nothing left.

As I wait for him to come back in to start his daily torture, I hear the door open. Both my eyes are swollen shut so badly I don't know who it is.

"I have food for you." I hear Amanda say as her footsteps approach.

"Let me go, he's done enough, I can't walk, I can't see, please," I plead.

"If I let you out, then he may turn on me." She says as I feel food against my lips. I shake my head until she gives me water to drink.

"I understand," and I do, when someone like Nick is done or bored with who he was torturing and killing, he will find someone else.

"Please eat," Amanda begs as I keep shaking my head. Just as she is about to stuff food in my mouth, I hear a gunshot and screaming. Four more shots come one after another before it goes quiet, other than yelling. So much yelling.

The chair Amanda is sitting in, I assume, falls back. I think maybe she runs out, however, soon I feel something cold and sharp against my neck. The door slams open, and two voices yell at the same time.

"Let him go, Ms. Reeves. There is nowhere you can go." One voice I know is familiar, but not at the same time.

"No, he abandoned me and our son, he left us, and I didn't do this. Nick did."

"We know Nick is responsible. Your son is fine, he is unharmed, but if you hurt him, you may never see your son again. Do you want that, Ms. Reeves?

"No, are you sure? Abel is okay?" She sounds frantic after the voice tells her about her child.

"Yes, he is watching a cartoon right now on the steps. He has headphones and doesn't know anything is happening. Do you really want him to be abandoned, like you were?"

Amanda sobs, "No, I never wanted that for him, that is why I kept him, it wasn't his fault."

"I know, it is okay, drop the knife, and I will take you out to him." The voice remains at the same distance away, but I can hear footsteps approaching.

"I can't. Where is Nick? Nick told me that if anything happened, I was supposed to kill Abel, Where is he?"

I can tell the person is about to lie before they even open their mouth, by the intake of breath they take. "He is outside too, you can see him."

"No, I want him in here, I want to see him." Amanda digs the knife in a bit more.

At this point, I don't care, kill me, don't kill me, just do something.

"Amanda, do you really want to kill Abel? Wasn't he good to you when you were together?" Whoever is talking to her knows enough to know how to manipulate her.

"Yes, but then he left."

"He did, because he had very important jobs overseas, and you knew that, just like Nick did."

"Yeah, they both left, and I was all alone." Amanda sobs, the knife trembling in her hand.

"Look at me, don't worry about them over there, Amanda, look at me, it will all be okay, just drop the knife." I feel the knife move down slightly, and then all the pressure is off right before I hear a slam behind me and a muffled humpf from someone.

"Get off me, I wasn't actually going to hurt him. Why are you putting handcuffs on me? I want to see my son. Where is Nick?" She screams as they move her out of the room. I then hear a wailing as she yells, 'Nick' repeatedly. It doesn't take me long to figure out what happened, but my mind is trying to stay awake, so I can't focus on his likely death, not yet.

Suddenly, it is brighter behind my eyelids, and I hear voices everywhere. I think one is Tech, but I can't be sure. I hear someone yelling for the ambulance. Someone is behind me, cutting off the zip ties. Then my legs loosen right before I pass out. I may have hit the floor, but it feels like hands holding me up.

CHAPTER TWENTY-FOUR

It is a week after I am admitted to the hospital when I finally wake up. They put me into a medically induced coma to help my body heal, and it needed to heal. The final count is four broken ribs, four bruised ribs, a broken tibia, and a fibula. I needed two blood transfusions because of blood loss. I had four broken fingers, over 100 stitches for all of the places that Nick cut me. And finally, a broken orbital socket and a missing tooth.

"Hey, handsome, are you feeling?" I weakly open my eyes to see Tech sitting next to me.

"If by any indication on your face, I am not great."

"Yeah, it was bad, I made sure that Stacy didn't see you."

"Bad bad?"

"Yeah, like worse than having my legs removed, bad."

I grimace, which hurts even more, "ouch."

"Yeah, but you are all bandaged up now, so you could definitely be the mummy in a neighborhood theatre somewhere."

"Good to know. How is Stacy?"

"She is good, she is working. After the first two days of you being in the coma, she couldn't just sit around, and there were some issues with her manager, I guess, so she went back to work." Tech shrugs.

"So what happened?"

"Well, long story short, since you are drugged up and won't remember this in 10 minutes, we went to the building, it is great by the way, don't worry, I signed the agreement. We started worrying because you weren't answering your phone. Stacy didn't know where you lived, a real gentleman there, and so I had to find the tax records for your place. Once I did that, we drove up there, and found your garage open, the front door wide open, your security system armed, and your car sitting in the driveway running with the driver's door open."

"I remember getting home and dumping stuff off, and then it all went black."

"Yeah, doctors said someone hit you in the back and then curb stomped you, apparently you had a nice bruise of a boot on your head."

"Okay, then I woke up in some room." My head is still fuzzy because of the drugs, but I can remember some of it.

"Yeah, so once we saw that, we called the police, who were less than helpful. Stacy called K and told him, and then he called an officer in Kansas City. Younger kid. We met up at our new office and discussed what we knew."

"Likely Officer Smith, good guy, young but solid officer."

"Yeah, that's him. Well, it took a couple of days, sorry about that, to find records of where Amanda or Nick may be. We tracked down Nick's family, who live out in California, and boy, did they have a story to tell. Apparently, Amanda was Nick's sister, and when she was young, she was abandoned by their mom after their parents split. Nick moved to California with his dad, and Amanda stayed here with her mom. After she was abandoned, they put her through the foster system until she ran away at 16 and was on her own since then."

"I was with her off and on for years and never knew that."

"Yeah, apparently she didn't remember her brother until he came back after getting discharged and looked her up. Enemy of my enemy and all that. She saw you right after you moved here, supposedly saw you at the airport, and called Kyle to tell him. He came out, got a job, etc, etc."

"Okay, I am tracking now, so it was Nick I saw at the park."

"Likely since he killed a guy and took his identification."

"So did he use that identification to get a job at Ares?"

"Oh no, they knew who he was. Officer Smith walked right in and asked them point-blank, and they admitted to knowing him, but not knowing what he was doing. Smith didn't believe them."

"Yeah, neither do I. Okay, so two days, then you found me?"

"Yeah, Amanda went out and bought something for the boy, and we tracked her back to the house. Speaking of the boy, he isn't yours."

"Yeah, tell me something I don't know." I try to roll my eyes, and they hurt.

"He isn't Amanda's either. She stole him when he was three months old from a hospital."

"Oh no, was he given back to his parents?" I feel horrible for the boy.

"Oh yeah, they showed up within probably 20 minutes of the police finding him. They live out in Leawood, and I am sure broke all the speed laws. He looks just like them. He is going to need therapy. So far, so good, from what Officer Smith says, he has been checking in on them."

"That's good, so what happened at the house?"

"Oh, you are going to enjoy this one. I drove out there, followed the police, and Stacy forced me to let her come with me. I should have said no, but well, you know Stacy. So we get there, and they are setting up, and she goes to the front door and knocks. Everyone is literally staring at her as she acts like it isn't a thing."

"Yeah, that sounds like her."

"Well, Nick answered the door, and she said something, and then he said something, and she pulled out her gun and shot him. Then all hell broke loose."

"Is she going to be in trouble?" I didn't want her in trouble for shooting someone because of me.

"No, the cops played see no evil and said that they deputized her and that her plan was to distract while the rest went around back."

"Was it? Did they?"

"I don't know for sure, but the official report says yes, so yes is what we are going with."

I laugh, it hurts, but it feels good to laugh. "How is she? I mean, most people don't take a life ever."

"She is surprisingly okay. I think there is much more to her than you or I know."

"Likely, she is pretty special. So you signed the lease?"

"Yup, and I was able to secure your credit card from your house, so I bought stuff for the new office, hired K to work at the front desk, and we have four more clients."

"How long have I been here?"

"Just over a week," Tech says proudly.

"What about the existing clients?"

"Oh, they are great. Reggie's family just moved in, and they love the house. Ruban has had no issues. Oh, I figured out what was going on. I was right, they were coming in from the roof."

"That's good to know. Did we fortify any areas people could get in?"

"Yup, all done. Everything is good. The doctor told us you are going to be out for about six weeks, so get used to hearing updates." Tech pulls out his laptop to show me the new clients. Two more NFL players and two businesses, excluding the one we are working with, in exchange for our office.

"Why didn't you tell me?" Tech closes the laptop, and I see tears forming.

"Tell you what?"

"What you named the company."

"I was going to, actually, I was planning on it before our meeting, but then the whole kidnapping and torture." I laugh a bit, trying to break the tension.

"It is a good thing, I think he would approve."

"I felt it was the right thing to do, and I didn't even have to think about it that hard, it just came to me. So you approve?"

"Absolutely, let's just make sure we don't let him down."

Stacy didn't even know why I named the security firm Mongoose. When it came to me while I was on the air, it felt right. We all had names when we served, nicknames, call names, names that our buddies called us. Marcus was Tech; well, Kessler was Mongoose. He was tall and thin and could sneak around like none of us could. He also had a bite, just like a mongoose, so we named him that, I think, during the first mission. It felt right to name the company after him because he was the reason I started the company, well, the reason I left the military, the reason that Marcus is sitting next to me now. It still feels right, and with Tech agreeing, it feels good.

***

After the first two weeks in the hospital, the staff are tired of me causing issues.

"I need to walk," I complain to the nurse helping me.

"No, Mr. Williams, you need to lie there because your lower leg is broken and you have screws holding it together." I can tell she is getting fed up, but I am literally on the verge of dying of boredom.

"Just a quick walk down to PT, even?"

"You are nowhere close to being ready for PT. This isn't a military hospital where you can boss people around." She put her hands on her hips.

"I couldn't boss people around there either, so not much is different," I laugh.

"Well then, get used to it, because the doctor wants you not to move for at least another week before they check the screws again."

"Fine, can my partner bring in my work so I can at least do something?"

She narrows her eyes, "What do you need?"

"Only a couple of monitors and maybe a desk, and a keyboard."

"I will have to check in with the doctor, but I don't think they are going to allow that."

"Nurse Rachet, you're not any fun." I flop against the bed.

"You know that isn't my name, and I am fun, just not with patients who try to make all of my wonderful black hair turn gray. Now get some sleep, Mr. Williams."

"Fine, but I am going to leave a bad Yelp review," I shout as she leaves.

***

A week passes before the doctor even considers letting me escape the prison that is my hospital room. On the promise of death, I am able to leave the hospital as long as I don't work out, run, put weight on my leg, or do anything that may cause my ribs to move oddly. So pretty much everything. I can't even go to the office because I have to be in a wheelchair when I am not in bed with my foot up, so I can't ride in a car. I can technically probably ride in a car, but the way the nurses look at me when Stacy signs me out, I know they have a mole. Stacy is going to tell them everything; she probably already has a spreadsheet somewhere that she is using to track how many times I move my leg.

"Ready?" She asks, smiling as she walks back into the room.

"Yes, so back to my house, right?"

260

"Absolutely not, you are staying with me for the next two weeks."

"Are you taking leave? Aren't you like running the radio station now?" Stacy's manager was implicated by Amanda in helping them coordinate the entire thing, hoping Stacy would quit. He hadn't planned on them going as far as they did, but he wanted to bring in someone else who would cost less.

"No, I am not taking leave. You will be at my house by yourself. Tech may be able to run over and help if you need it, but don't worry, I have a plan with Ethel to come check on you a couple of times a day. I am even giving her a key."

"Oh, so she likes me now?"

"No, but she loves me, so she will pause her soaps and knitting to make sure you don't die upstairs." She helps me into the wheelchair.

"That warms my heart. Well then, fine, but can I at least have a laptop?" I sheepishly grin at her.

"Maybe." As she pushes me toward the entrance. All of the nurses are clapping as we travel down the hall. I want to believe they are happy to see me finally moving, but I have a feeling I have been a bad patient, and they are happy to see me go.

"Hey, Abel? How are you feeling?" Stacy pauses just before leaving the hospital.

"Good, glad to be leaving, why?"

"Officer Smith wants to meet with you and his detective to give you an update on the case and get your statement if you are up for it."

"Absolutely, he can meet me outside your apartment so I can get some fresh air before I am put into another prison." I put the back of my hand on my forehead.

"Stop being dramatic," Stacy says as she unlocks my car and puts me in the passenger seat. I sniff as I slide in, making sure she hasn't been eating food inside. All I can smell is her citrus perfume, and I smile.

"Did you seriously think I ate in your car? I brought yours because mine is too tall, oh, and Tech's will be done in about a week."

"He really is going piggy wild with my credit card, isn't he?" I need to check the balance because I have a feeling I am going to be paying it off for a while.

"No, that was the initial payment from one of your jobs, he didn't tell me which one, but it was enough to get his car going."

"Maybe I should just retire and let him run the business." I ponder as she leaves the hospital.

"He will likely kill you, people aren't his thing, and he has been doing a lot."

"I know, and I feel bad, but it wasn't like I could talk to people while I was in the coma."

"True, do you want to call Officer Smith and let him know to meet you at my place in 30 minutes? He is in my contacts under Smith."

"Can do." Stacy hands me her unlocked phone, and I find his number. After the second ring, I hear his voice.

"Hey Stacy, how is our patient?"

"Our patient is now free, for the next hour probably. Stacy wanted me to call you and see if you were free. I am released, and she is making me stay at her place like the warden she is, so I figured I could sit outside for a bit to talk about what happened."

"Absolutely, let me get the detective looped in, and we will be there soon. Glad to hear you are out." Officer Smith hangs up.

The drive is slow as we talk about what has happened since I was hospitalized. Between Stacy and Tech, they both spent a considerable amount of time in the hospital, more than I had expected. I feel bad because they are both putting their lives on hold for me when I was in a coma, but they both say that I would do it for them, which is right. When Tech was hurt, everything stopped. I stayed by his side the entire time, until he pushed me away.

Arriving at her apartment, I see two cars, a police cruiser and an unmarked vehicle, parked near her front door. As we pull up, both cars' driver's doors open, and Officer Smith, along with a woman, step out. He is in his patrol uniform, and she is wearing slacks and a button-up shirt. She screams, 'I'm a detective,' even if I didn't know already.

They wait as I move to the wheelchair and make my way up to the landing by the front door.

"Thank you for meeting with us, Mr. Williams. My name is Detective Moss, and I am the lead detective on your case." She shakes my hand before pulling out a notepad.

"I don't know if anyone has updated you on the case, but I wanted to get your statement and then let you know what is going on."

I answer, "I know that the boy that Amanda had wasn't hers, I know I was tortured for days, I know that my business partner Tech and friend Stacy helped track me down. Other than that, everything is a bit of a blur."

"Okay, that is a good starting point. Can you please go over what you remember, all the way until you woke up in the hospital?" She stands posed with a pen.

"Absolutely," I tell her what I remember, starting with dropping them off, all the way to opening my eyes in the hospital. After I was done, she nods.

"Thank you, it is mostly a formality to get your statement, but if anything happens in the future, we want to have it, you understand?"

"I do, I am not new to statements." I smile, already feeling a bit tired.

"I will keep it short since I am sure you are tired. Nick Reeves was killed. He attacked someone, and they shot him in self-defense."

I don't look at Stacy because Tech already told me what happened there.

"The boy, whose real name is Jason, was returned to his family, who lived in Leawood. He was kidnapped during a routine hospital visit. His parents want to personally thank you."

"I did nothing."

"Directly, maybe not, but indirectly, you did. Finally, Amanda was arrested, and she was charged with two charges of kidnapping, attempted murder, confinement, and then all of the charges connected to her involvement in the burglaries, bomb threats, destruction of property, etc. She is going to be undergoing a psychiatric evaluation because of some things she said after being arrested."

"I figured I couldn't determine who was controlling who between the two of them."

"We think it was a bit of both, she wanted you back, and Nick wanted you dead, so they had a push-pull sense of control on what happened and when."

"Thank you for telling me. I am tired. Do you need anything else before I get my pain meds and she puts me to bed?"

"I don't, thank you for taking the time to speak with us. If you think of anything else, let Officer Smith know, and he can relay it to me, okay?" She shakes my hand again before walking to her car.

"Wait, I do. You may be a smidge upset, though." I grimace both from the pain and the fact that I had withheld evidence.

"Oh?" She turns around and walks back.

"Stacy, can you go grab the box that is in my car trunk? When Stacy's office was broken into and vandalized, I was able to get a print and a hair sample; there was also a box. I planned for Marcus to look into it before coming to Officer Smith, but then the whole kidnapping and everything."

"I am understandably upset, but did you at least collect it according to protocol?" She stands there with her hands on her hips as Stacy brings the box over to her.

"Absolutely, not my first rodeo when it comes to evidence." I open the box and lift out the bags, and hand them to her.

"Do you know what is in the box?" Detective Moss gently holds the bags, looking at them.

"No idea, but it is now your problem." I smile while she frowns.

"Any other surprises?"

"No. It was nice meeting you." I wave slightly as she gets in her car.

Officer Smith stays, "I am glad you are going to be okay. When I walked in and saw Amanda and you, I thought you were dead until I saw your chest rise and fall. It was rough."

"I'm sorry you had to see that. I knew the voice sounded familiar, but I couldn't place it. As much as I enjoy working with you, I hope to never be in that situation again." I smile as he does as well.

"Same, and by the way, my name is Mike, stop calling me Officer Smith, it is so impersonal."

"Sounds good, Mike. Have a safe night tonight."

Mike looks at Stacy, "Make sure he behaves."

"Oh, I will have a good night." Stacy waits until Mike is back in his car before she pushes me into the building.

She gets me upstairs, and her having little furniture makes moving the wheelchair around much easier than if she was properly decorated. Pushing me into the bedroom, she locks the wheelchair and then pulls the covers back. Unlocking the wheelchair, she pushes me to the bed, and I pull myself onto the bed.

"Do you want your pants and shirt off?" Stacy asks, and she moves the wheelchair to the side.

"Yes, please," I don't even have the energy to be snarky.

She takes them off before giving me a cup of water and two pills.

"What are these?"

"Pain pill and sleeping pill."

"You aren't staying? I thought maybe tonight you could."

"I have to go back to the station, we have a new host I need to help. You will be fine, you will have Sir Fur, and Ethel will come up to check."

"Great, a cat and an old lady." I take the pills and lay back on the pillow.

"You'll be fine." Stacy pats the top of my head and kisses my forehead before giving me a finger wave as she leaves. She doesn't even have a TV in her room. I didn't either, but that's not the point. I can feel the meds working, just as I feel a weight on the bed. Opening an eye, I see Sir Fur slinking up toward my face.

"Yes, can I help you?" I ask him as he approaches. Crawling onto my stomach, he does two little paw biscuits before laying down, his eyes slowly blinking as he watches me. He is lying lower than my ribs, so it doesn't hurt, but I still narrow my eyes at him.

"Don't eat me while I am asleep, okay?" I say as I fluff the pillow and lie back into it. I feel him purr as I fall asleep.

***

Over the next week, I began to feel better, and Ethel checks on me twice a day, or at least I see her that often. I did what I could to help my sore muscles and joints after lying in bed for weeks. Sir fur never leaves my side, either curled up beside me or on top of me. I will not admit to Stacy, but I am liking the cat. His presence helps me stay sane, even if I am talking to him most of the day. He seems to listen, so it is better than some people I know.

Stacy seems to flit in and out of the apartment, being there when I need meds and to sleep, but otherwise at the station.

"You need to take a break. I miss seeing you."

"No, you want me to take you out and about, but I miss you too." She kisses me on her way out the door in the morning. Coming back in quickly, "I forgot, Tech said he would be here at 1 to bring you a laptop and some stuff for you to sign."

Before I can ask her what he has for me, she is gone. I nap on and off, checking my phone to make sure I am awake for when he shows up. At 12:45, I hear the elevator ding. Sitting up straighter, I watch as Tech walks in with a laptop bag. Pausing to pet Sir Fur, who went to see who arrived and if they have treats for him, he walks into the bedroom.

"How are you feeling?" He asks as he lays the bag down.

"Bored out of my ever-loving mind, I have been talking to Sir Fur, and I swear he knows what I am saying."

"He may, anyway, I brought you a laptop, and I have a stack of paperwork for you to sign."

"Thank you for the laptop. What do I need to sign?"

"Permission to give me access to stuff as a partner, your kidney, the lease agreement, which I tentatively signed but he wanted you to also sign, the confirmation on my car being delivered, some receipts for furniture, new contracts for you to initial just so I know you saw them, hiring paperwork for K. I think that's it." Tech hands me a pile of documents.

"My kidney? You know I need both of them."

"Potato Pototo, and no, you don't. The company is doing well, and I am thinking about getting back into PT."

"You should, I am tossing around an idea of a call-in segment on Stacy's station to help veterans, and a meeting space, before you say anything, not a VA-type space, but a space with coffee that people can come and go and just be themselves and talk if they need or just sit if they need."

"Good idea, I may have a place."

"Tech, you have been here what? A month, and you already may 'have a space'?"

"What can I say, I am a man of the people." Tech smiles as he pulls the sheets I sign and stacks them next to the bed.

"You hate people."

"That doesn't mean I can't be a man of them."

"Okay, well, let me talk to Stacy tonight about it, and then we can go to your place."

"Sounds good, now hurry, I need to go meet a new client, a yoga studio, wants cameras everywhere, but nothing illegal."

"Obviously, well, here is the last one, wait, how did you get here?"

"I drove," Tech rolls his eyes like it is obvious.

"But I thought I signed a document for your car to be delivered."

"No, it was for the car's delivery. I took possession last week. Since you were the one paying, I explained to them you almost died, and they gave you an extension."

"Well, thanks, I am glad that my injuries allowed you to dodge some responsibility, especially when it comes to money." I laugh as he gathers everything and puts it in the envelope he pulls from the bag.

"Oh, I am having some food delivered. I heard Stacy is getting off work early, so I figured that Mongoose Security could buy you both a dinner." Petting Sir Fur one more time before leaving, I hear the elevator announcing his departure.

"Well, I guess it is just you and me until your mom gets here," I tell Sir Fur, who blinks before laying his head on his paws between my legs.

I fall asleep and wake to Sir Fur vaulting off the bed. Looking in the doorway, I see Stacy walk in with a bag of food. I whistle as she takes off her shoes.

"Hey, you're up I didn't know if you would be sleeping or not." She smiles as she sits next to me.

"Sir Fur woke me up when he ran to see you."

"I'm sorry."

"No, it is okay, I want to be up. I see you brought food. Is that what Tech paid for with our business?"

"Yeah, he got us Thai, I hope you like Thai."

"I love Thai, he better have ordered what I like." The food was too far away from me to sniff out what he bought.

"Don't know, I haven't looked yet, but it smells good when I grab it. Oh, he told me you wanted to talk to me about something?"

"You and he are awfully chatty." I hold up my hand. "I don't care, he is a great guy."

"He is, but there is nothing like what we have between us. He is a good friend and has helped me a lot since you were kidnapped, and I think it helps him. I feel a sadness in him similar to what you have."

"Yeah, we both lost a person, but he lost more." I frown, thinking about what Tech lost. Sometimes I am so self-centered that I don't think about those around me. Tech didn't just lose his legs, or Kessler, he lost me. The person who was always there, always telling him it was okay, that just another day, and we would be home. I realize I wasn't just the leader, but the cheerleader for them.

"Do you want to sit at the table or for me to bring the food to you?" She stands up and walks over to her dresser to take her jewelry off.

"Table, please. I need to get up." I sit up and move my legs around to the side of the bed. She smiles as she pulls the chair over so I can sit in it.

"Table it is then, let me change, and then we can eat." She pushes me to the table.

"Um, what are you doing?"

"Taking you to the table, and then I will change." She stops and looks down at me.

"No, no, I can sit right here when you change. I am not that much of an invalid." I put my good foot on the ground.

"Fine, but don't hurt yourself with how hot I am."

I roll my eyes and sit back to watch her change out of her slightly more professional outfit to a pair of basketball shorts and a tank top.

"Happy? Can we eat now?" She stands behind me, ready to push my chair.

"Yes, thank you." I can almost roll myself in the chair, but my broken fingers still hurt when I try.

As we eat, I lay out the plan for having a short, maybe once a week, call in to help other veterans, and the plan for an open table meeting area.

"I love it, let's do it. But not until you can walk on your own, I will not be your servant while you roll around the greater Kansas City area." She laughs as she eats.

Thankfully, Tech bought me exactly what I love, and so I eat as I think. "Oh, Tech says he has a place for me to have the meetings, any idea?"

"I keep forgetting you never met the owner of the building you have your office in. His name is Erik, and he met you at the park."

"The Erik who helped me after the shooting?"

"The one and the same, he is a veteran, and he has a conference room on the first floor that you could take over, no strings attached, I am sure, especially if it helps other veterans in the area."

"So, Tech wasn't a man of the people, he got lucky," I say more to myself than to her.

"What?"

"Nothing, Tech just being Tech, so you like the idea?"

"Absolutely, are you done for now?" I look down at my food when she asks and realize I haven't eaten much.

"Yeah, I think all of the sleep and pills aren't making me hungry."

"That's understandable. Ready to go to bed?" She winks as she puts the food away.

"Absolutely, you know I am feeling a lot better."

"Oh, you are? And what should I do about that?"

"You should ride me, just don't touch my leg or ribs, and I am sure the doctor won't even know."

She pulls off her tank top at the table. I watch as she walks over and leans into me, her chest right in front of my face.

"If you are teasing me, I am going to sleep on the couch," I mutter as she straddles me.

"Is this okay?"

"More than okay, in fact, this is perfect, but first you need to get off so you can help me take my boxers off."

"Oh yeah, my bad." She stands and pulls down her shorts before helping me take my boxers off. It has been a long time since I was in her, and my dick is ready, precome already on the tip.

"Like this." She bites her lip as she lowers herself down on me, already wet and so tight. I wrap my arms around her, careful not to pull her too tight against my ribs.

"Yeah, just like that." I run my good fingers up and down her back as she uses the foot pedals of the wheelchair for leverage. I move my back a little off the chair to give her access as she leans against the table and rides me. It isn't fast, but it feels so good, and she looks amazing riding me. Smiling, she leans forward into me, resting her head on my shoulder, her hands on the back of my chair.

"You know, hard sex is great and all, but this, this is so good, it feels different and so good." She whispers in my ear as I hold on to her as she rocks against me. I know exactly how she feels, but I can't voice it, the emotional pull she has over me is focusing on her enjoying herself.

We rock against each other for a while before she leans back. I use the palm of my hand to rub her clit as she slowly lifts herself up before sliding down. As I rub, I can see in her eyes that she is enjoying herself, especially as she rocks against my palm harder. She is moving less up and down on my dick and more against my palm. I brace myself as much as I can and let her grind against me. Her walls tighten as I watch her eyes roll back. I grind harder as she braces herself on the table before shuddering around my dick.

Leaning against me again, she whispers, "You know I may be falling in love with you."

I pull her back slightly so I can see her, "I feel the same way." I kiss her hard, one of the only body parts that isn't hurting right now.

"Okay, while that was great, please get off." I try not to sound in pain, but I am.

"Fuck, did I hurt you?" She scrambles off me.

"No, I hurt myself, I wanted this, now can you help me take a shower so we can get to bed, oh nurse."

"I will slap you, I am nobody's nurse, I am a caregiver, get it right." She laughs as she pushes me into the shower. Yeah, I am definitely falling for her, and fast.

CHAPTER TWENTY-FIVE

The call light blinks like a pulse, as urgent as the fear I once knew. I watch Stacy reach for it, her fingers brushing mine, her touch as soft and sure as her voice. The line fills with static, with the tension of silence and memory. Then a hesitant voice breaks through, a veteran, his words cutting in and out, cutting and edging with uncertainty. "The flashbacks," he says, and I hear the familiar strain. "How do you stop them? I need them to stop." My hands tighten on the desk, the edges of the past clear.

"You don't," I reply, steady. The studio is a cocoon, intimate and dark, the walls padded with soundproof panels and stories. I lean into the microphone, slightly away from Stacy. "You don't stop them. You learn to work through them."

Her eyes stare at me, as full of belief as they've ever been. I feel the power of it, feel the strength it gives.

"We as a nation don't talk about it enough, we as battle buddies and comrades don't talk about it. It is time that changes, we need to, we have to. Not just to save ourselves, but to save our friends, our family, the men and women who stood next to us on the battlefield." I continue, my voice even as I continue.

"We need to hear you, man, you are anonymous, but your voice can and will help others," I say, more urgent now, more sure this is the right thing.

The line fills with his breath, with the indistinct sound of doubt, a second from hanging up. "It's … a lot, too much."

I feel the pull, the echoes from my past. The veteran, regardless of how old he is or what he says, needs the certainty I've found.

"Yeah, it feels like it is," I tell him, my tone cutting through the weight, "It's not. It's like basic, when at the beginning you don't think you can make it, but then day after day, step after step, it gets better."

"I don't know where to start."

"It doesn't matter, because you aren't alone." It is as if I took the first step again, the first step in trusting Stacy.

"Stay with me, and listen, okay?" I hear him softly agree.

"It's the fear, the flashbacks, they hit, and they hit hard. It can be mundane things like running in the park, or cleaning a car, and something triggers it."

"Yeah, that happens." The voice is slightly stronger, but only by a slight amount.

"Stay grounded," I say, the advice familiar, a learned mantra. "It's so damn easy to get lost, to fully embrace yourself in the past, but that won't help. You can think that if you get lost there, then it will just make it better, that it is too much to handle, but it's not."

I hear the veteran's breath, the weight of all he carries.

"What if I can't? What if I succumb to the past?" His voice back softer, a whisper.

"Then reach out," I say, letting the strength I found break through, "Don't wait, Don't let it build."

A deep breath and then a voice, "Yeah, but I don't want to talk to someone who doesn't understand, I can't repeat the past again and again and have blank stares back at me."

"Trust me, I get it, but you know what, we have a group now, before you say anything, it's not that type of group. We have a place, you can drop in, drop out, heck, if you need, you can stay the night, and there is coffee and food, and you can just sit in a safe place and watch the present."

"Really? There's a place like that?"

"Absolutely, and this goes out to everyone who is struggling. It is open 24 hours a day, 7 days a week. Cascade Parkway, first floor. You walk in and tell the guard at the front that you are there for a meeting. He won't ask names, details, or anything. He will take you to the conference area, and you can stay. If you need to stay the night, please ask the guard, and there is a designated area available, safe with a bathroom and shower. Stay a night or a weekend if you need to."

"Thank you," the voice on the call says. "Thank you so much." He repeats before hanging up.

"He needs to know it gets better." Stacy's voice is an encouragement, a mark of pride.

"He will, they all will," the words are more than a promise, more than just a sound byte.

I look over and see her whole panel light up. It is going to be a long night, but I am ready. Tech and K are handling the building and clients, and we hired two more security guards, two veterans who recently left the military and are unsure about their next steps. This is where I am supposed to be.

"Hi, caller, you are on the air." Stacy clicks the button, showing that another veteran has been selected.

The rest of the evening is steady calls, 19 veterans of all ages, genders, wars that needed to know it would be okay, that not everyone gave up on them. I talk to men and women who lost limbs, who lost family members, who lost themselves. Every single one wanted to come back, but it is almost impossible to do it by yourself. For some, I reach for Stacy to ground me when the call is too close, when the past creeps in, when a voice sounds too much like Kessler's.

Finally, the board lay silent. Stacy takes off her headphones. "Are you ready to sign off tonight?" Her voice is bright with promise to all we've done in just a day, all we can do.

"Think so," I say, old doubt no longer a threat.

"This is Stacy Reynolds and Abel Williams signing off tonight. We will be here next week, same time, same place, and remember Cascade Parkway. For those out there who can support, we are always looking for donations to help veterans in your community. Even if it is homemade cookies once a year, or help wrapping Christmas presents, please come down and speak to the front desk guard, he or she will give you the information on how to support your veterans and your community. Have a good night, everyone." Her voice carries a warmth, it cuts through the night, softly cuts through the radio and the static.

"Ready to go back to my place?" Stacy asks as she puts the headphones away.

"You know, at some point, I should probably go home, since I do own property and a house."

"Yeah, but it is so much closer to work for both of us at my apartment. Also, Sir Fur loves you, and your property has wild animals that would make a snack out of Sir Fur." She shudders at the thought.

"Oh, so we are moving in together, are we?"

"I mean, we could." Stacy comes over and kisses me, her hand holding my head in place.

"I may have to think about it, I do really enjoy having property, and you share a three-story with two other tenants."

"That could be worked around." She grins.

"I will come to your house, but first, can you drop me off at the office? I have something I need to do."

"Yeah, everything okay?"

"Yeah, this is a me thing, not a work thing."

"Okay, your car is there, isn't it? Be as late as you need." She kisses me again as we walk out of the sound booth.

Arriving at the building, I get out and walk around to the driver's side.

"I love you, Stacy Reynolds." Kissing her, I run my tongue across her lips.

"Love you too, Abel Williams, now go do what you need to, I am sure I will be up, and if not, wake me up, okay." She winks as she rolls up the window and drives off.

Nodding to K, I walk toward the conference room. I'm not sure if anyone will be here this late, but if they are, I need to talk.

Walking in, I see a group of 11 sitting around talking. Some wear fatigue jackets, a reminder of what still holds them. Others wear street clothes, attempting to start a new life, but are pulled back into the past. They see me walk in and bring a seat over to the group.

"If you want, no pressure," the individual I take as the group leader says as he places the chair.

"I want to; I can wait to speak if you were all in the middle of something." I don't want to break the rhythm if they have one.

"Absolutely not, we were talking about the Chiefs and Royals. Name's Tank."

Sitting down, I brace myself. I need to do this, but it is still hard.

"My name is Williams, and I have only told a few people about this, and it almost ruined my life." I see a couple of veterans nod, as if they, too, hold things that tear them apart.

Letting the words come out, knowing tears will follow, but I need to say it. "I lost someone on my last mission, well, not me, my entire unit lost someone," the memory is sharp and precise. "I carried him, I wouldn't let the medics take him, I carried him in my lap all the way back to base."

"Kessler was his name, but we all called him Mongoose. He was a kid, selected for special forces right out of basic. He was good." My voice shakes with the effort, the truth. "I was supposed to bring him back home."

A few heads bow, the understanding immediate, the understanding too much.

"The bomb went off, a mole in our military tipped the enemy off, I saved them from the bullets, but I couldn't save him from the bomb."

I take a deep breath, "I thought I left it there. Left the loss and the guilt when I came back stateside. But it almost ruined the best friendship I ever had. He blamed me, I blamed myself, and I couldn't let it go. I was wrong, I left nothing in the sand other than the blood."

"It followed me back, and it followed me off base. The real battle? Not in the desert, no, it is here." I point to my head.

"I thought I was alone, I thought that my life was worth nothing, and things got bad, really bad, but I found a connection, a small one that grew. It worked, that connection brought back my best friend, that connection saved me from the hands of a mass murderer, it saved me."

"It isn't perfect, it isn't easy, but I am getting better, every day is a step, and sometimes there are steps back, but I realize that as a community we build ourselves up, we help each other, and we keep each other alive."

I look up at the fellow veterans with tears in their eyes. Looking toward the door, I see Erik, who nods and then steps out. He saved my life in the park, and I never feel I can repay him for that.

After speaking to some veterans one-on-one, I say my goodbyes. Walking out, I stop to see K.

"Every time I am here, you are here."

"I like the overtime," he laughs, "Really, I go home, you just only come when I am working."

"So how many today?" While we don't take names or situations, K keeps track of how many veterans come in, whether they stay the night, and any donations made. Erik and Stacy created a not-for-profit to help, which helps him with his building, and the radio station is helping with good publicity. Mongoose provides the food and good donations. I choose not to be on the committee because I don't want people to think I am taking advantage of anyone.

"We had 120 today, three are staying, one is rough, so I am glad he is staying. We also had a woman come by and drop off a check for $2000 and a basket to give to Mongoose Security. Said that it was the least she could do."

"That's great, thank you. I am off, call me if you need anything." I wave as I walk out to the covered parking where I left my car.

As I start the car, I realize I am heading home to my connection — the piece of the puzzle that has saved my life in many ways. Regardless of where we end up living, Stacy is my connection to the world, my grounding post. Smiling, I turn on the radio and blast hard rock as I drive to her house.

ABOUT AUTHOR

Flo Journey is the pen name for two authors who have come together to write in a variety of genres they enjoy. Look for more short stories and novels in the future from them. They genre hop among the genres they love. They write non spicy books under F.L. Journey.

Follow us on Facebook, Goodreads, Bookbub, and Amazon. Look for announcements about future projects. Please review and share.

If you read this far, please leave a review on your favorite platform

By signing up for our newsletter, you will be sent exclusive content.

Website: https://fljourneywrites.com/
Facebook: https://www.facebook.com/FLJourney
Tiktok: https://www.tiktok.com/@f.l.journey

OTHER BOOKS BY AUTHOR

As F.L. Journey

Ancient Resurgence Series

Ancient Resurgence: Daniel's Story

Ancient Resurgence

Cerberus Brothers Series

The Cobalt Warrior

The Crimson Scholar

The Jade Commander

Matching Galaxies

Princess and the Pirate

Once Upon A Midlife

Forgotten Echoes

Cursed Mirror (2025)

Anthologies

Illusions – "Death Awaits" – July 2024

Little Witches – "Growing up Teen Witch" – October 2024

Dark Descent: Whispers from Beyond – "Night Terrors" – June 2025

As Flo Journey

PNW Syndicate Series

Carlina

Beatrice (2026)

Mongoose Security

Abel's Savior

Marcus' Script (2026)

Anthologies

Snowy Escape – Merry Little Romance (Nov 2025)